Destroyer of Worlds

G. Daniel Gunn

Other Road Press
www.otherroadpress.com

Destroyer of Worlds

ISBN 10: 0-98373-292-2
ISBN 13: 978-0-98373-292-1

Published in January 2012
by Other Road Press, Princeton MA

For information, please contact:
www.otherroadpress.com

Cover Design by Elderlemon Design

Printed in the United States of America

Short Story Collection:

Christmas Trees and Monkeys

Other Novels

**Margaret's Ark
Solomon's Grave**

G. Daniel Gunn

For Linda

Welcome back to my newest, and probably darkest novel yet. Always, there are people who've had a hand in shaping the final product, from answering questions to proof-reading to supplying much-needed inspiration (and, sometimes, all of the above). Special thanks to Linda Busby, Fran Bellerive, Deb Reilly, Michelle Pendergrass, Sara Camilli and Nate Kenyon for their support in getting this dark tale out of my head and into your hands. And as always I thank God for this humble little talent with words, my kids: Andrew, Amanda and Audrey; my parents Joe & Marilyn and the rest of my family, friends and fellow authors who've been so supportive of my writing over the years.

I hope you enjoy the story.

Dan

Destroyer of Worlds

G. Daniel Gunn

G. Daniel Gunn

Corey
Saturday

I

On the last weekend before the world came to an end, Corey Union carefully lifted the shed door's clasp and let it drop. It swung silently back and forth on a single remaining screw. The woods around him were thick with midsummer humidity, cooled only by puddles of shadow from the crowded canopy of mountain laurel and elms overhead. Corey wiped rust from his fingertips onto his jeans, then gripped the door handle. It had been in the sun and was hot against his palm. The air swarmed with gnats. No mosquitoes yet, though they'd be out in force later this evening when it cooled.

Why would anyone have a shed this far back on the property? According to the realtor, most of the six acres had never been used. The old man who'd sold them the land had another hundred acre parcel on the other side of town. Until the sale, he'd let both remain *old growth* – that term was used a lot in this town. Corey thought a better expression would be *going to seed*.

The door was twisted in its frame. He pulled gently. When it did not move, Corey stepped back and gave a quick, hard yank. It opened, the bottom dragging along the thick growth of green along the forest floor, hinges grinding and snapping in protest.

After opening the door a few inches he waited, listening for the sound of bees. He'd heard them earlier: a distant buzz, soundtrack to a life outside the city. No swarm came charging out so he pulled the door the rest of the way open, having to lift it and step down on the clumps of moss and teaberry to give it room.

He stood in the doorway, letting his vision adjust to the gloom inside. The shed was no bigger than a one-car garage, at least from what he could see through the mountain laurel rising on either side of the structure and hiding the back from view. A sheen of black mold grew over every board. No one had come back here in a long time.

The idea of bringing a flashlight in the middle of such a bright day had never occurred to him. Corey hadn't been this far into the property before, but supposed since he now owned the land, the shed was his, too, and whatever might be inside. *Old places begat old things*, his wife Samantha would say.

His shadow stretched along a dull, gray dirt floor. Aside from an s-curve left by a snake at some point recently, no other prints, no other sign it had been disturbed for some time. Corey stepped further inside, moving slowly to avoid kicking up dust.

The interior was hot and stagnant, though an occasional wisp of air circulated through cracks and fissures in the walls and roof. A lone ceiling timber ran the length of the room. From this hung an old length of rope, like shed snakeskin, probably once used for hauling stuff to the sagging loft. Most of the room was lost in a dull charcoal murk while his vision adjusted. Corey crouched, letting light spill in from outside.

The object was barely discernable, save a half inch of exposed metal reflecting back the light from the doorway. It could have been anything, a piece of half-buried rock, an old nail (though any nail in here, he reasoned, would have long rusted over). Corey rose slightly, still stooping to keep the object in the light. His crouching steps were silent on the dirt, small breaths of dust kicked up with each. He glanced to the right side of the shed. There must be a concrete foundation; otherwise the building would have long ago fallen in on itself. Hard to tell. He reached the object and crouched beside it.

A key. An old fashioned sort, judging from the long neck and ornate metal loop at the exposed end. He dug away at the dirt with two fingers, hoping it might be embedded in something... but no. Once enough gray earth had been cleared it fell soundlessly on its side to expose the two-pronged end.

He thought of his father's ugly old clock, currently buried in one of the dozens of boxes yet to be unpacked in the basement. Corey picked up the key, brushed it clear. Some rust along the prongs and the handle. Nothing he couldn't clean up. Once upon a time it might have fallen from someone's pocket, but minor gusts blowing in from the cracks in the walls had long buried any tracks from its former owner.

Corey looked around from his new perspective, ignoring the growing ache in his ankles. His pupils were probably so dilated he'd have to shield his eyes when he stepped back outside, but the shed's interior had finally begun to reveal itself. Empty, no treasure chest or Pandora's Box which might be opened with the key which he held in his palm. Heavy. Cast iron? He thought again about the silent, old clock in his basement. The odds of the key fitting were so astronomical he almost let it drop back onto the dirt.

In that moment, the wasps chose to announce themselves. Corey looked up at the ceiling. Nothing but the single beam and dead rope, lines of sunlight peppered with motes of snowy dust, swaying green shade beyond. Still, the unmistakable whirring of a nest. He looked around with only with his eyes at first, then slowly turned his head from side to side. The sound was growing louder, filling the small room.

He thought, *Shit, shit, shit....*

Corey clenched the key into his right fist and moved only his feet, toes first then the heel, pivoting on the dirt floor until he faced back towards the door. He raised his left hand to block out the light.

The edge of the nest was a massive growth pushing out of the wall two feet from where he'd stepped inside. It spread upward from the floor into the darkened eaves, then stretched back into the corner. The nest was taller than he was, and wider, filling the corner of the shed like a disease on the trunk of an old tree. There *had* been a window on the front wall, but Corey hadn't been able to see through it when he'd arrived. What he'd mistaken for an old, opaque curtain had been a small fraction of this nest. Gray, papery, crawling now with tiny dark objects which had apparently waited until Corey moved as far into this damned place as possible before springing their trap.

Some of the wasps rose from the nest, tentative recon patrols of ten or twenty, drifting a few feet from the safety of the nest before returning, replaced by twenty or thirty more, back and forth like this until the bright, taunting daylight outside the doorway was dimmed with their presence. The lower half was still clear. Could he crawl out without being stung? Out to clean air, and maybe another forty years of breathing? He wasn't allergic, but that wouldn't matter with a hundred or a thousand tiny drops of poison flowing through his system.

He waited, heart pounding so hard he began to worry it might incite the swarm to attack, and tried to get a read on what type of wasp he was dealing with. Hard to tell in the gloom, but no yellow that he could see. That was good, wasn't it? Did plain old black wasps have poison, or just a bad temper and painful bite?

A drone landed on the dirt in front of him. It skittered across the ground in a slow motion dance. Its fat, white-striped black body showed Corey just how screwed he was. *Fucked Royally,* as his coworker, Robert Schard, might say. The creature skittering along the dirt in front of him, an advanced scout most likely, was a Paper Wasp. Known for their aggressive, *sting first and ask questions later* attitude. He'd had a few run-ins with them in the past, most recently at the old house in Worcester when he was trimming the hedges. Get too close, they stung you. Simple as that. Left unchecked, their nests could swell to horrific sizes. This one had been unchecked for *years.*

The scout finally lifted off the floor and joined the growing swarm filling the upper half of the doorway and now the rafters. Like a blanket about to drop on top of him. *So many of them, thousands!* The sound of their anger became a roar, the pathetic label *buzz* long obsolete. A thousand pissed off lions pulling together into a ball, getting ready to explode over him like a thunderstorm.

Now or never, he decided. With the key digging into his palm – knowing it would be his only reward for the pain he was about to suffer – Corey rose again into a half crouch and ran directly into the cloud, trying to keep as low as possible.

The cloud lifted before he reached the door. Only the *tap, tap* of a few slow-movers bouncing off his forehead. Then he was through and running upright, watching the ground as the sun poured into his expanded pupils, casting everything in a wash of white and yellow. He'd caught them off guard. They were probably grouping themselves into a giant fist behind him like in those old cartoons. Corey jumped over, and sometimes through, the gauntlet of mountain laurel through which he'd come to reach the shed, praying that he wouldn't miss the threadbare path he'd followed from the house to get here. He almost tripped when a branch grabbed his ankle. Instead of falling, he hopped on his free foot, keeping a jerky forward motion until the plant gave up the fight and released him.

Only when he found the path at the edge of the property did he risk stopping and turning, ready to sprint towards the house if even a single wasp gave chase.

A dark cloud circled the shed, but nothing followed.

He leaned forward and rested his clenched fists against his legs, trying to breathe the hot summer air. All the while he watched the shed. The wasps spread like ink across the front wall, covering the useless window, filling the door frame. But they traveled no further. Corey took another deep breath, tying to get his body to calm down. His face ran with sweat and his right hand hurt.

He opened his fists. The key had pressed so hard into his palm its impression remained when he plucked it away with his left. There was a small cut at the bottom of his hand, barely bleeding but enough to make him double check that it wasn't from the rusty section. He opened and closed his hand, trying to work loose the impression in his palm while he tried, more successfully now, to slow his breathing.

His system was not yet ready to shut down the flight reflex which had probably just saved his life. *Breathe in; hold it. No, can't hold it, so just breathe out and try again.* Slowly, slowly, his pulse calmed. The air drifted more leisurely into him instead of pouring like magma.

At some point, he'd closed his eyes. He opened them with a start. The wasps were gone. With the exception of the door which now hung drunkenly open, the shed looked much as it had when he'd first wandered back here to explore his new land.

Where the hell had they gone? He'd expected the wasps to linger after chasing a giant from their cave.

He took another long breath, let it out. Maybe he'd take a nap when he got back to the house. He'd had enough excitement for the day. *Wishful thinking,* since Sam had her *Hundred Things To Do This Weekend* list waiting for him when he returned, near death experience or not.

Corey stood up, keeping one eye on the shed, and stretched muscles that were now stiff with an over-abundance of adrenaline. He hoped the wasps *had* gone back inside and weren't creeping through the underbrush, getting ready to spring on him while his guard was down.

That was stupid, but the image was enough to make him pocket the old key – he'd give it a better look when he got back to the house – and turn towards home. He glanced behind him, further down the path. It wound through the rest of the property and beyond. A roof and one white-shingled wall were visible through the foliage. Maybe his neighbors enjoyed walking through the woods. The path was overgrown enough to give him the sense it wasn't a frequent occurrence. Did they know about the nest? He'd mention it if they ever got around to meeting.

Hopefully they were decent people. With such a limited choice of neighbors, it took only a single crappy one to ruin your day for a long time.

Corey gave the shed one final glance then headed for home.

II

Hank Cowles enjoyed Saturday mornings, especially the hour just before noon. *People-watching.* An odd pastime for one of his ilk, but it gave him an ironic sense of belonging. Here he was, an old man, sitting in a wobbly folding chair on his front lawn, watching families scurry to the next big event in their vans and SUV's and feeding his fascination. On occasion, Hank would attend Saint Malachy's church, sometimes even served as usher. He loved that, passing the collection basket from one cheapskate to the next and watching them squirm when he lingered beside their pew after they dropped in a measly dollar or two. Not that he gave two shits about the church, he just liked screwing with the people inside.

"Fucking crow-bar wallet heads," he muttered. Nurse Charles looked up from her spot beside the chair, decided he'd only been talking to himself and laid her small head back onto her paws.

Fucking crow-bar wallet heads, Hank thought, smiling. Amazing what nonsensical gibberish came out of his mouth when he wasn't being careful. But he enjoyed the nuances of human language. Cursing, especially. Something therapeutic about telling a person to *fuck off* and get away with it for no other reason than that he was a doddering old man who probably didn't have complete use of his faculties.

The sun was hot. Hank ran both hands over his face and balding head to wipe nonexistent sweat away. He did not perspire, not unless he chose to and as a rule he did not. Still, his palms were cool against his overheated scalp and he did enjoy touching himself. During these rare, hot, New England summer days someone invariably walked past on their way to the *Greedy Grocer* – one of six ridiculously small shops crowded together in Hillcrest's only strip mall – and commented that perhaps he should spend a little less time in the sun. He particularly looked forward to that idiot Josh Everson who managed the *Grocer*. The kid would drive past on his way to check up on his unreliable employees. If Hank was out front, he'd stop his car dead center in the road (something only possible in a sleepy little town like this). The moron would wave, look at Nurse Charles and ask how Hank's little "Shit Sue" was doing. He never spelled it out, but Hank heard it in his voice, in his mind. The kid was insatiably amused by the dog's name, but made it a point never to ask how she got it. Hank would never tell him, anyway. Still, of all the assholes in town, Everson was OK. Nurse Charles wanted to rip his balls off with her little teeth, but she wouldn't. Not if Hank didn't want her to.

No sign of him this morning, and that was fine. Hank had other matters to ponder. The wasps kept zipping past, telling him over and over, *ad fucking nauseam*, that the game was afoot. The clock would soon be ticking. That probably meant Vanessa would be making an appearance soon. She always did. Key in hand, Corey Union would get things moving along quickly. No wasting time, putting off what could be done tomorrow, no, sir. He wasn't that kind of guy.

Hank opened his eyes and laughed softly. Nurse Charles continued to lay on her paws and pretended to doze, dreaming of death and blood and pain and...

...and the same shit he, himself, had begun to dream. Last night, only a snatch of memory remaining of a bright white cloud burning into orange, then red. A close up of one child's eye widening in wonder, then terror at the sight...

The Shih-Tzu growled.

"Yea, yea, fine," Hank muttered. "What do you care?" He closed his eyes again and turned his face towards the sun. "It's a beautiful summer day, Charlie, and hot. I'm allowed a little reflection."

The dog did not reply.

Hank lowered his head, waved absently as Agnes Lewis drove by in her LeSabre. She didn't see him, too intent was she on not *quite* remembering which side of the road to drive on. Looking at Nurse Charles, Hank decided, *Tomorrow, maybe.* Or the next day. They'd go for a walk across town and pay a visit to the nice family who had bought his property. Between the dog and the wasps, he'd keep tabs on them, including Vanessa, and make sure the clock was wound and kept on ticking....

III

Samantha Union spread peanut butter across the white bread, then paused long enough to close her eyes and breathe in the sweet presence of rose petals and green leaves. The scent drifted into her nostrils, cooling her head. The flowers bloomed from the white vase on the window sill, a gift from Corey, picked up on his way home last night. *Add some color to the place*, he'd said with a smile. He'd been right; the place needed more color. The house, a raised ranch with a full basement just waiting for Corey to finish some day, still smelled of new egg shell paint – *sterile,* she thought, *no history to seep into its walls* – and the lingering tang of hardwood shellac at the back of her throat. They had moved in last week, the first weekend spent unpacking some of the boxes, relegating others to the empty basement until their contents were needed or missed. They had plenty of time to pick and choose what to hang upon the monotonous white of the walls. Maybe in the Fall, when the weather began pushing them indoors, they'd paint a few of the rooms something other than the same, same white. *All is new,* she thought, *a blank slate on which to write the scratchings of our lives.*

She had to stop writing poetry in her head if she was ever going to finish Abby's sandwich. She took a second breath, reluctantly opened her eyes and finished with a little peanut butter on each slice, gently-spooned grape jelly on one side. The peanut butter kept the "jelly juice," as Abby called it, from leaking into the bread.

Sandwich on the plate, knife to the crust. Eating the crust herself Sam moved away from the window and laid the food on the table in front of her daughter.

The four-year old sat quietly twirling two fingers around her left braid, paying no heed to her mother.

Sam followed her gaze. Of course, what else? On the kitchen wall beside the phone, one of the few adornments too big to bother storing away, a glass-framed painting of a pasture, impressionistic rendering of a cow grazing atop the first of many fading hills. The image was colorful, though the years had faded it – originally painted eighty years ago, according to Corey, the self-proclaimed art expert currently wandering around the woods. He said it was only a reproduction, which was how they could afford it, but nearly as old as the original. At the moment, it was bathed in sunlight pouring from the picture window facing the back deck and woods beyond.

Sam tried to see what it was about the sparse painting that so absorbed her daughter every time she sat at the table. *Always in that seat, night or day; no one else could take her seat.*

"Mom," Abby said, blinking back to reality, "do you think Moomoo is lonely?" While she waited for an answer, Abby lifted the sandwich and took a bite. Sam gave the lone cow a prolonged gaze, then shrugged.

"Maybe, but he looks happy enough."

"I'd be low-ly," she said through a mouthful of peanut butter.

Sam touched the girl's head before returning to the counter, ostensibly to clean the knife and jelly spoon in the sink; slowly breathed in the roses; let her gaze linger on the green leaves, red petals. Smells and colors blended in her "poet's mind," a term her mother once used for her unique way of seeing the world. Red – that of roses; subtle smooth petals giving warmth, love, not the bright red of Cayenne pepper or valentines. *That* pepper-hot red was spicy, stressful. Yellow was frightening, though she never understood why, regardless of how often Doctor Reilly had tried to dig into those days gone by. Green was giving, life.

Outside, tired wooden footsteps ascended the porch.

"Daddy's back!"

Thank God, Sam thought and, as usual, cursed the relief at seeing her husband rise past the railing, knowing he was close again. Doctor Reilly had once accused her of being addicted to Corey, to his presence. No, that wasn't the word. *Dependant.*

Was that so bad?

Sandwich forgotten, Abby watched her father through the thin curtains at the edge of the picture window. Last weekend, Corey had pushed the table against the wall for a better view of the woods. There were only the three of them, after all. *Just three.* Her daughter moved away from the window and opened the door, ran outside. In her excitement, she hadn't noticed the large, black and white wasp on the screen door. It flew over her head. Sam was certain it would land and sting Abby in retaliation but it disappeared beyond the railing. She would need to look under the porch later, see if there was a nest. Abby wasn't allergic; she'd been stung last year at preschool with no bad effect; but this wasp had been a bit too big for Sam's liking. Probably every insect out here in the woods of northern Worcester County would be like that. Big, intimidating.

She didn't like wasps, or any other stinging creature.

Standing by the door, she tried to catch a whiff of color, but was too far from the vase. Instead, Samantha followed her daughter outside to see what their hunter-gatherer had discovered. He held out something small in his hand to Abby, who stared at it with wonder as if it was a diamond. Probably another *Big Bug.*

IV

Corey spent the rest of the day making a dent in Samantha's *Hundred Things* list, clearing away mountain laurel on the southern end of the yard with his newly bought chainsaw. That had been fun. Hacking and slashing was going to be one of the perks of living out here. After tucking the various implements of destruction back under the porch, he wandered into the basement. The room was refreshingly cool, drying the grime and sweat on his body. Before jumping into the shower, he wanted to find the clock.

The house's foundation was built mostly above ground – water table too high, *so sayeth the building inspector* – with the only windows facing under the back porch. He flipped on the lights. The basement was cluttered with everything they'd trucked in from storage, boxes scattered across the floor with no real organization.

The key was upstairs on the sill above the kitchen sink. Corey had given Sam an abbreviated version of his adventure – had to give *some* explanation for why his palm now had a key-shaped dent. But he kept the story light, not wanting to scare Abby too badly. Sam's face had paled, then tightened. As he'd expected, she insisted Corey stay away from there. No objection from him. More importantly, they reiterated this to Abby as she turned the key over in her hand. Their daughter nodded absently; the concept of wandering into any dark, scary woods was the furthest thing from her mind, anyway.

Corey closed the box labeled *Misc Knick-Knacks* and shoved it aside, fairly certain he'd packed the clock in *one* of the boxes marked with a *Misc*. On the second try he found it, wrapped in an old quilt his mother had given them the first year they were married. No sooner did he have it out than Corey wondered why he'd been so eager to find it. The base was a foot and a half wide, and the clock rose an equivalent height. On one side of the base was the clock itself. Standing on the opposite end, arms outstretched as if presenting the clock's round face to the world, the *blue boy*. The only truly-*blue* feature was the figure's baggy blue pants, but the name had been bestowed by some long dead relative. The boy wore a white peasant shirt over bright pink skin more fitting to a lawn flamingo than a human.

The face was the most disconcerting, to Corey at least, caught halfway between a laugh and a sneeze. Maybe a scream. Looking at it now with adult eyes... no, definitely a sneeze.

The clock itself was a gaudy piece of work, at its core wood but with polished iron accents at the corners and painted bright gold. Much of its sheen had been retained over the years, probably because it spent most of its life stowed away, out of sight. This was an ornament which never took much of a place in his childhood home. Mostly it lived a useless life on the shelf of his parents' closet. The face of the clock, with its delicate Roman numerals, was pleasant enough to look at, its round glass intact except for a hairline crack near the six. The minute-hand was bent a little. Corey turned the adjusting knob in the back. It moved freely past the other hands. It would work, if the key fit. Which, of course, it wouldn't. The odds were a million to one against it.

He frowned. As a child, on those rare occasions he'd take it down from his father's shelf, the thing was uncomfortable to look at and touch. Still was, for reasons he could never work out, except that it was an ugly, strange thing. Maybe someone in the past had thrown away the original key as an excuse to squirrel it away. Truth was, down the Union line, everyone probably hated it but never had the heart to toss it in the trash.

He privately hoped the key wouldn't fit as he tromped upstairs, leaving his saw-dusted work boots on the top step before emerging into the hallway with the clock tucked under one arm. It wasn't something that blended well into a room. But it had survived all these years to become the Union family's most cherished, or at least *honored*, heirloom. For all Corey knew, it was also the family's most honored joke.

Sitting cross-legged on the living room floor, Abby didn't look up from the television when he passed. *Can't interrupt the cartoons.* As long as her TV time didn't get out of hand, they let her set her own schedule. As long as it was the Cartoon channel, not CNN. Corey had used the parental control on the remote to block any news channel. His daughter didn't need to hear about other people's misery. Well, *none* of them needed to hear it. Better to let stupid mindless cartoons fill your head than real monsters. Corey pushed these thoughts aside. He wasn't going to ruin the day.

Samantha was in the kitchen pressing thick burger patties onto a plate for a late barbeque. He set the clock in the center of the table and walked to the sill above the sink. Sam flipped the last patty between her hands and stared back over her shoulder. "I forgot how ugly that thing is," she said, smiling in spite of her words. "We used to have a grandfather clock when I was a kid. It dinged at all hours, every day. It was nice, though. Do you think Blue Boy will do that?" Her brows furrowed in mock concern. "Or maybe it'll just cough and gasp."

Corey laughed. "I doubt we'll find out, but it's been eating at me all day so let's find out one way or another so we can tuck the thing back into its box before supper." He reached past her and scooped up the key

"You need a shower," she said.

He gave her a gentle bite on the neck. "Join me?"

"Maybe after."

He returned to the table and turned the clock around so the back faced him. The pink-skinned boy stared with his screaming sneeze out towards the woods. Corey slipped the key into the hole in the back. "So far so good. Ready?"

Samantha smiled, dropped the patty onto the plate. It landed with a smack. "Wind and see, Toy Boy."

Gently, he twisted. The key turned, just a few clicks. It was stiff, but it *was* turning. Dust had likely gotten into the housing over the years. Nothing a little oil wouldn't cure. Three more clicks. The works inside were probably snapping apart. One more click, then the key turned more easily.

No way, he thought. This could become the first time in generations.... Corey continued turning the key, slowly until finally meeting some resistance. No telling how fragile the springs were in there. He stopped.

And waited.

The clock began to tick.

Vanessa

The crow tilted its head, watching her first with one round eye, then the other, moving with a jerky, nervous motion. Vanessa ran a finger along the smooth handle of the coffee mug, stared back at the bird perched on the railing across the porch from her. Slowly, the crow opened its beak, leaving it open as if frozen in a yawn. Vanessa opened her own mouth, for no other reason than she liked how it looked on her companion.

An intangible whiff of shadow rushed past them. The crow closed its mouth and flapped off from the table, leaving a small pile of turd on the boards as a parting gift. It sailed out of sight in the opposite direction from where the shadow had passed. Away from the woods.

She remained in her chair, staring at the vacated spot. The shadow was likely one of the many hawks living in this wooded town, passing between the house and setting sun. How Corey might have interpreted it, had he seen or sensed it racing past, well... he would have given it a far darker origin, an omen or portent to the end of the world. It might have taken on a significant role in his world.

But he hadn't seen it. The shadow was for Vanessa alone, and the crow.

She'd relaxed long enough. Corey had not been in the house long enough to establish many behavioral patterns. She needed to keep close tabs on his actions. Vanessa got up from the chair, a stiff-backed number she'd dragged outside to avoid displacing the wicker furniture already here when she'd moved in. Things pre-established in this house needed to remain as they were. She enjoyed being outside. It was warm, and the bugs didn't bother her too much.

She wandered to the railing, flicking the dried turd off the deck with her sandal and leaned forward. The wood felt cool under her bare arms. Last night, so late it was actually *this morning*, she'd quietly come out and lay naked on the painted boards, enjoyed the cool under her like running water with a million stars above. So many more stars than could ever be seen under the city lights of Worcester.

This is what it is to be alive, how it feels to be human, she'd thought then, and for a few moments everything was going to be all right. Corey would be OK. His world was not going to end in a few days. The illusion lasted for only a few moments, but it was nice, until she regained some sense and put her clothes back on, moved inside.

Now Vanessa turned around, leaned back on the railing, thought of the man she swore to protect. Twilight spilled across the woods behind the house like slow running ink. Unpainted toes curled under her sandal straps. She closed her eyes, breathed in the cool summer, and listened the symphony of nature around her.

Ticking, too, faint like a wristwatch held to the ear, the clock sound floated above and below the thin current of the world, an underscore to everything. Not a true sound, because what Corey had wound was not really a clock, just an illusion, just an empty box, but the ticking... the ticking was there, always, a metaphor become reality in his world and in Vanessa's simply confirmation that the story had begun.

The clock would be the instrument of the world's destruction. Leave it to the old man to choose something so clichéd. The proverbial *doomsday clock*. But of course, it was Corey who'd chosen it, as unwitting as the choice might have been. *The chosen choose the tool for their own destruction...* something like that, might have been from *Ghostbusters*, though.

Tick, tick, tick....

She breathed deeply, pulling evening air into her lungs, expanding her chest to hold as much as she could, let it out slowly, fighting the desire to pull more in before the last had been expelled. Deeper, faster, Corey's clock was ticking. Vanessa wrapped her arms in a slow self-hug. Too much to do. Her role in his doomed world was beginning soon whether she wanted it to or not, and she had to be ready.

Corey
Saturday

"Good night, Sweetie," she said, and kissed Abby gently on the forehead. The girl's eyes were heavy, struggling to stay open. She was probably asleep already. Samantha had let her help today marking the borders for the new garden, holding the small stakes while Sam hammered them in, helping her turn the soil over. Not much would grow this late into summer, but the process was important. Both Abby and Sam loved turning the soil over and digging in with their hands. Outside all day, sun and heat, sometimes stopping to watch Corey from a safe distance as he defoliated the yard with his new toy. Abby would sleep all night, always did after a day outside. She'd adjusted to the new house faster than her parents.

Sam leaned forward until her lips brushed the girl's ear, whispered, *"Turn the earth over like a secret message; feel its response; speak to it like a friend; learn what lessons it has to teach; renew it with seed. We are all its lovers; we are all its family."*

She'd written that in her spiral notebook earlier, while Abby gobbled a midday snack in front of the TV and Corey hacked and slashed outside. Samantha had sat on her bed, writing, crossing out, trying a new word, tucking the book back under the mattress – *hidden away like a lover,* she'd thought absently. Sometimes, on nights like this, with Abby drifting away to dream on her own, Sam would whisper these secret poems, feed her child's dreams. Share her soul.

She couldn't do so with Corey, not share her writing. Even now, as she straightened and checked that the night light was on before closing the bedroom door, Samantha did not understand why this was the case. Afraid Corey might say something, react the wrong way, or *not* react, confirming for her that these secret words were nothing more than a whim, a pastime of his cute little wife. Nothing deeper. Nothing sacred. He knew she wrote them, knew also she preferred to keep her words, her small pieces of soul, private. She should trust him not to read it, but it felt safer, hiding them away, keep them safe from exposure.

Doctor Reilly thought it was her way of controlling a part of her life, holding onto a piece of her soul no one else could touch. One of the many reasons Samantha stopped attending their semi-weekly sessions. Reilly had moved from being a helpful confidante, helping her through the miscarriage two years ago, to someone too intent herself on controlling Samantha, how she thought, labeling and categorizing her behavior with a series of *why*s. Samantha didn't need to be told *why* she did anything. Not anymore. She did things because she did things, and she was fine with that. Now, at least. She loved her husband, loved her writing. Maybe she feared the two wouldn't get along if they ever met and she'd have to choose; feared the choice might be harder than she cared to admit. She found some comfort in the knowledge that they shared the same room.

The same world, the same woman.

The bedroom door clicked shut. Sam waited; no sound from inside. Abby was out for the count. When she stepped from the hall, a freshly showered Corey hunkered by the clock in the living room. He stood when she approached.

"She asleep?" Arms moving around her, rubbing her back. Sam leaned into him, smelled clean skin. Ivory soap, no cologne, not this late. He hadn't seemed to mind her suggestion that he take his shower a little earlier, without her.

"Like a rock," she said.

The arms tightened, hands moving down over her rump, squeezing.

In her ear, Corey whispered, "Think the bugs are bad outside?"

She shrugged, turned slowly, leaned into him for a heartbeat before stepping forward, taking his hand. He had big hands, palms rough and calloused from the work he'd done today. She led him through the back door onto the back porch. A quick memory of this morning's wasp returned, but she let it drift away. She'd checked. No sign of a nest. Just a stray, wandering too far from home.

Abby's room faced the front of the house, a deliberate maneuver to allow nighttime conversations out here without waking her.

Samantha's slippers hissed across the wood, moving to the edge of the porch. Corey's bare footsteps were quiet but heavy. His arms moved around her again, this time from behind, pulled back against him.

She whispered, "There are so many stars," leaning her head back onto his shoulder, letting his hands explore her. "We should have turned off the kitchen light. I'll bet we can see the Milky Way."

He grunted in agreement, hands teasing along her shirt, fingers finding the topmost button. She was wearing an old flannel shirt. She called it her "ratty outside gown." Buttoned front, sleeves rolled up her thin arms. Corey worked the top button free, then the next. The air was cool against her skin and she liked it, felt her body responding to the air and his body hardening against her back.

"First clear night since we got here," he said, voice rough, eager. She pressed her butt against him, felt his arousal growing. He worked the remaining buttons loose with less tenderness. She had removed her bra earlier. His touch through the open shirt was gentle, but insistent.

Without turning, she reached around, her fingertips working over the front of his jeans, then loosened the belt. She did this with her eyes closed, feeling his presence around her, aching for him to be inside her. *Soon*, she told herself, *soon enough*....

When the clasp came free, she pulled the belt through the loops and turned around to face her husband, the strong wonderful man she'd married who was now pushing the old shirt completely off her shoulders.

Vanessa

Vanessa lingered on the path at the edge of the woods. The line of trees was close enough to see every detail of their lovemaking, every muscle in the man's bare legs as he held his wife by the buttocks with one hand, stroked his erection with the other. Vanessa imagined the woman was a writhing china doll in his arms as he thrust inside her, the two of them clinging to each other in passion and fear.

She watched, an observer in her long black dress concealed by the darkness around her and the silence she held so close, watching them, watching *him*. She fought the urge to undress, share in his sex, knowing her stark white body would practically glow under so much starlight. She couldn't risk that. She only watched, enjoying seeing him, imagining the couple together, if only briefly, celebrating the sensations life could offer. There was so little time left. It would be a sin to distract him, tip the scales when he seemed so happy. Vanessa would become the wedge between them soon enough. It had to happen, to save him before an old man named Hank Cowles roared in and tore it all apart.

She imagined that their bodies might fit well together.

Postures eventually loosened; Corey lowered his wife from the railing, mumbling soft words Vanessa tried not to hear. The two collapsed against each other, spent. She didn't move, let Corey enjoy his private happiness one final time.

Naked, satiated, he smiled in the glow of the kitchen light spilling across the porch. When he collected his cast-off clothes and walked into the house, the two came together inside with a less hurried embrace. Vanessa watched him a while through the window, rubbed her hands along her arms and finally turned away.

It hurt too much to watch any more.

Corey
Sunday

I

A buzzing whine drew Corey from a thin cloud of sleep. It didn't take much to wake him these days. A sudden gust of wind, the creak of a floorboard. The new house shifted and settled, keeping his mind always alert. He hadn't dreamed since moving here.

The sound continued. Corey opened his eyes, half-expecting the window to be black, middle of the night. What he saw was a thin coat of dust across the glass, illuminated by a slant of sunlight. He blinked, realizing that he'd slept all night. At least he *thought* he had. Another sign that things were normalizing, that they were settling into the new place. The buzzing continued from the clock radio beside him. *Not* truly a buzzing but a man's voice fighting for clarity from the poorly tuned station. Corey set the dial this way on purpose. Enough noise to wake him without resorting to the heart-stopping electronic shrill, but never clear enough to find its way into his rested (this morning at least) brain and filling it with mindless chatter or news. *Especially* news, bad as it always was. Just a flickering cadence or the occasional hissing song to get him out of bed.

Eight-thirty. *That's right... Sunday....* He'd never been much of a church person, not until he met his Catholic wife. She rarely missed mass. In order to be married at her home parish in Providence, Corey had to endure weeks of classes, molding him into the good Catholic man he now pretended to be. He didn't mind. It never hurt to expose

Abby to as many positive influences as possible, even if only once a week, and she enjoyed going.

Corey reached out and tapped the snooze button, rolled over and slid his arm under Sam's, letting it rest between her breasts. She was awake, but only just. He pulled her closer.

She muttered, "Good morning," before rolling onto her back, stretching, turning until they faced each other. He loved watching her do that. She must have noticed because she whispered in his ear, "Down, boy. It starts at ten and we can't be late the first time."

He pressed himself against her, but going too far would only frustrate both of them. Still, he would enjoy these few minutes. He bent his head and kissed her neck. She moaned in pleasure, caught herself, slapped loudly against his back.

"Ouch!"

"Time to get up, sleepy-head."

He sighed and rolled onto his back, stalling long enough to watch Sam pull free the sheets and slip her body into a robe. When the show was over, he got up, turned off the radio and slipped into his own robe. Sam had already claimed the master bath so he wandered into the hall to use the other. The television volume rose suddenly from the living room. Corey bypassed the bathroom and followed the sound. Abby sat cross-legged on the floor, nightdress pulled over her knees to support two Barbies reclining in its makeshift hammock. The remote control in her hand told him she'd waited until they'd gotten out of bed before turning the sound up.

"Morning, Daddy!"

"Morning, Sweetie." He leaned down, kissed her on the forehead before wandering into the kitchen to start the coffee. He called over his shoulder, "Oh, and don't forget, we've got church in a little while. Time for some breakfast."

"Fruit Loops."

As soon as the coffee was perking, he looked back into the living room. Abby was paying more attention to her dolls than the show, switching outfits between them. He said, "Clock still ticking?"

She scrambled onto her hands and knees, letting the dolls fall, and scurried over to the fireplace. Corey had decided to leave the clock on the hearth for the time being, until they chose a more appropriate location or followed tradition and shoved it into some closet. After a few seconds with her ear against the face, Abby nodded. "It's ticking. I can hear it!" She pulled her head away, began inspecting the details of the blue boy, his small arms out in a sideways "V" holding up the clock. Her fingers traced the folds of the sleeves, details of his hair, losing herself in the study. Corey had to admit the work was amazing, even if the end result wasn't very pleasing.

The show on the television faded to a commercial. Corey couldn't see it, only the sudden fade of light against his daughter's nightgown as she studied the clock. A quick news blurb – even on Sunday mornings kids weren't safe from these intrusions. The media rattled their sabers in your face when all you wanted to do was to live your life, be happy.

His chest tightened. *They won't let you. They'll tie you down, lock you in a room and sound-byte you until you bleed and thrash, until you become something they can hold up to the rest of the world, force feed your pain to someone else who doesn't want to....*

Corey tried to close his mind as he shuffled back into the kitchen, having no real destination, simply not wanting to hear what was being said. How the world was going to hell, careening too fast to stop. He wished he was back in college, twenty years old and not caring what was going on outside his small life. The world had become much darker since then. Corey knew enough about what was happening. He simply didn't want to hear about it. He leaned against the counter, trapping his hands behind him. The coffee maker gurgled. It was hard enough at work avoiding conversations, the skittering, frightened look in everyone's eyes. This was the weekend, alone in the woods with his family, getting ready for *church,* for God's sake. He shouldn't have to...

"Daddy?"

Corey looked up. Abby was in the wide entranceway where kitchen, living room and hall converged. He swallowed, stood straighter. "I know, Sweetie. Fruit Loops."

She walked up and wrapped herself around his legs. Her head barely reached his waist. "The bad news is gone," she said. "Just commercials now."

He swallowed, felt his face burn. Barely five and already she was taking care of *him*, already understood that her father was broken. *The monsters are gone now; you're safe, Daddy.* The idea warmed him, and hurt. Corey ran his hand over her uncombed hair. Children rarely got enough credit for how quickly they picked up on things. Maybe they picked up *too much*. Abby shouldn't have to worry about her father.

He was frightened enough for both of them.

All he could say was, "Thank you, Sweetie. I'll bring your cereal in a minute."

She gave his legs one last squeeze before running back into the living room.

Corey poured the cereal and milk, brought the bowl into the living room. Sam would complain about Abby eating on the carpet and, yes, there would be a few drops of milk spilled, but her show was back on. She was hungry, and she'd earned the right this morning. He put it on the rug in front her, looked at the clock and frowned. *Not right.*

Corey went back into the kitchen to check the microwave's time. The clock had lost five minutes already. Probably should wind it more.

Later.

They managed to eat, shower, dress and get out the front door by nine-forty. Mass was at ten. The drive across town shouldn't be more than ten minutes but, to Sam, sitting in the pew a few minutes extra was better than stalking in behind the opening procession.

Not until they'd reached the minivan did Corey notice the woman walking up their long driveway. Her beautiful, angled face was framed by short black hair. She wore a long, black print dress, buttoned in front up to the neck. No car in sight. *Our first neighbor*, he thought. As if to complete the picture, she held out a pie. They came together in front of the van.

"Good morning," she said, a little out of breath. "I'm sorry for bothering you; looks like you're going somewhere." She raised the pie higher. It was wrapped in cellophane with a small piece of masking tape stuck to the top. "Just wanted to bring a little house-warming present." She met Corey's gaze with wide, blue eyes before turning to Samantha. Meanwhile, Abby shifted behind Corey's leg. She never did well with strangers. He took his daughter's hand and Sam took the pie.

"Thanks," Sam said, half-turning to show Corey. She had that look which screamed, *I have no idea what else to say*. Their neighbor waved a hand.

"I'd like to say I made it, but the Congregational Church had a bake sale yesterday so I stopped in and picked this up. I don't want to keep you. Is that where you're going?"

"Almost," Corey said. "Saint Malachy's next door." He extended his free hand. "I'm Corey Union, this is Samantha and Abby," always introducing his wife using her full name to avoid confusion.

"Call me Sam," Sam added, her usual addendum.

The woman took their hands in turn. Her touch was cool, dry. Abby allowed her own hand to be taken, though she leaned into Corey as she did so. Before the woman straightened, Corey realized that her hair was actually quite long, woven into a braid along her back, not cut short as he'd originally thought.

"I'm Vanessa," she said. "Our properties abut." She waved loose fingers in a general direction behind them, "Out back."

Corey nodded, too aware of the time and Sam's growing panic about being late. He gave Abby a nudge. "Why don't you get in the car, Sweetie?" To Vanessa, "Yes, I think I saw your house yesterday when I was out walking the woods."

She glanced at Samantha (pie still in hand) and Abby moving cautiously to the passenger side of the car. "I'm going to make you late. I'd really love to have you all come by the house soon, so we can get to know each other." She followed his wife towards the doors. "I think it's so important to be friends with your neighbors, don't you?"

Like Abby, Sam was normally quiet around new people, letting Corey plow through the requisite small talk. She surprised him by saying, "That would be really nice. Maybe you could come back here tonight for supper? We could share the pie."

Vanessa clasped her hands against her chest, an act which, to Corey, seemed wonderfully country-ish. "That would be wonderful. You're sure it wouldn't be any trouble?"

Abby had climbed into the van. Sam slid the door closed behind her and opened her own. She might be playing the role of good neighbor surprisingly well, but hell if she was going to be late because of it. Corey tried not to smile. "No trouble at all. I think it'd be great. Seven o'clock all right? It's going to be lasagna."

Vanessa laid a hand on the door as it closed. Her braid was gone. Corey had been right the first time, short hair, not long. But the braid... probably just the folds of her shirt.

She smiled through the window. "Seven. Perfect!" Vanessa looked doe-eyed through the car at Corey, who had climbed in behind the wheel. Sam laid the pie on the floor between her feet. Vanessa said, "Would you mind if I took the shortcut home?" She nodded towards the back yard.

Corey thought of the path, and the bees. She must know about them, and he didn't want to drag this talk out any longer. "Go ahead. Thanks for the pie!"

Sam added, "See you tonight!"

Vanessa smiled and wiggled her fingers goodbye before heading towards the path out back. Corey started the car and said, "That was odd, but nice."

Sam laid her hand on his leg, gave it a squeeze. "Welcome to Green Acres." When she laughed, Corey thought it was the most beautiful sound in the world.

II

"It's not exactly a family recipe. I always use the one on the package of pasta. But," Sam shrugged, blushing, "if it works, why change it?"

Corey didn't think his wife had ever talked this much during a meal. *Gushing* was never a word he'd attributed to her, but that's what she was doing in her way after

Vanessa's compliment. Their neighbor wore the same dark dress as this morning, still buttoned to the neck. Her hair, he was relieved to notice, remained short.

"Well, my compliments to the *packagers* then." Vanessa took another forkful into her mouth, chewed slowly. She sat at the corner of the table nearest Samantha, Abby beside her and Corey at the far end. She'd moved her chair a bit closer to Sam before settling in to eat. Corey had to resist the urge to read any meaning into this, other than simple neighborliness.

"My Mom's a good cook," Abby said as she cut a too-big slab from her lasagna and tried to shove the whole thing into her mouth, leaning over the plate to let whatever wouldn't fit fall back safely. Vanessa laughed, laid the tips of her fingers on the girl's shoulder.

"I guess so. Those stuffed cheeks are the best compliment any cook could want."

Abby began to laugh but realized she'd lose the glob if she did, so only nodded. Vanessa turned her attention back to Sam. She wasn't ignoring Corey, not exactly, but her focus was primarily on his wife. Sam enjoyed the attention. When Abby was born, she'd left her job as executive secretary, trying her hand at the stay-at-home-mom career. Corey's programming job at the same company paid well enough, and they had good benefits. Since then, her interaction with the adult world was limited to the occasional visit from friends. Maybe this would be a good thing, seeing how she spoke so easily with Vanessa.

He swallowed his final bite and asked, "So, do you work in the area?"

Vanessa turned cool blue eyes at him before her smile returned, warm as ever. "I work out of my home, actually. Freelance." She shrugged, and at Corey's blank nod she tapped her fork on the plate and said, "I do websites for people, sometimes maintain them. I dabble in jewelry, too."

Sam chimed in. "You make jewelry? I was thinking of trying that some day." She looked around the kitchen. "Something other than laundry all day would be nice."

Corey may as well have disappeared after that. Vanessa and Sam talked for fifteen minutes about the process, their neighbor offering to come over one day and give Sam a few tips. Now and then her hand alighted on Samantha's when making a point, never lingering. Corey focused on the spoken words rather than any nonverbal cues. In truth, he would have been more interested in her web work but said nothing, pretended to be interested in settings and wire shaping. Abby listened intently, interjecting her own comments on necklaces and earrings. These were welcomed by Vanessa with an interest too intense, in Corey's mind, to be more than polite inclusion in the conversation. Corey settled into collecting plates, rinsing and settling them into the dishwasher.

When he had nothing left to do, he said, "Coffee?"

Vanessa thought about it a moment, said, "If it's decaf, that sounds wonderful."

He nodded, lost himself in measuring enough for all three of them. He leaned against the counter, watching the women talk until the coffee belched its completion. Sam got up from the table as he poured, kissed him on the cheek with a, "Thank you, Honey," (three words he appreciated more than he could have expressed at the moment).

"I want one," Abby said. Samantha took down a fourth mug. Into this she poured some apple juice out of the fridge.

Corey turned to Vanessa. "How do you like yours?"

"Black," she said.

"Three blacks, then," relieved he didn't have to explain why there was no cream in the house. "How about we sit in the living room?"

So, they moved into the other room. Vanessa took the smaller chair by the fireplace, Abby its twin across the room near the door, which allowed Sam and Corey to share the couch. He noticed Vanessa staring at the clock, wondering if she would offer a compliment on it. If that happened, he'd know she was full of shit.

There he was, being cynical again. Why couldn't he just take her at face value? She was a nice person; that was it.

She has a crush on your wife, he thought. So unexpected was the idea, he must have made a face. "Corey, you OK?"

His back stiffened. Rolling his shoulders, trying to force himself to relax, he said, "Sorry, back's a bit sore from all the yard work." Not a total lie, but he still felt like crap for needing an excuse.

Vanessa looked at him with half-closed lids, as if to say, *I know what you were thinking.*

What the hell *was* he thinking?

Sam said, "Corey, the clock's a bit slow, isn't it?"

He nodded, grateful for the distraction. "Yea, I noticed that this morning. Probably need to wind it better."

Vanessa looked back down at the clock, "It looks like an antique. Does it take batteries?"

"A key," he said, deciding then he didn't want to mention where he'd found it, though unsure *why*. "I didn't wind it much last night. Meant to do it this morning but we were in a rush."

She nodded absently, staring intently at the ugly thing. She still hadn't told them how beautiful it was. One point for the neighbor.

Sam asked, "Do you attend the other church?"

Vanessa looked at her, smiled. "No. I'm a Druid, actually."

"A Druid? What's that?"

Vanessa laughed and waved one hand as if to dispel interest. "Mostly touching trees and having sex in the woods." His wife laughed and covered her mouth in embarrassment.

"Mommy," Abby whispered, "she said a bad word."

Vanessa leaned towards the girl. "You're absolutely right, young lady. I apologize."

Abby nodded, please with the apology, or perhaps simply with being called *young lady*.

Sex in the woods, Corey thought, finding his brain moving in a dangerous direction. He looked back at the clock. "Maybe I should try winding - "

"I really should be going," Vanessa said, then abruptly stood. "I've sponged off your hospitality too long."

Everyone else rose from their seats, though more in reaction to the suddenness of her movements than in agreement. Vanessa pulled Samantha into a loose embrace. "Dinner was wonderful. My turn next time."

Sam hadn't blushed this much since their honeymoon. She nodded, said, "That would be nice." Vanessa ruffled Abby's hair, then gave Corey the same loose hug. She was feather light in his arms, barely there before moving away. Maybe it was because of her Druid remark, but he had the impression of fallen leaves, the smell of Autumn surrounding him, fleeting, now gone. Probably some brand of perfume.

They walked her to the kitchen after she insisted on using the backyard path again. "I have good night vision, and it's almost a full moon."

Not until they'd stepped onto the porch did Abby remember dessert. "Wait! We didn't have pie!"

Sam stopped. "That's right! Can you stay just a little longer?"

Vanessa considered for a moment, then, "How about I come by..." she looked sideways at some invisible planner in her head, "...Tuesday afternoon? We could share it then? It *should* keep. I really have to get back," again a pause and sideways look, "some maintenance I'd promised to do for the town website."

Corey wanted to ask more about that, but his role had been relegated to the background so much tonight, he stayed quiet.

"Tuesday should be OK. Abby and I will be puttering around the yard, planting. Can you come for lunch?"

The woman looked about to hug her again, but only nodded. "Lunch Tuesday then." She wiggled her fingers at Abby before trotting down the steps. They watched her shadow move onto the path and disappear. Corey would be working Tuesday. He explained this when they got back inside and cut himself a slice of the pie over the half-hearted objections of his wife.

He'd completely forgotten about the clock.

Vanessa

"Druid," Vanessa whispered to no one. She allowed herself a quiet laugh. The idea would have been funny, if it hadn't been such an unexpected statement. The imaginative mind could go into overdrive when it was needed. She looked up at the stars, so brilliant out here away from the lights of the city, free of the constant sheet of haze lingering over everything like a bad odor. She looked down, stepped along the path, breathing slowly and bringing herself into better tune with the stillness. What the hell was she doing out here? There were coyotes, snakes, God knew what else. She *needed* to be here, though, *away* for a while. She'd head inside soon, start it all over again. The Unions had such a perfect plot of land here, a corner of paradise tucked away, only for them. The idea was calming, and a little sad.

This sadness was nothing Vanessa could dwell on. She had a job to do. As real as the leaf she held between the fingers of her outstretched hand – hoping it wasn't poison ivy – the world Corey Union knew was an illusion, a veneer laid over a reality of death, blood running like an underground river, coming soon to the surface. She imagined it would break loose over them, directed in a macabre way by Hank Cowles. The old man should have no power, *deserved* no power. Not like this. As much as she felt the need to protect Corey, it was a struggle to remember that Hank Cowles had no real influence over her, or her actions. *Corey*, yes, there was no question Cowles – if not the man himself then certainly his existence – had an influence, like a wound that would reopen if she let it.

And Corey *was* going to let it. The simple act of eventually winding the damned clock again would be like unlocking the door for the old man to step inside. At least, Corey's interpretation of the old man. Vanessa needed to know the real Hank Cowles better. Hopefully Thursday, if Chen approved. Of course he *had to*, he'd *promised*. This was her week, her time.

She rubbed her hands across her arms, looked around at the forest's dark shapes wavering in front of other, darker shadows. Why was she so afraid to be outside like this, away from the house even for a little while?

Samantha Union's reaction to her presence was interesting, an eagerness in her attention, almost desperation. Maybe, deep down she understood what Vanessa had planned, who she truly was. Part of Samantha *wanted* to be pulled away from the family. Maybe Corey understood more than he let on, feeding some line into the river, seeing how it played out.

What would he do when it became obvious that Vanessa was going to destroy the paradise he'd created, almost as thoroughly as Hank Cowles had done before and will again? Corey would never see her as a friend, let alone anything *more* than a friend. Vanessa turned around, looked at the lights of the Union house distant through the trees. He was going to *despise* her.

Her chest felt like it was folding in on itself, over an empty center where her heart used to be. A black hole sucking her in until there was nothing left but --

Stop it! You're no better than his wife, hiding poetry under the bed! This is a job and nothing more. Grow the hell up and get to work!

Get to work.

That was the final sentence, no matter what she thought about the man. She needed to get to work destroying Corey Union, with *love*, before Hank Cowles could do the same in his own terrible way. He was the *Destroyer of Worlds*. Cowles did it with hate, arriving like a distant thunderstorm rising on the horizon, and there wasn't a damned thing anyone could do to stop it. Except Vanessa. Maybe this time she could reach in and save *someone* before the storm passed over and wiped everything clean. Like it did before. Over and over, the cycle never ended. Vanessa wouldn't be able to save Samantha or her beautiful daughter. When this ended, they would be dead, but Corey had a chance, always had a chance, if Vanessa kept her head and remembered all of this was for him. *Him*, not her.

She fiddled with more leaves, thought about the clock. Nothing but an empty, ugly box but Corey would wind the stupid thing, eventually; nothing she could do about it right now. She hadn't insinuated herself into his world enough, yet. He could wind it one more time. After that, however, it had to unwind and die, forever and ever.

A buzzing sound pulled her attention away from the house lights. She turned towards the gloom beyond the path. Just some wasps sending out a warning before settling in for the night. Probably from the old shed, lost and forgotten out there somewhere at the edge of the property. Not *entirely* forgotten, she remembered. Corey knew about it. That's where he'd found his little key.

Something shifted up ahead on along the path. A white blur, like a miniature ghost. *Nurse Charles*, she thought, then cursed under her breath. It could not be the dog. Why was she acting like such a frightened child?

The white shape growled, two lights glistened and reflected the rising moonlight. Small eyes, on a small white dog –

"Stop it!" she shouted, too loudly, recoiling from the sound of her own voice. More quietly, she said, "Get a grip on yourself, for heaven's sake. The dog is not here! Not *anywhere*. This is *your* time, now."

Stating the obvious made her fell better. Vanessa was in control and if it took talking to herself in the woods to remember that, so be it. She looked again. No white blur ahead. No growling, no glowing orbs, no eyes.

Even so, she'd be a fool not to recognize the danger in what had just happened. She had less than a week to do what she had to do. Every moment she needed to be alert and rational. If she couldn't, she might as well dig a hole now and bury Corey Union in it. Because if she failed, he would be lost forever.

Corey
Sunday Night

Samantha watched him undress from her side of the bed, sheet pulled to her mouth like a little girl. Even so, Corey could tell his wife was smiling from the glint in her eyes. When he slid under the sheet, she let out a contented sigh and curled onto his chest. Her leg hooked around his, his arm under her, sliding lower, realizing she was naked. *Jungle Boy and Jungle Girl*, he thought. He tried not to get too worked up and end up not being able to sleep when she rolled over. But her fingertips slowly caressed the fine hairs on his belly. She wasn't helping matters.

Sam whispered, "She was nice." It took a moment before Corey understood she meant Vanessa; he was too distracted by those wandering fingertips.

"Yeah. You two got along well." His arousal became stronger, more urgent. *Down, Boy*, he thought, then understood it was okay. Sam slid on top of him, raised herself up and stretched her legs down the length of his own, moving slowly back and forth. She covered his mouth with kisses, moving to his neck, hips always in motion, sending him into mad gasps. She was breathing deeply, too, when she reached down, guided him into her. She leaned back, nails digging into his chest.

He came quickly, *too* quickly maybe, though he had the impression she'd already climaxed herself.

She collapsed on top of him, arms and legs snaked around him, not letting him out, kissing and making contented sounds against his skin. He resisted the urge to say something stupid like, *Wow*, settled on running his hands along her back and legs, enjoying her presence, the softness of her on top of him.

Eventually they moved apart, and an hour later, she was fast asleep beside him. Corey lay awake, right arm wrapped around her. The world drifted in and out of focus. He should have collapsed into sleep; he always *did* after sex but this time, as soon as he began to sink lower something pulled him to the surface. A memory, a nagging feeling that he was forgetting something.

He slowly pulled his arm away from Sam's body and rolled over, reluctantly checking the time. Just after eleven-thirty. He closed his eyes, tried to relax. That was when he heard them. With one ear muffled by the pillow, his sense of direction was skewed. It sounded as if the wasps were outside the bedroom window. It was open, but the sound through the screen should have been louder if they were there. He waited, wondering if they were in the attic.

Wasps slept at night, didn't they?

Their heady noise reminded him of the shed. The key. The clock.

I forgot to wind it.

Not a thought that would send him jumping from the bed, however. He could always wind it tomorrow morning, reset the time. He let the sound drift past like the wind, imagined his body sinking into the mattress, legs liquid, muscles relaxed....

Sleep came, but only as fitful flashes of dreams. Abby running in the back yard, the sun blazing, the scene shifting, the decrepit barn's roof collapsing, Sam's body on top of him, the walls of the barn folding in, Vanessa's body on top of him, replacing his wife, black and white swarms roiling out of the destroyed shed like smoke, buzzing in rage –

His eyes opened with a start. Corey focused on the digital clock beside him. Three Twenty-One. He swallowed, still dreaming, still hearing the wasps.

Not a dream. The sound was still going, louder now, angry and...

"Shit." He pulled the dead weight of his body out of bed, feeling around for his bathrobe. The sound's direction was more focused now that he was standing. Down the hall.

Corey hesitated in the doorway. If the wasps had gotten inside the house he didn't want to stir them up. The hall nightlight revealed nothing moving along the walls. He walked forward, head cocked to gauge where the sound was coming from. Past Abby's closed door. The sound remained ahead of him, keeping its distance. It had to be coming from the living room. He hadn't opened the fireplace flue, but someone might have.

What was it about this place and wasps?

On his left, the kitchen was vaguely illuminated by the blue numbers on the microwave. Corey flipped the light switch controlling the lamps on either side of the couch.

The living room filled with light, and the sound of the wasps stopped.

Finger still on the switch, he scanned the room for movement, waited for the sound to return.

It did not. He resisted the urge to turn off the lights again to see if the buzzing started up. If that happened, Corey didn't like what that might imply about his sanity. He left the light on and walked across the room, tapped the glass doors of the fireplace. Nothing. Giving the clock only a cursory glance, he knelt down and opened the doors.

Nothing but new bricks, black smudges where they'd lit a small fire last weekend to cure the concrete. He considered, briefly, reaching up to test the flue trap, but decided that wouldn't be the smartest choice at the moment. Maybe in the daylight, when the world seemed less surreal. He closed the doors.

Content for the time being that the wasps were gone, Corey sat on the hearth, finally giving the clock and its silent, screaming boy more attention. He picked it up. Again his hands moved under the base rather than try to hold or touch the figure presenting the time with such enthusiasm. He rested it on his lap and wound the key, stopping only when resistance built to the point that any more might damage the mechanism. He adjusted the time ahead a few minutes, as well. The ticking was louder, now, almost happy, *like a dog finally getting water*, Sam might say.

Corey laid the clock back on the hearth and watched it for a few more seconds. At least it didn't chime every hour. Nothing else moved on it save the hour and minute hands. The creepy figure kept to the same position unlike his dancing Swiss cousins. Even so, Corey wished his Dad was still around to see the thing working after all this time.

Something tapped against the glass behind him. Corey turned around and pulled the brass handle, opening the rightmost door.

The fireplace was full of yellow wasps. They crawled inside the house, thumb-sized yellow bodies with short, stubby wings and pulsing abdomens, blending and contrasting with each other as they spilled onto the hearth. Corey fell backwards onto the carpet and crab-crawled a few feet away. The flow of insects poured over the clock, covering the face and the screaming figure.

The inside of the fireplace was an undulating mass of black and yellow. The angry buzzing he'd heard earlier did not return, save a quick flit as one or the other shook its wings in some indefinable language. The did not fly, merely marched out silently, groggy, perhaps, from the late hour.

Corey didn't want to wait for them to realize he was there. He moved slowly backwards, keeping his motion as fluid as possible. He should close the fireplace door, but that wasn't possible. Not right now. A few minutes ago he'd considered reaching up to check the flue. His arms crawled with the thought of them over his arms, covering *him* instead of the figure on the base of the clock.

When he reached the juncture of the living room and kitchen, he got to his feet. He thought, *Now what?*

Abby... he couldn't let her wander out here without somehow containing these things. Their flow had ebbed. A few remained, wandering across the hearth, but the clock supported the bulk of them, turning it into a fat yellow box, undulating with a thousand small bodies, all of them crawling, exploring, buzzing lightly as they moved.

They suddenly stopped, frozen as if time had been paused. Corey didn't know enough about wasps to see this as a good or bad thing. *Bad*, probably. He imagined thousands of multi-faceted eyes fixed on him, tiny stingers pushing in and out, filling with yellow poison, preparing to –

"Aw, shit." He reached out and found the light switch for the kitchen, heart pounding too fast, too *loud*. Always watching the clock, wondering if their combined weight might topple the thing off the hearth and shatter their calm, send them into flight to finish what had started in the shed. *These aren't the same bees*, he thought. *These are yellow.* He turned on the kitchen light, then waited. If they swarmed, where would he go? *Abby's room. Protect Abby.*

How he'd protect her wasn't a question he wanted to think about.

The wasps remained motionless. Maybe they'd fallen asleep. Maybe they'd worn their little bodies out crawling to the clock, like exhausted penitents reaching a temple, falling to their knees...

Stop it; just move!

Corey stepped into the kitchen, listening intently for any changes behind him. Nothing yet. He opened the pantry door, moved aside a stack of rags and plastic *Stop N Shop* grocery bags until he found the can of wasp spray. It was old, unpacked from the house in Worcester and tucked far back on the shelf. In his hand, its half-full weight offered minimal comfort. But it was something. There was no way in hell he'd spray them, not unless they attacked. At least then he could take a few out before....

OK, focus. Next step, get Abby out of her room and into his to make sure she didn't wander out here alone. He returned to the hall and gave the fireplace a quick over-the-shoulder glance.

The wasps were gone.

The clock and the figure shone in the lamplight with no sign that a swarm of wasps had a moment earlier covered every inch of them. Corey didn't move, except to pull the red cap free from the spray can. His hand was slick with sweat. He looked around. Nothing crawling along the ceiling, nor on the couch or chairs or tables. Not that he could see everywhere from this vantage point. The right glass door was open and the fireplace's back wall was visible. Nothing.

Where the hell could they have gone? To get back up the chimney so quickly they would have had to fly. He'd have heard it. Wouldn't he?

Corey let the cap fall soundlessly to the carpet and switched hands, wiping his right against the bathrobe while he walked around the room, holding his only line of defense before him like a crucifix. Nothing. Not a single bee.

The buzzing returned when he approached the fireplace, echoing down from the flue. They *were* in there. Going back outside? He knelt with the can in front, opened the glass door on the left. He leaned forward and looked up. The buzzing was getting louder again. *Coming back.* Corey thought of Abby, mostly to give him the nerve, whispered a curse then reached up, into the flue. Expecting the crunch of their bodies under his fingers and a hundred hot jabs of stingers, he found the handle, felt only cold iron and the loop of the handle. The whine of the bees was loud and urgent.

He yanked the flue closed, dulling the approaching sound.

The room was silent. No *ping, ping* of the them hitting the trap.

Now that the immediate shock had passed, Carey noticed how fast his heart was running. They may be out of the house, but they were in the chimney, no question. He closed the glass doors. It was all he could do until someone could come and spray with something more potent than six year-old *Raid.*

After a quick exploration through the kitchen's *stuff* drawer, Corey returned with a note written on the back of Sam's shopping list pad with thick black marker.

BEES! DO NOT TOUCH DOORS!

Abby wouldn't be able to read it, but he'd have Sam explain what it said. He taped the sheet across the doors, then sat on the floor against the couch for another ten minutes, making sure they couldn't find another way in. His eyes began to close, open, close again. Corey shuffled back to bed just after four o'clock only to be jolted awake by the radio's static at six. Sam stirred, then rolled herself back into sleep. Corey didn't have a problem getting out of bed. Before starting his morning routine, he went back into the living room.

The sun was up, but not Abby. Morning light played through the front window, across the clock and fireplace doors. The note was there, and no wasps. Corey crouched down, listened, heard nothing but the cacophony of birds' songs outside the windows.

Seeing the note, taped a bit cockeyed, at least proved he hadn't dreamt the whole thing. He re-taped the note straighter and let out the breath he'd been holding. *Living in the country*, he decided. Something he'd have to get used to. It had been a bizarre experience, but that could be attributed to the insane hour when he'd had to deal with it. Maybe a little stress, too, new house, world going to hell. *Keep it together, Corey. People need you to be strong, remember?*

He tightened the sash of his robe and headed back down the hall. He'd wake Sam after his shower, let her know what had happened. Meanwhile, time was wasting. The drive to work was twenty minutes longer from here. He'd been late the first couple of days. Not today. Wasp-haunted clock or not.

Monday

I

"Time is ticking and she keeps on licking," the old man sang, tunelessly, as he walked. His eyes squinted whenever the sun flashed bright through the green canopy above him. Hank Cowles still enjoyed visiting this part of town, although less so than years earlier, when the paved road he and Nurse Charles currently traversed was nothing but a thin vein worming through the woods. Like the path which snaked between the Union property and that of the sex-starved nymph who thought herself his rival. Maybe she *was* the angel sailing on feathery wings to save the day as she proclaimed. Maybe, in a twisted sort of way. To Hank, Vanessa was nothing but a meddlesome bitch who would get hurt if she kept sticking her pouty lip where it didn't belong.

The small dog beside him sneezed in agreement.

A cloud of gnats drifted around Hank's head in a lazy drift. Their season was ending. These days belonged to the flocks of dragonflies having a wonderful time decimating the gnats' ranks. Hank casually swatted aside a particularly thick clump in the air before him, for no other reason than he enjoyed disrupting patterns of any kind.

The driveway up ahead was discernable only as a break in the trees along the road. The Union family home, its owners squatting on this once primal land. They'd been personally chosen by Hank Cowles and his dog from over thirty potential buyers who'd walked eagerly along its uneven landscape, making an offer, then a second and third.

Hank had chosen this family. As a result, the lovely, lonely creature Vanessa immediately began slithering her way between them like the garden serpent she was. No doubt working her charms on Corey, or his wife. Maybe both. Hank raised an eyebrow at *that* picture. He often wondered how a creature like her could have such a screwed up sense of love, physical or not. Life was like that, he supposed, no matter what part of the ground it wormed itself up from. Life began with individuals; individuals formed groups; groups to civiliz –

Something wet splashed on his ankle. Hank looked down. He was standing in the middle of the road, lost as usual with his philosophizing. Nurse Charles's small back leg was raised up as she pissed against his ankle. Hank watched this little attention-grabber and tried to decide why the act seemed so wrong. Anatomically, perhaps. Did bitches pee like that? He was pretty sure they squatted, and was equally sure Charlie was female. This question was far more gripping in his mind than the fact that the dog was peeing on his sock and pant leg in the first place. Still, he considered kicking the thing into the bushes, stomping on its little chest, then again on its head, crushing its neck....

The Shih-Tzu lowered the leg and sat on its haunches. It opened its mouth and began to pant, the dog pantomime of a smile. She looked so cute, Hank thought, sitting there smiling. Hank understood the look, as clear as if the animal had spoken. *Fantasize all you want*, the dog didn't say, *but go any further than that and I'll tear your head off, you damned waste of breath.*

Something like that. He laughed, the act no more than a twitch at the corner of his mouth and a quick exhalation of breath through his nose. For him, it was a guffaw. Hank raised his own leg, slowly, gave it a shake. The stain wasn't too bad. Not the first time Charlie had done something like this. He tended to drift in his mind, never focusing on the task at hand for very long.

"Thanks," he said. Along this quiet street, even in this modern time with the occasional house marring the old forest like a zit, there was rarely a car passing by at eleven o'clock on a weekday morning. Anyone with any place to go was already there.

Much like him and his dog.

"OK, Charlie," he said, "go do what you do best, eh?"

Nurse Charles wagged her stump of a tail and trotted towards the driveway. Hank lowered the foot he'd been holding aloft and added, louder, "I'm going home to wait for my call, and to change."

The dog continued merrily up the long driveway. Behind it, the road was empty, a deserted stretch of asphalt dappled in summer shade.

II

"What does this one say?" Abby held the piece of torn notebook paper out to her mother. Samantha took it between two gloved fingers and read the passage, to herself first, smiling at the image she thought she'd captured so clearly. She leaned back on her heels and read, "*Black soil, the soul of the earth, fed with water from sky and heart.*"

Abby smiled and took the paper back. "That's pretty." She stared at the pen scratches as if trying to decide which words were which. She'd be able to read them soon enough, Sam knew. Maybe even write her own.

Samantha leaned forward and dug a narrow groove in the dirt with the spade. "Right here, Sweetie." Abby hesitated, reluctant to give up her mother's words. "It's all right," Sam whispered. "They'll still be there, and here."

She poked the girl lightly on the forehead with her fingertip. It left a smudge of dirt like ashes.

Abby giggled, then laid the strip of paper reverently into the small grave. Samantha covered it with loam. Already her daughter had taken the next slip. "This one?"

Sam read that verse, then the next. For each, she allowed her daughter time to stare at the words as if committing them to memory, before prodding her to bury them in the garden.

Abby never asked why they did this, what the point of the ritual was. If she ever did, Sam wondered if she could honestly answer. She'd written the nine-line poem this morning over breakfast, once Corey was off to work. It was always easier to write when she didn't have to worry about him accidentally glimpsing something over her shoulder. She had to stop worrying so much. Her secret words, *secret life, secret dreams, secret strife*, was therapy. Her own, not Doctor Reilly's.

Why Corey could not be a part of it, Sam never completely understood, nor why *Abby* could be included. Of course, hiding the words from her daughter would prove impossible. To Abby, it was a game, a secret shared between them. Maybe that was wrong – Samantha was sure it *was* wrong to ask her daughter to not to repeat the poems to her father – but for now, it was right. She was more afraid of Corey learning that she was allowing Abby into her *inner sanctum*, but not him.

Finishing the poem this morning, she'd impulsively torn the page from the spiral notebook and on a whim, no conscious plan to do so, ripped each line into its own existence. Abby was impatient to get outside to the garden, and Sam at once understood her words would be fertilizer, growing into new life around the tomatoes and cucumbers – *if* she could get the plants to grow and mature in time. All of this, the writing and planting and growing of life, an artistic endeavor; maybe a way of secretly sharing it with Corey at the same time.

She wasn't crazy. In fact, she would *go* crazy if she didn't do it.

When they'd finished with the last strip, *the final literary funeral*, she thought, Sam sat fully on the ground in front of the small garden and nodded to Abby. The girl was holding an open packet of carrot seeds. They wouldn't grow very big in only half a season, but it would be good practice for next year. It would be fun to see how much they matured. Here she was, a grown woman, hiding her poetry under the bed, burying it line by line in the garden. And there was Corey, a grown man, with a recent, and at times quite extreme fear of the world.

A small white dog poked its muzzle against Samantha's left wrist. She jerked sideways in surprise. The dog didn't run away. It looked at her, small pink tongue sliding back and forth over white teeth, a smiling pant. She thought, *Corey's afraid of dogs, too*, a fact neither of them wanted to admit openly in front of their daughter. The stub of their visitor's tail wagged joyously.

Abby said, "Mommy! A doggie, a doggie, a doggie!" The girl dropped the packet of seeds. They spilled onto the grass beside the low stake-and-string fence. *Seeds scattered and sown*, Sam sang in her mind.

With no concept of *strange dog protocol*, Abby immediately scooped the Shih-Tzu into her arms like a doll. The dog raised its muzzle and pelted the girl with licks, tail wagging faster. "Hey, girl! You're so cute! Can we keep her?" The dog raised its front paws in a tangled half-dance. Abby laughed. Sam decided the poor animal was probably trying to free itself rather than be cute.

"Abby, don't squeeze it so hard. And no, we can't keep her. I'm sure she belongs to someone."

Abby let the dog drop back onto four legs but did not stop patting it, scratching it, running her hand along its curly white back. She whispered into its ear, "What's your name, Sweetie?"

Sam smiled. Abby was using one of the nicknames she and Corey had for her. She ran her own fingertips over the soft, slightly tangled hair, found the collar and worked the tags around to the back of the dog's neck. The animal didn't mind, too intent on playing with its new friend.

Sam read the ID tag. Her brow furrowed.

"I think she belongs to a nurse..." Then she saw Hank Cowles' name and realized *Nurse Charles* was the dog's name. "She belongs to Mister Cowles."

"Who's he?"

"I don't remember." Sam recognized the name, but couldn't remember exactly.... She double-checked the dog's name, just to be sure, before continuing, "And this," she released the tag and gave the mutt an affectionate, highly amused tousle on the head, "is Nurse Charles!" *What a stupid, wonderful name*, she thought to herself.

Abby put the dog's face between her hands and said, in all seriousness, "Nice to meet you, Miss Charles."

Sam didn't bother correcting her, but looked around the yard, expecting to see the dog's owner coming their way. No sign, though. She said, "Mister Cowles must be looking for her. Let's go around front, see if he's there."

They stood, Sam more slowly as her muscles worked out the stiffness from kneeling so long, brushed the dirt off the front of their jeans. Nurse Charles walked merrily around the girl, wanting to play.

The air smelled wet. A few dark gray clouds drifted amid lighter, whiter ones. It was raining somewhere. Not here. Not yet.

The threesome walked around the house. No sign of the owner. Then she remembered that Hank Cowles used to own this land. In fact, he'd sold it to them. With this came the memory of how abrasive the old man had been the one time they'd met, when he'd insisted upon a face-to-face before accepting the offer on the property. They'd never met him again, not even during the closing. Still, he'd be happy to know his dog was OK. They let Nurse Charles come inside only long enough to call the number embossed on her ID tag. She had to make sure the dog was outside again, preferably back with her owner, before Corey got home.

Fear of bombs, she thought, *fear of dogs. Cerberus' multiple heads rising over the horizon to devour the world.*

She found her notebook, still open on the kitchen table, and wrote the thought down before making the call.

III

Corey closed the electronic file he'd been reviewing, realized he'd forgotten to make the update needed for the next test cycle and opened the file again. All morning he'd been distracted, thinking of clocks and bees and bad dreams. Mostly of dreams. What was real? What had he only imagined? In the light of day with other normal, *real* lives flurrying around him, he'd begun to consider that most of the morning's nightmare with the wasps had been just that, a nightmare. A waking dream, though he could not deny the bees' existence. They *had* been real, but to what extent? Probably a nest stuffed in the chimney like a lost Christmas toy. The note was taped to the glass doors, *and* he remembered writing it. He'd been awake through it all but.... But reality didn't step sideways like that, not in the sun-bright world that he lived in. That's exactly what it had felt like. A twisted dream crawling though a tear in his world, swarming over the clock. So, then, he'd been asleep, or half-asleep. His addled brain twisted the events to fit how it saw the rest of the world - dangerous, looming like a thunderstorm. Nothing about how his mind worked lately was much of a surprise. Spend so much effort avoiding reality and it'll find other cracks to seep in, like gas.

This revelation had come when Corey tried to condense what had happened to a sleepy-eyed Sam this morning. As a child, his mother used to tell him that if he told the details of a nightmare, it would become less frightening. It would not come back. And it worked. Like this morning. The more details he remembered the more ludicrous it sounded. He'd edited most out before they reached his lips, telling her there was probably a nest in the flue and that Sam had to make sure Abby didn't touch the doors. Nice and normal, the way things would always be from now on.

"...count fifty-two dead, a hundred hospitalized in what had been dubbed the worst –"

"Headphones, Andrew," Corey said over the half wall of his cubicle. He may have spoken too loudly but didn't care. They weren't supposed to have radios at their desks without headphones. Rules were rules. He was tired of people assuming everyone else gave a shit what misery transpired the night before.

Andrew Booth's deep voice returned over the wall, "Wasn't me." Then, louder, "Rob, headphones..."

"What?" Robert Schard's more distant voice from the cube next to Andrew's. "Oh, sorry." The news report cut off at the words, "...president has reit-"

Silence. *Before the storm*, Corey thought. All his life he'd had little phobias: dogs, spiders – he probably needed to add bees to that list – but this one had taken such a tight hold on him recently. Sam knew about it. Apparently, so did Abby. They did what they could, but it was easier to avoid CNN and MSNBC at home, especially with the *Hundred Things* list to distract him. Not here, surrounded by over thirty-plus coworkers with instant access to bad news on the Internet.

Corey could remember the moment he'd picked up this new hysteria. Just over two years ago, not long after Sam's miscarriage. Flipping the car radio to NPR after kissing his two year old daughter and beautiful, sad wife goodbye. Another school shooting followed by the requisite death count of troops overseas. As the reporter counted the bodies, Corey heard another meaning lurking under the words. *You're next, and everyone you love.*

Every third world country seemed to hate Corey Union personally, and half of them were developing nuclear capability. That day, the talking heads taunted him from the mounted television in the W&G employee cafeteria, debating between themselves when the first mushroom cloud would appear on home soil, smiling and spewing half-truths with so much eagerness.

Maybe it wasn't a phobia. Maybe he was simply afraid. Everyone was. Unlike them, Corey didn't want to waste the time he had left, a year, a week, watching the world's destruction approach, staring like a deer caught in a train's single-eyed light. All he wanted was to spend a happy, normal life with Sam and Abby. His parents had done that, and their parents before them.

Corey tried to focus on the contents of the file on his screen. He made the change he was supposed to do last time, double-checked himself then clicked *Save*. He submitted the batch job, sent the resulting file as a spreadsheet to Kathrina in the QA group.

"How's the new house coming?"

Andrew's voice was so sudden above the cubicle's half wall, Corey visibly flinched. The black man standing over the wall smiled and raised his hands before him. "Shit, C. Sorry." He laughed. "Deep in thought planning the deforestation of Hillcrest?"

Corey managed to smile back. Andrew knew better than to talk current events around him. "Not deforestation," he said in reply. "Up there, we call it a controlled burn."

Andrew folded his muscular arms over the cubical wall. He looked tired. Corey said, "You look like you had a busy weekend. Sleep much?"

A shrug. "Not much last night. My mom's into painting lately, and gave me her latest one Saturday for the apartment. A monkey hanging on some branches. Creepy thing-- eyes that follow you around the room."

"Put it in the attic."

"Don't have one. Besides, man, she's my mother."

Corey nodded. "I miss her hot dogs."

Andrew nodded and said, "Me, too." Booth's parents were locally famous. For decades they ran the *Hot Dog Dandy Truck,* parked every day between eleven and twelve-thirty outside the building, proudly directing customers' attention towards the W&G building and their successful son who worked on the fourth floor. After Max Booth died in a bizarre accident with the truck one morning, Andrew's mother drifted into lonely retirement. No more *Hot Dog Dandy* dogs.

Corey absently tapped the keyboard's space bar as he talked. "Abby's enjoying the open space, I guess. Hopefully she'll make some friends soon." He thought of their new neighbor. Before he could stop himself, he added, "Sam's got a new friend, too. Some woman who lives behind us on the adjoining property." A flash from the dream, not his wife but Vanessa on top of him. Just a dream, and a semi-normal one at least, not the half-waking kind with bees. He hoped it was only that and not some lurid fantasy.

Andrew's smile faded a notch, reading something into Corey's statement, maybe. Then he nodded and the world, which had tipped for a second, righted itself once more. Corey was reading too much into *everything*. The guy was probably bored with the conversation, itching to talk about the war or the latest bombing, the back and forth saber rattling between the Powers, the latest child wrapped in explosives running into a crowd.

Andrew said, "Wow, look at that." He was staring behind Corey, at the bank of windows overlooking Main Street.

Corey heard the *tap-tap-tap* against the glass and swiveled around in his chair. Hundreds of fat, round bees were colliding with the window. Black and white bodies hitting the glass then spinning, confused, trying for purchase on the smooth surface. They were quickly knocked free by the new wave, and more after them. A cloud of bees raining towards him, striking the invisible barrier, bouncing off –

Corey covered his face with his palms, bit his tongue to keep from shouting.

Andrew laughed, "What the hell? You the Wicked Witch or something?"

His statement was so bizarre Corey lowered his hands and looked up. Andrew nodded his head sideways. "Since when are you afraid of rain?"

Corey looked. No fat bees. Raindrops, angled by some breeze unfelt inside the building, splattering against the glass before sliding away and making room for the next wave. *Rain.* A heavy downpour, so thick that details of the bank building across the street blurred away. Already it was thinning. A passing cloudburst.

Just rain.

Corey took in a deep breath, held it while he looked down between his knees. His face burned. What the hell must people think of him? He let the breath out.

Andrew shifted uneasily behind the wall. "Sorry if I spooked you, guy. It's just that we weren't supposed to get rain today... you OK?"

Corey nodded. "Sorry. Didn't sleep much last night, either." Andrew didn't appear to need more explanation. After muttering that they both needed to go to bed earlier tonight, he sank into his own three-walled world.

Alone again, Corey tapped the space bar. His computer beeped; the spreadsheet had finished downloading. He tried to remember who he was supposed to mail it to while trying his best not to look behind him, at the rain fading to an occasional wet tap against the glass.

IV

Barely twenty minutes after the call, Hank Cowles emerged around the side of the house. Sam had been poking holes along the tilled and mulched garden while they waited, dropping seeds into the holes and carefully covering them over. Abby had become frustrated that Nurse Charles would not come inside the garden with her. She was currently running around the yard with the ecstatic little dog, waving a stick over its head. The dog barked and chased her, trying to jump high enough to get hold of it.

"Mommy! Miss Charles's daddy is here!"

When Sam looked up, Hank Cowles was smiling and waving, whether at Abby or the dog she couldn't tell. He was a tall man, stooped, with unseasonably long polyester sleeves buttoned at the wrist. What little hair he had was grouped in tufts along the top and back of his scalp. Nurse Charles barked and ran excited circles around the old man before returning to Abby, jumping up and finally getting hold of the stick. The interchange gave Samantha time to brush herself off and extricate herself from the garden. Hank met her halfway.

"Mrs. Union," he said with an odd expression: half-smile, half-snarl. She remembered that look from their other meeting, suggesting perhaps a minor stroke in his past.

"Mister Cowles," Sam said, smiling widely as if to make up for the man's own incomplete grin. "You got here fast."

His grip was cool and dry compared to Sam's heated, sweaty palms. A wasp circled his head a moment, large like the one she'd seen on the door Saturday. It flew away but another, or maybe it was the same, took its place. Where were these things coming from?

Hank reached into the pocket of his chinos, produced a cell phone, waggling it between his fingers. "My only phone," he said, slipping it back into the pocket. "I was merely on the other end of your road. I enjoy taking walks, especially in the good weather."

"The tag said you live on Main Street," she said. "That's quite a long walk."

"What else is an old man like me going to do with so much time in the day? Besides, a trip across town to visit my property," he bowed his head, "actually, part of it is now yours, isn't it, has become a ritual for us. Charlie and me, I mean. I hope you don't mind."

"I don't blame you. It's so beautiful here."

His smile rose to something more genuine, revealing gaps where a few teeth had long fallen out. "It certainly is. I promise not to intrude on your privacy. But we do enjoy the road." He gestured towards the front, turned to Abby. "I see Charlie has a new friend. That's nice. Children need pets, don't you think?"

She watched the pair for a few seconds without replying. Finally, "Yes. Unfortunately, my husband's allergic." Not a lie, not really. He was allergic to pollen, ragweed. Not dogs. Not physically.

Hank made a noise in his throat. To Sam it sounded like a stifled laugh. "Allergic, or afraid. Many people have phobias, more so lately it seems. Everyone should have a dog."

Sam blinked. What the hell was he talking about? "He's allergic," she replied in a weak voice.

Hank turned, a small move, but now that he faced her, his height loomed. "He's afraid." The smile was gone.

Sam shook her head, not knowing what else to do. Hank counted off his next points on gnarled fingers. "Of dogs, cats, any animal, in fact, which displays a sentient thought. Anything he cannot control. You didn't know that, did you, that his eccentricities aren't relegated only to the canine family?"

A step back, putting more space between them. "Why are you saying that? Lots of people are nervous around dogs. Did he tell you something? When would you have talked?"

As if bored of the topic, Hank raised his arms towards the house and the slowly developing yard. "I see you've settled in well." He narrowed his eyes. "How much more are you planning on opening up?"

She assumed, *hoped*, he realized his rudeness and was trying to change the subject. Accusing Corey of being some frightened child, afraid of more than... *was* he afraid of cats? *Don't give his ranting any more thought!*

And what they did with the property wasn't any of his business, either. The land was thick with old trees, choking and competing with each other for room. A half acre was now cleared and usable; the other five and a half surrounded them like a tangled hedge. She shrugged and, with a stammering voice, hoping if she answered the question he'd just go away, *Hiding like a bird in the bushes, chirping its plea to go away, go away,* "We might go back a little more, if we decide to get a pool. But it's nice like this, p-peaceful." *Damn it!* She hadn't stammered since she was a child. She was taking him too seriously. The man was old, probably senile.

But was he dangerous? Samantha's throat was dry, legs heavy. *Don't show fear lest the wolves attack.*

The book of poetry was on the kitchen table, open and exposed.

"That it is," Hank said, nodding. "I don't suppose you've met anyone from town yet? Any neighbors?"

An image of *her*, the scent of Autumn filling her head. "Vanessa," she said, almost to herself. When she realized she'd answered his question aloud, Samantha took a full step away from him. Something was very wrong with all of this.

Hank stared past her, towards the rear of the yard. "Ah, Vanessa. She lives behind you, through the trees that way?"

Sam found herself picturing the woman's eyes, deep blue, almost black. Maybe they were black. Smell of the woods around her, dress buttoned to her neck.

What the hell was she doing? She and her daughter were alone with a crazy man. Hank stared down at her, again with that half-snarl. He pursed his lips, added, "Well, actually she doesn't *really* live there. It's all a rather complex illusion built and fed by - "

"She brought us pie!" She had to interrupt him, even if it meant talking gibberish. His words were confusing, making her dizzy. She blushed partly from embarrassment but mostly a growing frustration. She needed to make him go away, then get inside, write down the flitterings in her mind. *He stood judging me, judging us, like God over Adam, knowing too much, while the nurse circled and wrapped her child with strings that bound. Stop it, stop it!*

Any semblance of a grin on his face dropped, as if he'd run out of strength to maintain the pretense. "I don't mean to imply she's not real, of course." He shrugged his shoulders. "Anyway, can't say we've had much to do with each other. I'm a rather private man, after all. And, since I never actually *lived* here myself...." Two wasps zipped across the lawn toward him, veered away at the last minute. Sam followed their progress, and he followed her stare. "Bees and wasps, the workers of the world. *They* couldn't give a rat's ass what's happening in the outside world. Until, even for them, it's too late."

He knew about the wasps. She thought of the key, cradled a sudden protectiveness for Corey's little discovery.

He stared after the bees, towards the woods. His pale, almost colorless eyes were unfocused. "The bees are your friends, if you let them. If you don't bother them, try to squish them with a newspaper, they won't bother you." He blinked, looked down suddenly. "Right?"

"I suppose." The wasps were gone. She wanted *him* to be gone.

He clapped his dry hands together a couple of times. Nurse Charles bounded to his side. "Well, Charlie and I should be going. Don't want your husband to start... sneezing when he gets home." He laughed, a paper sound more like a wheeze. "Thank you for keeping an eye on the dog." He sighed. "Unfortunately, she loves to explore these woods. I have a feeling this won't be the last time you see her."

Abby ran up to them and hooked her arms around her mother's left leg. She said, "Miss Charles can come by any time!"

"That's good to know." Hank began to turn but suddenly stopped and snapped his fingers.

Please leave, Sam thought.

"In a moment," he said. She gasped, realizing she must have said the thought aloud. Hank leaned towards her. His breath was minty. "You need to remind your husband when he gets home to keep winding the clock, every day. He can't let it stop now that it's been started. It *cannot* stop, do you understand? He wishes he had control over his universe; well, now he's got it. All things move forward. All things come to an end." He straightened, raised his arms a little by his side. "You can write that one down in your book."

His smile was full now; no signs of stroke. His shoulders shook as he turned to leave, Nurse Charles at his heel.

Samantha was frozen, unable to move or stop herself from whispering, "What the hell are you talking about? How can you - "

"Mommy! Bad word!"

Hank laughed, kept on walking. He was nearly to the front corner of the house and out of sight when he shouted back to them, "Bad word, Mommy. Bad place." Then he and his dog were out of sight.

"Mommy?"

It took Samantha a few seconds to look down, kneel beside her daughter and give her a hug. Her head felt tight, daylight flashing around her like anger. "It's OK, Sweetie, I stood up too fast, that's all."

Abby was quiet for a moment, but finally accepted the excuse. "Miss Charles is a cute dog."

Corey was afraid of dogs, afraid of many things. The old man knew about them. And her book of poems. How could he know?

She squeezed Abby closer, wishing she didn't care, wishing she understood what was going on in that terrible man's head, and in her own. In this quiet moment, this vacuum left in Hank Cowles' absence, nothing felt real. Everything felt like a bad dream about to blink away.

V

Corey turned the key until the tension returned, tipped the clock back onto its base. He'd considered letting it wind down, just to spite the old bastard for terrorizing his family. Then he remembered the bees, didn't want to worry about them coming back. Just a dream. Any connection, no matter how thin, between them and the clock was only a remnant of that. But he was exhausted, and didn't want anything to keep him awake tonight. The clock was wound, the flue shut; no sign of the bees. Things were locked down and wound tight.

He looked up at Sam. "You think he was in the woods, spying on me when I found it?"

She'd been standing in the middle of the room, arms crossed, foot absently tapping out her frustration. At Corey's question, she moved forward and sat beside him on the hearth, leaned into his offered arm.

"I don't know. He *had* to be, but he also knew other things...." She looked up and around the room as if checking to make sure Abby wasn't around. But she'd had another fun day outside and gone to bed with no argument, after giving Corey all of the details of the visit over dinner. The dog and its owner, working in the garden with Mommy (giving Samantha a quick, smiling glance as she did, some secret passing between them), moving on to what she had eaten for lunch, when she took a nap. Not until she was settled in bed did Sam give him the truth of what had happened, what had been said. Most of it, at least. More than once she would stop mid-sentence, like now.

"Knew what?" he said.

"About how you feel, about dogs and such. He knew you were... that you didn't like dogs."

He quietly rocked for a minute, saying nothing, looking across the living room. "You mean that they scare the shit out of me for some reason I don't understand?"

She nodded, trying to hide the smile which crept across her face.

Corey cleared his throat. "I'd wager he knew about the nest in the old shed. All that talk of bees, not bothering them. Would have been nice to give us some warning."

"I think he's crazy."

"Sounds it. From what I remember of him, he was pretty old."

"Maybe." She stifled a yawn, then followed Corey when he moved to stand up.

He said, "Well, I wound the clock. That should make him happy." He bent down, gave the small, screaming man a tap on his head before moving towards the couch.

Sam hesitated, watched him plop down on the end by the remote. She was exposed now, on display as she'd been with Hank Cowles. *Like I will be...* she thought.

He finally noticed, put down the remote without turning on the TV. "What's the matter?"

"I'm sorry." Too late to stop, because he'll want to know what she was sorry for. And why would he care? He hadn't complained before. But... she was shaking, for heaven's sake. It made no sense. *No sense!* "I'm sorry that I don't let you read my poetry." She said it quickly, the words coming out without any thought. It was the only way. As soon it had left her mouth, it felt as if the statement would have spilled out on its own whether she'd changed her mind or not. "I love you, you know that right? I'm just... it's just private, something personal. Don't be angry." Tears welled but she dared not blink and make this a worse scene than it already would be. Even now, Samantha wasn't sure why any of this mattered. She pressed her lips together, feeling like an idiot, waiting for the scorn.

Waiting for the yellow.

What did that mean? *Yellow.* That was the color in her mind. *Scorn, sharp ridicule. Pain.*

Sure enough, it began. Corey was smiling.

He leaned against the side cushion, laid one arm along the back of the couch in invitation. "I'm not angry, Sam. It's personal, something you prefer to keep private between you and Abby." She sucked in a breath. He added, "I think it's kind of cute, a little secret between mother and daughter...."

Her world stopped. Everything was silent, like cotton in her ears. He knew about Abby? How? *Well, how else?* Too much to expect a four year-old to keep secrets from her Daddy.

Corey stood up, took her hand. "Sam, what's the matter? I swear it doesn't bother me. Why is this coming up now?"

She stared and let the tears fall free. Her face burned red, embarrassed. "She told you what I wrote?"

He shook his head, led her to the couch. She followed, but left some distance between them, sitting on the edge, ready to run. She stopped wondering why it mattered, only that it did. Her world, her mind, her secrets. "No," he said. "Just little comments she's made over the past few months, nothing specific. Enough so I understood. And I haven't read any of it myself, not intentionally." She stiffened, and he added quickly, "I mean, last year I was making the bed after doing laundry. I was going to flip the mattress over, saw the book. Looked through, then realized what it was. I assumed it wasn't something you wanted me seeing, though I can't say I understand why, so I put it back. Decided we didn't need to turn the mattress over after all." He shrugged, his own face red with the admission.

Flipped through, she thought, *like fingers through the underwear drawer, sniffing through her garbage.* No.

"Look, it's nothing. Writing is a private thing. I respect that. I'd be lying if I said I haven't been tempted to peek now and then but I swear I didn't!" He was about to say something else, caught himself, fell silent.

She didn't know what to say.

He wasn't laughing. *Sometime last year*, he'd said. She suddenly wanted to ask if he liked what he read, but then his true *face in yellow* would press forward from the mask, choking off her oxygen. It would be so close, tell her it was funny and isn't that cute and why didn't she cut her fingers so they wouldn't stain the paper any more than they had; *here let me help*....

She fell against him with loud, gasping sobs, lost in spinning thoughts which made no sense, no sense, until she was so far into it there was no turning back.

VI

Corey held his wife, his body shaking in time with her crying. His own tears were falling now, but he would not let her see them. Was she crying because he'd admitted seeing her poems, or that he knew she shared them with Abby? Maybe the simple fact that he made contact with her book, her *secret*, as unintentional as it was.

What *secret*, though? It wasn't a big deal. He'd never say that out loud; obviously, it was a big deal to her. He wanted to tell Sam how much he'd enjoyed what he'd read before he'd tucked the book away, dark as some of her lines might be, but she'd been traumatized enough for one night. No sense rubbing salt in the wound.

What troubled him most was *how* upset she was. Flashbacks to how things had been two years ago, when she'd lost the baby near the end of her first trimester. Statements from the doctors, how this was common and would not affect future pregnancies, did nothing to quell the sudden outpouring of grief. Such intense sorrow was normal, according to the therapist she'd seen a few times. Sam had fallen into a sad, lonely place which Corey could never fully visit as a father, painful as those days had also for him, too. Her reaction had been partly physical, hormones slowly getting back into a normal rhythm, but none of that mattered to her, not then. Only patience, *infinite* patience sometimes, and a few sessions alone with the therapist to pull her out. The spiral notebooks she'd kept hidden – he would check occasionally to see if it was still there, noticing how sometimes the cover was a different color – were obviously good therapy. More than her visits to that faceless women every Tuesday for the first few months after losing the baby. Before Sam had decided to stop going to see the woman out of the blue.

Out of the yellow.

What the hell did *that* mean? One of her cryptic lines of poetry, no doubt.

Samantha fell quiet in his arms. At least Abby hadn't woken. Bad enough her father was an emotional wreck. To find out both her parents were loose in the gears would be too much for a girl her age to bear.

A half hour had passed since Sam's oddly-timed confession, if an actual confession it was. She hadn't spoken, and her body weighed heavier against his chest. An occasional, deep sniffle. Why had she mentioned this now?

He also knew..., she'd begun to say, but never finished the statement. Talking about Hank Cowles, of course. The crazy old man liked playing sick games like *Spy on the Union Family*.

Did he know about her poetry? Corey looked around the room, careful to do so only with his eyes. Did Cowles come in here at some point? Corey tried to remember if they'd locked up before heading to church yesterday. Probably not.

Too much going on. Too much of a change all at once. Best not add paranoia to his own growing symptoms.

Corey's arm was falling asleep. He squeezed his wife's shoulder. "You OK?"

She nodded.

"Want to go to bed?"

Another nod.

"It's OK," he said, not sure what he meant by it. Maybe *everything*. Everything was OK. Here in the house. Everything in the world might be falling apart, but they were safe here, nestled away in a magical wood.

"I know," she said, and sniffed. "I'm sorry."

"Don't be. Artists have a right to privacy. Right?" He turned on the couch until they were facing each other, Sam's embarrassed gaze struggling to make eye contact. He touched her chin and said, "Listen, it doesn't bother me, never has. OK?"

Sam stiffened and looked away, eyes down, mulling over what he had said, likely deciding if he'd been making fun of her. She finally nodded, *almost* smiled. "OK."

"Then it's time for bed. Sleep," he added, "perchance to dream."

She gave him a sidelong glance to imply he was drifting into dangerous waters. He raised his palm in surrender. She took it into her own and walked with him into the hall. They stopped in Abby's room on their way.

Sam on the side of Abby's bed, running a hand across the girl's head, a light touch. Abby shifting deeper into her blankets. Corey watched all this from the doorway, the pangs of fear growing again. How could he protect them, take this one moment of peace and preserve it forever? He couldn't. The world wouldn't let him. It would pour down on them like fire.

"Corey?" He closed his eyes, took a silent breath in. *Don't start!* She needed him to be sane tonight. They certainly made an interesting couple, he decided, and smirked. It felt very good to do so. Corey stepped inside and joined his wife at the side of his daughter's bed.

VII

Hank Cowles stood on a hill as dark as the clouds which roiled overhead. They flashed red, like lightning but sharper, brighter. Over and around him the air seemed to burn. He stretched out his arms, looked out over the world. Down the hillside, trees bent from the force above, bowing in homage amid the small Rockwell village nestled like a sleeping child in the arms of the valley. From that place, drifting across the curling brown grass were terrible screams, the quick, reflexive hushing of parents and those who looked out the windows or up towards the ceiling as the roaring inside the clouds and beyond grew louder and more fierce. The storm rumbled overhead like a massive, angry machine, screaming in its final death throes, an unseen, multi-wheeled tractor-trailer careening off the interstate, an airliner with broken wings spinning and falling in death, demons opening their mouths to feed while screaming in pain and delight. All of it rolling above and past the houses, coiling in on itself then surging outward, burning the clouds. The fire spilled free and rained like melted plastic over Hank and the hill and the houses and the people.

The sound intensified, became a frenzy, as Vanessa watched from her small porch. Knives of glittering steel slammed into the street then through it, kicking jagged chunks of asphalt into the heated air. The blades pulled free of the earth and rose back towards the clouds only to slam down in other places, other roads and lawns and homes. Roofs folded under their weight with sharp, metallic thuds. This time, when the blades lifted, people were impaled on their tines. God angrily eating a dinner of souls, or maybe feeding them to the screaming demons like a parent to a child. Vanessa gripped the posts on either side of the steps and leaned out, laughing and crying, pleading to be killed like the others around her. The wind in this place, this dream, had fingers of its own, jagged nails that ripped at her dress, tearing it, preparing her body for feeding, for its own impaling and rising into the unseen, howling mouth. Someone stumbled from a broken door of the house next door, ran drunkenly across the street, pajama pants falling around his ankles. Mister Possey, her neighbor. Vanessa moaned aloud when his legs were severed by twin steel blades which rose a few feet then pushed their points through his belly from behind. Blood and screams and feces and intestines spilled around his gurgled pleas for mercy. Vanessa screamed as well, not wanting to be abandoned. She ran onto the dead grass. Something glinted in front of her; a metal flash slammed into her midsection, heavy weight twisting, flinging her wildly into the air. The pain was hot pepper inside her body, exploding in a thousand small spots of agony. Her head slammed onto the ground before lifting again, pulled upward. A new blade pierced her throat. She could not scream, only wave her arms in dying ecstasy as she rose higher and higher into the burning air.

Corey Union watched Vanessa's body slide along the blade, defying gravity before it split in half. Her upper torso, soaked in blood, fell to earth, only to be caught by another of the monstrous blades. He pulled his wife and daughter closer as they cowered at the edge of the forest that now burned out of control behind them. They'd been running through the dense growth of laurel and sumac, tripping, falling, watching the sky and treetops burn, trying to pray for mercy as they ran. The clouds twisted into grotesque shapes, laughing clowns, before the trees exploded and popped like gunfire around him. Flames licked at their backs while the neighborhood they faced was a broken plate from some dark god's hurried meal. A thick metal blade, glinting blue and red, slid soundlessly into the ground six feet away. Up it rose, down again a few feet closer. Corey looked up to see the smiling clown face of the world's end squinting its red eyes down at them, laughing, playing with its food. He pulled Samantha close with one arm, Abby with the other.

Sam wanted to break free of her husband's grip but he held on, as if offering his family to the insatiable demons. *Take them*, he might be thinking; *spare me*. No, Corey *could not* be thinking this. The ground shook. She fell with him to the ground then resisted when he tried to pull her up again. Her view of the ruined neighborhood was cut off by a blade, digging into the ground inches from her knees. It went in deeper than before, deeper and deeper with no end emerging from the cloud-choked sky above them. Though Abby cried against her father, resigned to dying, Samantha would not accept this. This was only a dream, a bad one, but still she had to run. She leaned forward then rolled, colliding with the hot metal of the blade. Its smooth surface slid deeper into the ground against her, like a claw looking for grubs in the earth. It burned. Corey grabbed her foot, but she kicked him away.

Why was she running? Corey wanted to pull her back so that if his family had to die, at least they could die together. Why did they *have* to? He couldn't stop what was happening, but had to try, had to save them. Sam had regained her balance and ran into the burning woods, soot-coated head glancing back only once before the gleaming blade which had been digging into the earth tore upward below her, burying its point between her legs. Her body twitched and convulsed with the red and yellow flames of the world her backdrop. The blade broke through her skull. Corey curled away from the fire and his wife's desecrated body. Abby was no longer with him. He raised his head and shouted but no human voice could compete with the ripping and tearing of the planet. Far, far up with a magnified vision, which could only mean this was a dream, *had to be a dream*, remains of their neighbor had nearly reached the edge of the cloud. A dozen more blades, like scissors held in the fingers of angels, emerged to snip the two halves of her body into smaller and smaller pieces.

Corey jerked upright in his bed screaming and shouting words he didn't understand, if they were truly words at all.

Vanessa's eyes opened in the quiet dark of her room, thrusting her hips into the air, her body wracked in spasms of a dream-infused orgasm, all the while feeling light fingers across her legs, caressing her skin, gripping hungrily. She opened her eyes, realized she'd kicked the sheets off the bed, gasped suddenly at another gentle caress on her thigh, the naked form of Samantha on top of her, moving, kissing. The woman did not speak nor acknowledge her presence with any words, only a hurried touching, tasting, relentless motion growing in hunger and urgency. A part of Vanessa tried to pull away, shake herself from this continuing dream, but this was the weaker part of her in this moment. She reached out for the other with trembling hands, pulled Samantha against her, harder, guiding her, losing herself in the sensations of her body, spinning the world in a pleasurable rotation that she did not want to wake from. The feel of another wanting her, taking her, loving her.

Across town, Hank Cowles opened his eyes with a start, found himself alone in his small bedroom, heart pounding out the fear and excitement of the magnificent destruction. His face curled into a wide smile, looking like a grimace, or a wince of pain. He glanced sideway into the hallway where Nurse Charles sat in the center of the floor, eyes glinting in the hallway light, looking back at him. One of her three small heads panted happily in a dog smile, the other snarled, the other licked something from its stained chops. Hank blinked. There now was only the one head, emotionless, small tail quietly tapping against the floor. He leaned back against the mattress, let the muscles of his face relax while his heart continued to hammer. Was he afraid? He shouldn't be; he *couldn't* be. This was the bell, the tolling of the coming hour. This was what he was created for.

The dog watched dispassionately from the hall.

Corey had to force himself to close his mouth, grit his teeth to stop screaming. He was breathing fast and sweating, but alive. *A dream. Only a dream.*

Wondering how he'd explain to Sam what he'd seen, why he'd been screaming, Corey slowly realized he might not have to. She hadn't woken. No light touch on his back or shout of surprise.

He turned his head, still praying that what he'd seen was only a dream. Just a bad dream.

Her side of the bed was empty. He reached out, felt warm sheets, indentation in the pillow where her head had rested. His thrashing must have driven her out of bed and into the living room.

If so, why hadn't she come back in when he started screaming?

Eventually, his breathing slowed to a point where he could step out from under the sheet and not risk collapsing. He didn't want to faint, fall back through the veil of sleep into that hell again.

His robe had fallen to the floor. Corey wrapped it around his body and tied the sash tight. The feel of the robe tight against him had comfort, an artificial hug. The light in the master bath was off. She wasn't there. He stepped into the hallway and almost screamed again out of surprise.

Abby was standing in the center of the hall, Teddy hanging limply from her right hand, its stuffed feet barely glancing off the floor. Her other hand was raised to her mouth with thumb inserted. She hadn't sucked her thumb in over a year. Corey raised his hand and tried to smile. "Sorry, Sweetie," he breathed. "You startled me."

"Someone was yelling."

It was your father, he thought, *losing a little more of his mind*.

"It was just me. I got up for a drink and stubbed my toe."

Lie to the children, lie to the world.

Another line from Sam's poetry? The thought served to wake him completely.

Abby stepped forward, stared at his bare feet poking from under the robe. The thumb remained in her mouth, even as she said, "Did it hurt?"

"A little. Come on, let's get you back to bed."

He led her into the bedroom, hoping to see Sam lying on her bed. She was not. Abby scooted under the sheets. "I'm afraid to go back to sleep."

He sat down, caressed the top of her head and used a finger to move a lock of hair from her eyes. "Why's that?"

"I don't want any more bad dreams."

"You had a bad dream?"

She nodded, eyes already half closed.

"Well, remember the rule for bad dreams? If you tell me about it, it'll never, *ever* come back. Right?"

She nodded, the hand still planted in front of her face. He should probably tell her not to suck her thumb but had no energy for it. In a muffled voice, she told him a few details of the dream.

Corey managed to keep his composure, let her recite for him the same dream, more or less, that he'd just awoken from. Either her version was tamer, *no impaled mother or friendly neighbor snipped into pieces*, or these details were too much for her to retain. Even so, she seemed calm as she spoke.

Not until she was asleep and he stood outside the bedroom leaning against the wall did Corey allow himself to consider that they'd had the same dream.

The same *vision*.

The same *dream*!

The world did not work like that; no room for psychic connections or shared... shared anything. He closed his eyes, tried to close his mind. There was no room in his brain to consider this. He needed Samantha. Needed to lay with her, curl against her body even if he did not sleep another minute. He'd feel her with him, feel safe.

Samantha was not in the kitchen, or the living room. After a confused ten minutes looking in every corner of the house, including the basement and a quick desperate visit to the attic, Corey gave up and went outside.

Bare feet cool on the night grass – *living grass, living and green and not burned* – he circled the house, hoping he hadn't left anything lying around from the weekend which might pierce the bottom of his foot.

Sam was not out here. Both cars were still in the driveway. She was just *gone*.

Vanessa

Vanessa found Corey pacing in a small circle on the back porch, lost. He lifted a hand to his ear, as if listening for something, then lowered it to the railing. She took in a breath, trying to push away the lingering quivers of pleasure in her own body and focused on Corey, who was standing a few feet away, his back to her. She concentrated on him alone, not Samantha, or the vivid dream, the nightmare. She'd sort it all out later. She softly spoke his name. Corey turned around so quickly he almost fell back against the railing. Vanessa had put on her robe but left it hanging open, exposing herself to him, letting him see.

Corey mumbled something about missing his wife. Slowly, she approached him, reached out and touched his forehead. His eyes had followed the progress of her fingers, nearly crossing. With fingertips against his flesh, Vanessa whispered, "She's sleeping now, Mister Union, as should you. Come to bed." She leaned in close to his ear, his head turning a little to follow her progress. "You've taken such good care of her."

Even in his exhaustion and fear, he smelled wonderful. She could not resist pressing her lips against his ear. Her body warmed at the contact. Reluctantly, she pulled away, but her fingertips never left his forehead.

Enough for one night, she thought. It was time to go. She looked Corey in the eyes, waited until she was certain he was focused on her, then pulled her fingers away.

Corey
Tuesday

I

Samantha opened her eyes to a room flooded with clear morning light. She stretched out, luxuriating in the heavy, contented feel of an uninterrupted night's sleep. A rare event. A blessing. Usually, she'd have awakened a few times, long enough to turn over and drift away again.

But she'd been *exhausted* last night after her strange, emotional talk with Corey, and of course her crying like a baby. Like a *crazy woman*. She waited for the pain to return, the embarrassment to wind her up for another, stressed out waking. It did not. She felt too good. *Wonderful*, in fact.

The contented weight of an exhausted lover.

They hadn't made love. Not physically. Mentally? Maybe. Corey hadn't laughed at her, not the way she'd feared. He hadn't had much chance to react at all with her tirade of emotion. Instead, he'd held her in a long, loving embrace, even cried a little himself. He'd *loved* her.

She rolled on her side. Seven-thirty. Early, still. He might not have left.

Light footfalls on the rug behind her, the press of the mattress, then Corey's arm snaking around and finding its favorite embrace below her breasts. "Good morning," he whispered.

Samantha smiled, inside and out. She leaned into him as he kissed her shoulder. His lips traveled as she rolled. She pulled his face to hers and kissed him, hoping he wouldn't break the moment by mentioning she hadn't brushed her teeth yet. He didn't, returned the kiss, moved on to her cheek, then her closed eyelids, forehead.

Eventually, he straightened, one eyebrow raised. He said, "You haven't brushed your teeth yet."

Samantha laughed, reached behind her and tossed the pillow. It missed. Corey smiled. A glow inside her belly, music in her mind in her soul... *give it a rest*, she thought, then pulled him down into another kiss. He didn't resist, though his constant smile made the kiss hard.

When he pulled back a second time, Samantha sighed, "I slept great. Guess I needed it."

"We both did. I barely heard the radio." He absently straightened his clothes. "Abby ate breakfast. She's watching cartoons now. I told her to let you sleep, so why not roll over and catch another hour?" He tossed the pillow back onto the bed. It landed across her face.

She left it there and stretched again, long and slow under the single sheet. Peeking out from under the pillow she noticed, with great pleasure, Corey's gaze moving along her form. She waved her hand. "Go hunt and gather for your family."

When he was gone, she lingered, pillow still over her face. She looked sideways at the rectangle of morning light against the opposite wall. A few bits of dust speckled as they passed through it. She didn't want this oasis of calm to fade. A good cry last night, that was all. No other reason. She stared at one particular speck of dust when it entered the light, followed its angled progress until it disappeared. The sound of Corey's Honda starting outside, the slow crunch of tires down the driveway.

Today was Tuesday. Something was going on.... Vanessa was coming by for lunch. No, *pie*. Having some pie with Vanessa. Sam pictured the woman in that near-Victorian dress, her loose posture and easy smile a contrast to the conservative clothing. The image warmed her, comfortable like a freshly made bed. *Like a breeze coming through the window in summer carrying the scent of lilacs and roses. Purple and red, warm.*

She shook her head, rolled out from under the sheets. Too much sleep. There were scratches across her calves and the top of her feet. She stared, wondering absently when she'd gotten them. Not troubled, however; too calm was the morning, too deep had her mind settled. Nothing was going to get her going in the wrong direction. She must have gotten them in the garden; hadn't noticed until now.

She shrugged, not caring where they came from, letting the sheet fall away as she moved into the bathroom.

What did Corey think of their mysterious neighbor? He must have noticed her beauty, though he would never consider anything beyond that. Not to mention Vanessa had all but ignored him the other night. More interested in Samantha.

More interested in *her*. She paused in the middle of the bathroom, hand lightly resting on the edge of the sink, across her belly - smooth but a little soft. Sam closed her eyes. *Don't think; don't drift there.* As she expected, the contented blanket covering her mind slipped. Just a little. Nothing bad.

Something tapped on the window above the whirlpool tub. A yellow jacket, wings blurred. Its alien face tapped against the glass. Another joined it, then a third, all of them bouncing off the window, fading back, returning again. Three living spots of yellow, watching her, pattering like raindrops. The window was fixed and could not be opened. No chance of them getting in. She walked to the toilet and sat to do her business.

The drone of their wings drifted through the screened open window above her head. The tapping over the tub continued, sometimes faster or stopping all together. When Sam was finished, she washed her hands and reached for the toothbrush, not wanting to turn and see the yellow. Dab of toothpaste on the brush. The raindrop taps behind her were gone. Still, she heard their buzzing through the window above the toilet. The light in the room wavered like reflected water. Before putting the toothbrush in her mouth, she turned around.

The window over the tub was covered in yellow wasps. A hundred or more of them fought for space, swarming over each other as if in a nest, feet stepping soundlessly across the glass. She ran to the toilet and put her ear to the screen. No sound, nothing but birdsong from the woods at the back of the yard.

Samantha slowly stepped sideways to get a better look over the tub.

No bees. She closed her eyes, waited, opened them. Still clear; no sign they'd ever been there. The imaginary blanket of calm around her fell to the floor like the bed sheet. She couldn't have possibly imagined them –

The sound of the bees returned, louder, tinny. Coming from above.

She looked up in time to see the first few crawling out of the ceiling vent. More followed, fanning like smoke across the ceiling. Wings buzzing, but none of them flying. Not yet. They only moved aside in a yellow cloud to make room for more pouring through the vent slats.

They hadn't called the exterminator, yesterday. Sam backed up, whispering words of muttered panic. They would fall on her now, cover her and kill her and –

When her back connected with the door jamb she screamed and rolled out of the room, grabbing the door knob, pulling it closed behind her. In the last flashing view of the bathroom, the swarm dropped down. The droning exploded in volume to a buzz saw whine behind the closed door, colliding with it on the other side. Sam pulled harder on the knob, then looked down. A single bee poked curiously from beneath the door. She ran to the bed, pulled the sheet off the floor and shoved it into the open space, forcing the bee back inside.

Abby ran into the room. "Mommy, what's wrong?" She stopped, a smile bursting on her face. "You're naked!"

"Sweetie, go back into the other room, OK?"

The girl backed up, no longer smiling. "What's wrong?"

"Nothing, nothing. Something's wrong with the bathroom, that's all."

The girl didn't leave. Her head tilted to the side. "Did you stub your toe like Daddy did last night?"

"What? Toe? No. No." She'd missed that one.

Abby didn't looked frightened, just curious. As Samantha stood up, her eyes fixed on the sheet at the bottom of the door. The girl walked to the chair beside the bed and picked up the bathrobe.

"Here, Mommy." Sam forced herself to smile and took the robe. "Does Daddy need to fix it?"

Sam wrapped the robe around herself, keeping her eyes on the door. "Fix what, Sweetie?" The robe was smooth, satin, a gift from Corey a couple of Christmases ago.

"The bathroom. I had breakfast. Daddy made it for me."

"What? Yes. Good; I mean, thank you."

She laid a hand on Abby's shoulder and guided her into the hall, closing the bedroom door behind them. "Did you have breakfast?"

"I just said I did!"

"Ah, good. Come on, then. I'm hungry, and I need to call Daddy later."

"To fix the bathroom, right?"

She kissed her daughter on top of her head. "That's right, Sweetie."

"He can fix everything."

II

So far, the day was going well. This morning Corey woke more refreshed than any other since moving into the new house. Sam, too. The fresh country air had finally settled into their bones. Last night's emotional outpouring might have been Sam's way of purging all that stress from their old life. The more he thought about the past two weeks, the happier Corey was with the decision to move to Hillcrest. Away from Worcester's congestion, they were now surrounded by nature, which could be as noisy as the city but with a calmer, less frenzied cadence. Birdsong instead of car horns; looking at the sky instead of over your shoulder; deer droppings instead of discarded Dunkin' Donuts coffee cups. The biggest news would now be school budget debates, not murders.

Corey hesitated on the sidewalk. The small white CVS Pharmacy bag, a refill of Tylenol and Sam's birth control pills, swayed in his hand. Two cabs worked their way towards him amid the slow, lunchtime crawl on Main Street.

Yellow, he remembered. Something about last night, some odd consideration while Sam was wailing on his shoulder. The cabs crawled closer. The color yellow had been a common theme in his wife's notebook. It meant something to her, but...

When the first cab reached him, Corey recognized the old man behind the wheel, struggled to remember *how* he knew him. The man stared out the windshield, not at the car in front of him but directly at Corey. Even with its driver's attention riveted away from the traffic, the cab moved in time with it. As the taxi moved past, the old man glared through the passenger window with a stern, wrinkled face. Corey knew that face but had no reference, nothing to pin it to, nothing –

The curly white head of a small dog rose over the top of the passenger door, eyes wide and small pink tongue dabbing the closed window with spit. A large, smiling bumble bee adorned the taxi's door over the standard *Yellow Cab* moniker. The scene should have been cute, but Corey's chest tightened, bled into his belly. Rising panic. Pain. *Bringer of Pain. Destroyer of Worlds.*

He stepped back. The dog dropped out of sight. The man was facing forward again – not a man. A woman, wide flushed faced, tangles of unwashed hair. The sun reflected off the glass and distorted Corey's view. He'd simply misinterpreted what he'd seen. *Hank Cowles*, he realized, was who the old man had been – or *not* been. Sam's story had shaken him up more than he'd thought. He followed the cab's progress down the road. No small dog in the window. The second passing taxi was driven by a thin Indian man with a gaze locked on the woman's bumper.

Something buzzed in the pocket of Corey's slacks. He reflexively slapped at his pants, thinking of bees, fat black and white monsters crawling inside his pocket, pattering across the office window. Only his cell phone, set to vibrate.

Corey half bent, letting out his breath, feeling like an idiot. He stared at the sidewalk and tried to smile away the moment. There was no humor to find in it. The next time the phone vibrated, he fished it out of his pocket.

"Hello?"

"Corey?" The voice was instantly familiar, but the signal fuzzed away, Sam's words indistinct. He changed the angle against his ear, took a couple of steps down the sidewalk.

"Hello?" he said again. "Sam?"

"Corey, can you hear me?" Her voice was a little clearer. No one sounded themselves through these things.

"Better now," he said, turning to watch the twin cabs roll away like a funeral procession. His smile dropped. He was beginning to think too much like his wife.

"I think we've got a problem." She relayed her adventure with the wasps through occasional waves of static.

"Why didn't you call me earlier?"

"To be honest, I didn't want to deal with them, not before coffee; then things got...." A hiss, followed by her tinny laugh, so unreal from the speaker. "Anyway, I just checked. They're gone now."

Yesterday, the bees swarming around the clock. Now this. He'd almost convinced himself it had been a dream. In truth, he simply hadn't wanted to deal with it. "You're sure they were yellow jackets?" *Yellow*, again. *Stop it!*

"Well, no, not sure of anything. Is there a difference? Should we call Warren?"

Warren James was the architect and contractor who'd built their house. "What could he do? He's not an exterminator."

"No." Her sigh sounded like air blown through a straw. "Maybe they had bee problems during construction. Maybe they built the house on top of a nest."

"I suppose. Couldn't hurt to call. I'll check the attic tonight and see..." He hesitated. He'd just been in the attic, hadn't he? When?

The weekend before last, for a look around. It felt more recent than that. Corey had been looking for something, or someone.... no. They'd had no reason to go back up there since moving day.

"Corey?"

"Hi, yeah, sorry. Had one of those déjà vu things. Anyway, I'll check tonight. If there's a nest, we'll call a bee guy."

"Not Hank Cowles I hope." She laughed.

Corey looked up but the cab was gone. "Why did you …" then remembered her story of how bees kept flying around Cowles' head yesterday. Cory turned away from the road, his gaze landing on a newspaper kiosk. Large black letters spelled out the imminent end of the world. He blurred his vision so he wouldn't read any of it.

The peace of his day was gone, *dissipated like the fog of a good dream.*

Twice in one day he was writing poetry for his wife. This had to stop.

"Hey," he said, "we need a distraction. How about we try that restaurant in town? The *Grille* something-or-other. Get out and see more of our town."

Her tiny voice said, "That's a great idea! Oh, wait, that reminds me."

"What?"

"Vanessa is coming by for lunch... at least I think she is. Isn't that what we decided Sunday?"

Vanessa standing on the porch, half-naked, beautiful, fingertips on his forehead.

The sidewalk tilted. Corey stepped towards the *Bellerive Bank and Trust,* leaned on the bricks with an outstretched arm. What the hell was going on?

Silence on the line. He had to say something. "Is she there now?" Of course she wasn't. Otherwise –

"No. Not yet. I wonder if I should have called her. The pie's going to go bad soon – what's left of it. It's just about noon. Maybe I should call her."

The sidewalk steadied. How could he be fantasizing about his neighbor? It hadn't been the first time. He'd dreamt about her, too. This was worse, though, while on the phone with his wife. Corey swallowed. Last night he'd felt like the normal one in their marriage. It'd been a nice change. Now. *Now...*

"No, wait," Sam added, "I can't. I don't have her phone number. What's her last name?"

He almost had said "Reilly" but realized that was Sam's old therapist. That would have been a bad slip. But it gave him an idea. She hadn't done much for Sam, as far as he could tell. Maybe for him... a thought for another time, however.

What the hell *was* Vanessa's last name? Had she said?

"I have no idea. I don't think she – "

"Hold on. Someone's knocking."

The sound of the phone laid onto the kitchen table. Now Corey had a mental picture of where she'd been standing. He assumed she was calling from the bedroom, staring nervously at the door to the bathroom.

Voices, distant, drowned out by the sounds of traffic beside him. Another kitchen table *thunk*. "Corey, Vanessa's here. I have to go. See you tonight."

"OK. Have a nice time."

"I will. Love you; bye."

"Love you, too." But he sensed she'd already disconnected.

He closed the phone and stared at it for a while longer. It was good, wasn't it, that she had someone to visit with? He pictured Sam and their neighbor with no last name sitting on the couch, sipping coffee, eating pie. Abby would be there. She'd be having pie, too.

Knowing this gave Corey a better feeling about the visit, though he didn't understand why. Not exactly. Nor did he understand why another yellow cab, moving up the road, brought with it a renewed panic attack. He looked up to the patch of sky between the buildings. City air smelled like diesel and chewing gum. *Monster wads of Juicy Fruit buried beneath the asphalt.* The image made him smile. Another thing Samantha might have said years ago, when neither of them cared what was happening around them, only *between* them.

They would find it again.

He made it a point not to look at the cars as he walked back to his building, CVS bag renewing its pendulum swing from his hand.

III

Without a call from Sam the rest of the afternoon, Corey assumed things had gone well. He'd find out soon enough. Small town folk were supposed to be neighborly. Even so, Vanessa had so quickly worked herself into their lives. Corey enjoyed his privacy, assumed Sam did, too. Vanessa was nice enough, but he hoped she didn't make a habit of hanging around all the time.

Then again, Corey was at work all day, could talk to anyone he wanted. Sam had the same right. His chest tightened. Was he jealous? Ridiculous. Standard male paranoia, two women talking in secret, bringing up all his faults and foibles. What happened at home should stay at home, not be spread around as conversational fodder.

He steered the Honda onto the highway off-ramp. Sam wouldn't bring up intimate details with a stranger, no matter *how* charismatic she might be. He was being paranoid, another blemish on his soul to join so many others.

Entering Hillcrest. The drive home was a panorama of unspoiled beauty. The towns, nestled between the industrial cities of Worcester and Fitchburg, might have been culled from a Rockwell painting. *Bucolic*, he thought the word might be. Trees reached from both sides, sometimes opening to an expanse of hay fields soon to be rolled into oversized bundles by the rusty red tractor parked by the road.

He passed west through the center of town. Corey tried to remember if he was supposed to pick up milk at the *Greedy Grocer*. No, didn't think so. Milk was one of the few staples that could be gotten last minute without a twenty minute ride back into the city. Corey passed by the stores, then noticed the old man walking towards him on the sidewalk. Stooped, long sleeved flannel shirt buttoned to the wrist in defiance of the heat. A small white dog trotted beside him.

Both looked up to follow the car's progress. Corey's hands tightened around the steering wheel. This wasn't happening, couldn't be happening. Not an ancient cab driver this time but a tired old man walking his dog on a warm summer evening. Hank Cowles again.

Everything suddenly made sense. He must have passed him and his little dog on the way home another day but didn't remember it. He lived in town, after all. Then why did the sight of him fill Corey with such paralyzing fear? *Anger*, he decided, *not fear*. Hank Cowles knew too much about them, more than anyone, even in this small town, should know.

Hank didn't smile as the car passed, but raised his hand in a gesture which could have been greeting or dismissal. Corey's chest felt hollow. He waved back, wanting to stop, run from his car and grab the man by his unseasonable shirt, shake him until he admitted spying.

His palms squeaked painfully on the steering wheel. The car wavered in the lane. Corey let out the breath he'd been holding, took another in. He drove past the old man, glanced occasionally in the mirror to make sure he hadn't transformed into someone else again. He and his dog, walking away without a care in the world.

IV

The *Cabel Grille* was a modest-sized restaurant located on the east side of Hillcrest, a half mile from Interstate 190. The place was crowded for a Tuesday. Samantha hadn't called ahead. In fact, she'd forgotten about it as soon as Vanessa arrived for lunch. Regardless, after Corey had taken a few minutes to change into jeans and a clean polo shirt, they'd gotten into the car to see if the place was open. If not, Sam reasoned, they'd have an excuse to go somewhere else, seeing as they would already be in the car. Corey agreed with a smile, but Samantha couldn't help notice a distance in him this evening. She tried not to worry over it, nor assume it had anything to do with her confession last night.

She ordered a chicken Caesar salad, Corey an extra-thick cheeseburger, and for Abby, a kid's meal of macaroni and cheese with a cookie. Their daughter played with a twenty piece puzzle of a Labrador that came with her meal (*thankfully not a Shih-Tzu*, Sam had joked with Corey, then had to explain to Abby that she hadn't said a swear word). The restaurant knew how to cater to small town clientele with an elaborate array of vegetarian and low-carb plates alongside enough meat and potatoes to satisfy pretty much everyone.

Sam speared a piece of breaded chicken onto her fork and looked at Corey. He was currently bent towards Abby. She was giving him every detail of Vanessa's visit.

"And when she took a bite of pie it was too warm because Mommy heated it in the microwave so she said *ouch* and blew on it. She smiles a lot, you know. She's pretty, like Mommy. She works on the computer in her house for a job." All of this with as little breathing as possible. The girl stopped long enough to spear as many macaronis as possible with her fork, a game she played whenever *mac and cheese* was the meal. When she could fit no more on the fork she gave her mother a quick, sideways glance. Samantha's cue.

"Please don't put all that in your mouth."

"I can eat all this!" Waving the over-laden fork in the air like a scepter.

"If you do," she said, calmly, playing the game, "it's going to leak out your nose."

Abby laughed but still managed to get nearly half into her mouth before finally chewing. Samantha shook her head and poked a piece of lettuce, *real food*.

Corey watched their exchange with a wistful smile. He looked tired. "So it went OK?" he asked, an opening for Samantha to work any details in that might be worth mentioning while Abby was chewing.

She nodded. "Vanessa's very nice. A little intense."

"Intense?" He used both hands to raise the burger, watched over the bun.

Sam shrugged. "Not sure why I think that -- maybe because she always leans forward when she talks to you, or when she's listening, you know? As if whatever she's about to say, or what *you're* saying is the most important thing ever."

"Vanessa invited us over to her house for supper tomorrow night," Abby said, refueled for another run.

Before she could build up steam to add more, Corey said, "She did? So soon?" He didn't sound happy.

Samantha said, "Well, yes, she wanted to repay the favor, said she's booked for the next few nights after that and, to be honest, I think she might be a little lonely. Living alone like she does."

Corey's face had darkened. Not angry. Whatever it was, it was new for him. She didn't know what it meant, but something bothered him.

"O...K...," he said, drawing out the letters. "I suppose that's fine. I assume it'll be early enough for Abby to hit the sack at a decent time."

Abby tilted her head, twisting her mouth in a *what-does-that-mean* way. Corey noticed and added, "Hit the sack. It means go to bed."

"Why?"

He raised his burger in front of him and shrugged. "No idea." He was looking at Samantha again, not wanting to get off track.

Sam wondered why she felt so defensive. "We figured six-thirty. It would allow you time to change if you want, and for us to get home by eight. Nothing too elaborate."

"She doesn't have a dog," Abby said with a pout. "But she used to. She had a big black one named Blackie. It ran away when she was little. She said maybe some day if she got another one I could help train him and ... "

And she went on for a few minutes more. Samantha took advantage of the dialogue to eat more of her salad, grateful that Corey's attention was forced on their daughter. He watched Abby talk, nodding now and then, occasionally looking Sam's way as if there were a hundred questions meant for her alone but which he either couldn't or wouldn't ask. *Not in front of the child.* Words meant for adults, those who understand the cravings of the body.

She blushed, tried to cover it by taking a sip of her water. She never felt comfortable drinking alcohol in public. Maybe a glass of wine if one was offered. The water was cool going down, *washed clean as if from a baptism*, concentrated on the sensation to help fight the red she knew shone like a beacon from her cheeks.

Vanessa had been wonderful with Abby, never getting annoyed with her or put off by the constant interruptions. When Samantha and Vanessa could talk directly it was mostly about local events. Not much on that topic, however. *Hay Day* in the Fall at the Swayne Farm, local fairs and bake sales. That topic led to the pie, Vanessa casually wondering who'd made it. She was quick to point out she didn't know too many people in Hillcrest. She had, however, noticed a sign for *Story Time* at the town library. Every Thursday during the summer. Samantha thought it would be a good place for Abby to meet other kids her age, so she'd written it down on the calendar.

Throughout the visit, Vanessa's presence filled the room. She dressed conservatively again, similar to Sunday, but blue this time, subtle floral patterns reaching to the knees, buttoned to her throat. Her demeanor and expression were far from conservative. Wide, sweeping arm gestures, a sharp, brown gaze. Long black hair which sometimes -- perhaps because of the way she kept it closely braided -- looked as though it were no longer than the dress's collar.

Sam was swept up in the woman's spirit, *wrapped in it like a blanket on a cold night.*

It made no sense. She loved Corey and never once found herself attracted to anyone of the same sex. But this afternoon, Sam couldn't help wonder if, in some strange way, she wasn't falling in love with the woman. Probably a crush, drawn by the way her neighbor carried herself, how she sounded so comfortable with any topic. More than that. Sam wished she could *be* like Vanessa. If she spent more time around her, she might actually learn how.

She thought she understood Corey's reaction to Vanessa's invitation. He *was* jealous, of the sudden drawing away of his wife's attention from *him.*

Nothing more. Nothing.

Their table had fallen silent, the only voices that of other diners' conversations. Corey and Abby watched her. His expression had softened to the relaxed, amused look he got when Samantha said something "endearing."

She blinked and whispered, "I'm sorry. Veg'd out for a minute. What was the question?"

Corey said, "Nothing important. Just wondering how long that booger's been stuck on the end of your nose." He pointed to her face. She reached up, face filling with heat for the second time that night, and wiped at her nose. Abby grabbed her stomach and doubled over in laughter.

"There's no booger!" she screamed, drawing looks from other diners. "Daddy was just joking!"

Corey was laughing now too, though much more quietly, shoulders moving in time.

Sam wanted to laugh. She really did. "Very funny, guys." She gave Abby a poke across the table.

Corey's mouth stretched suddenly into a wide yawn. "Sorry. I'm suddenly exhausted. Slept like a stone last night, but maybe my body isn't used to it."

"Rocks don't sleep, Daddy."

He ran a hand over her hair. "Just an expression, Honey. It means I slept all night without waking up."

Abby narrowed her gaze. "You got up, Daddy. When I had my bad dream and you sent me to bed. You made me tell it. I went back to sleep and didn't have any dreams at all. Just like a rock!"

Samantha looked at him, but Corey was still staring at Abby. "Did I get up last night?" He looked at Sam.

She shrugged. "I don't remember. I was sleeping - " she leaned across the table and whispered, "– like a rock." Abby giggled. "So if *you* did -"

"Abby what was your dream about? I don't remember."

Sam closed her mouth and leaned back in her chair. He'd just interrupted her.

Abby's bottom lip stuck out. "Big giant forks, remember? Bad ones, sticking out of the clouds. It was scary." She sat back, crossed her arms in front of her, said sternly, "I do not want to talk about it. I already told you."

"Ok," he said. He looked to Samantha for confirmation. Of *what*, she didn't have a clue.

"Giant Forks," he said, to himself, then forced a smile towards Abby. "Sounds very silly. At least you know it won't come back ever again, right?"

Abby nodded, but didn't look convinced.

Corey
Wednesday

I

The morning was clear, still cool this early. Corey enjoyed driving to work when most people were only considering getting out of bed. Summer meant no buses or high school kids waiting on corners. Just him and the woods, then the slow merge into the human race as he rolled down the interstate towards Worcester. The real world rose ahead like a storm cloud.

He'd slept soundly again, after an extended session of staring at the shadowy wall across the room, thinking about his daughter's nightmare. Flashes of memory, nothing concrete. He could not remember getting out of bed the night before, settling Abby down. She'd been so certain. If her mention of the "angry forks" hadn't sounded do damned familiar, he would have assumed she'd dreamt his part, too. *Dreaming of waking*, as Sam might put it.

What had finally allowed him to drift away beside the steady breathing of his wife was the decision to accept that he *had* gotten up, tended to Abby, even listened to her story of the dream without waking up completely. When he returned to bed he'd simply incorporated what she'd told him into his own dream, only to be forgotten on waking like most of his others.

He did dream, last night, but preferred not to think about it. No giant forks. He'd dreamt again of their beautiful but mysterious neighbor standing over his bed, reaching down, touching him, a lost, distracted look as she

—

No. He wouldn't dwell. Dreams were only dreams. Nothing else. Time to settle his mind on the world rolling towards him. The clean country air thinned to a polluted sheen as he closed in on the city limits.

The clock wound more easily this morning. That was one aspect of these odd few days Corey decided he would embrace, Hank Cowles' intrusions aside. The thing had languished in his family for generations and now it had a chance for life. It ticked away the seconds for the first time in years, and would continue to do so as long as he took care of it. These days everything around him felt out of control. Doing this one small thing was a corner he could tuck in tight, have power over. It was still just as ugly, and in truth didn't keep very good time, but he'd keep at it, until things settled down.

A truck passed on the left, roaring like a jet. He slid the window up. As he approached the Ararat Street exit, more cars spilled from their private worlds onto the highway. The road widened into three lanes this close to the center of the city, an assembly line for daily worker bees, far from the peaceful stretch of road it had been.

Bees. No sign of them this morning; no waking in the night to their angry, insistent whine. He'd called the builder yesterday after lunch, but Wayne hadn't remembered any wasp issues when the house was built.

Not that it isn't possible, he'd said. *You want everything storybook, but bugs are the one thing you'll never completely control, especially where* you *live.* They *need to live somewhere.*

He'd given Corey the number of an exterminator. If they continued to poke their alien faces where they didn't belong, he'd give the guy a call. He'd forgotten about checking the attic. Tonight, though. He'd check tonight.

He moved into the right lane, heading for the downtown exit. The city always looked refreshed in the morning, clean. Corey was falling behind on his project. Time to focus, get stuff done, take his mind off the pending visit to Vanessa's house tonight. He wasn't looking forward to it. In some ways, everything had started to get weird once she had made her entrance into their lives.

Vanessa, the old man and his cute little dog. That was another battle Corey had no mental energy to tackle.

II

"Almost seven years, now," Vanessa said, in answer to Sam's question, "and hopefully another seventy." She tossed her head back in a gesture now as familiar to Corey as his wife's constant tucking of stray locks behind her ear, or Abby's habit of sticking out her lower lip when deep in thought.

"I can see why," Sam said, leaning back on the couch. "The house might be small, but it's so warm. And with the woods behind you, feels like it's hidden in a forest." She pushed aside the thin curtains drifting in the breeze over the double hung windows, looked out towards the neighborhood. The house was angled to allow a view to the trees marking the edge of the woods. The twilight glow, filtered through the sheer material, drifted across her face. Corey decided his wife never looked more comfortable anywhere, or more beautiful. The thought kindled a strange sadness in him.

"Like a gingerbread house." Vanessa laughed, ignoring Corey's discomfort or, more likely, missing it entirely.

"Yes," Sam said, "exactly."

That was when Corey realized what bothered him so much. Not how well Sam and Vanessa connected, on more levels than perhaps he and she ever had. It was, quite simply, that she *became* Vanessa, took on her relaxed, comfortable-anywhere persona when they were together.

He was losing her.

No, he wasn't. He was jealous. And selfish.

Their dinner had been a delicious meal of angel hair pasta adorned with shrimp, covered in white sauce. Everyone, including Corey, had nothing but compliments for the food. Vanessa had waved the praise away with a reference to a recipe she'd seen on the side of the box of spaghetti. Somehow, Corey didn't think that was true, especially since it was the same self-effacing comment Sam used the other day.

He sipped his coffee, a thick brew of decaf sprinkled with ginger. She'd added it without asking and, in keeping with the evening, it was the best cup of coffee he'd had in a long time. *The bitch,* he thought.

Corey smirked, wiped his mouth with his hand to cover it. Hand down, smile gone, he felt better. Abby's legs dangled over the edge of the couch, sipping a mug of hot chocolate with a generous dollop of marshmallow. She looked content letting the adults talk, but her eyes focused too much on the drink. She was fading. Almost bed time.

Vanessa regarded Corey with those piercing eyes of hers. He was entrenched in the thick cushion of a recliner. The living room was smaller than theirs, but laid out similarly. Vanessa said, "You've been rather quiet tonight, Corey."

He shrugged, forced a smile. "Sorry. Well-fed and warmed with coffee, I'm content to listen."

She stared a moment longer, reclining back against the couch like Sam was doing. For the moment, at least, he was the center of this woman's attention. It felt patronizing. "I know," she said, "next time you come, I'll show you my computer. You work as a programmer, don't you?"

He nodded. "Yeah. You do websites, right?"

"As a side. Lately I've been trying my hand at computer-based art." She laughed lightly, pushing her chin out as she did. She *was* quite beautiful. "I'm a bit flighty when it comes to the right side of my brain. Got tired of oils, and you can only get so much artistic satisfaction from making jewelry. In my mind, at least."

Samantha looked around the room. "Did you paint any of these?"

"All of them. Not great, I know, but they remind me of the moments I painted them. They were good times, so I keep them here." She leaned forward and looked at Corey with a mischievous sideways glance. "The *bad times* paintings are in the basement." She said this in mock seriousness, but Abby cringed.

"Really?"

"No, no. I'm sorry, Honey. I was only joking."

"They're wonderful," Sam said, looking around the room from her perch on the couch. Apparently, she was too comfortable to get up and browse. Corey could see five paintings from his seat. All but one were similar in size-- eight-by-ten, framed in aged wooden frames. The fifth was smaller, the size of a paperback. The painting closest to him was a still life, bowl of fruit, grapes spilling over the lip, a vase with two bright red roses. A long silver fork lay across the foreground, an odd element, but somehow fitting. The painting beside this, centered over a mahogany end table was of a long, sloping hillside, the image leading the eye down to a quaint church-steepled village glowing in darkening twilight. It looked familiar, this scene.

"These are quite good," he said, to no one in particular, still focused on the hillside scene. "That one," he pointed, "is it around here somewhere? Feels like I've seen it before."

"I don't believe so," Vanessa said. "I saw one like it on the Cape, and did my own version from memory when I got back. It's one of my oldest ones, too. Painted it in college, actually."

"Oh, where'd you go to school?" Samantha asked.

"UMass Amherst."

Corey stopped listening as they compared notes. Sam had gone to the University of Massachusetts, but in Dartmouth. The growing cynic in him assumed Vanessa knew this already and lied about where she'd gone, if she'd ever been to college at all. That was when he looked more closely at the last of the larger paintings. Another field, a pasture with a lone cow looking up from its meal of grass as if startled by the artist. The same painting was in their kitchen, or one close to it. He stared, eyes moving slightly to take in every detail. No, not *close*. Exactly the same painting.

What the hell was going on?

"You didn't paint *that* one, did you?"

Sam had been talking. She fell silent and stared at him. He didn't like the look, or the tone of his own question. But it was the same painting....

"Which one? With the cow?"

Abby turned around, suddenly awake. That was good, since her mug of hot chocolate had been tipping dangerously in her grip. "It's Moomoo!"

A flurry of motion on the couch as Sam turned, Vanessa leaned forward. Of course she must have known what the painting was about. "Oh, yes. Not my best, but I find myself always relating to that poor lonely cow." She smiled.

Sam temporarily forgot her irritation at being interrupted and whispered, "But, we have the same painting in our house. A lot like that one, at least."

"It's Moomoo," Abby said again, delighted. "He's in our kitchen. But our picture is bigger! Moomoo's bigger, too. This one is prettier."

"Why, thank you, Sweetie." Vanessa turned to Corey. "Are you sure? Was it hanging the other night? I didn't notice it. I'll admit, I based this one on a painting I saw in *The Artist* magazine. Maybe you have the original. Or a print?"

Sam said, "Oh, it's definitely a print. We got it at an art sale at the mall a long time ago. What are the odds of that?" She laughed. Corey wondered, *What are the odds?* Too many coincidences. He felt suddenly tired and out of place. Everything here was warm and comfortable. As much as he didn't want to, he had a sense of *being safe* here. The others felt that way, too. But with so many strange things falling in front of him, any coincidence bothered him. This house's sense of safety and comfort felt thinned, worn to a patchy veneer, revealing something behind the dark walls. A trap closing in on them. He looked back to the hillside painting with its village and evening glow and felt another sense of déjà vu. He'd seen that place before; in fact, he'd *been* there recently. But that was impossible.

He stared at the still life's long, silver fork in the foreground, tried not to think of Abby's nightmare. The clouds over the perfect village were yellow and purple in the sky. How many details had his daughter given him?

"Corey?"

He looked away from the wall. "What?"

Sam was standing beside his chair, laid a cool hand on his forehead. "You're sweating. Feeling OK?"

He reached up. His fingertips touched her hand, glad for its presence against his skin. He wanted to go home, be alone with his wife. Lay with her in their bed away from this strange woman with her contradicting details and intentions.

He took Sam's hand and lowered it to his mouth, kissed it lightly. "Good meal and warm coffee," he said again. He released her and added, louder, "But I'd say young Abigail has had enough excitement for the night. We'd better get you to bed, little one."

"I'm not tired," she said, but Corey knew she wouldn't put up a fight.

Sam said, "You're right. Thank you for having us over, Vanessa. Dinner and company were both wonderful."

Vanessa got to her feet. They embraced amiably. As friends. Anything else was only his imagination. Again, when Vanessa hugged him Corey was surrounded by Autumn leaves and apples, crisp air, dying grass. Then they were apart and the room came back into focus. After a prolonged squeeze for Abby, she walked them to the door.

"I assume you're taking the path back," she said, following them down the two steps to her back yard, "or do you think it's already too dark?" The woods were filled with shadow, but the path was clear.

"We'll be fine," Sam said. Corey nodded.

Vanessa took in a deep breath, her entire body lifting within the dress. "It's a beautiful night. Mind if I walk with you? It'll give me an excuse to get some exercise."

They walked together among the trees, Corey holding Abby's hand behind the two women and sensed they'd done this all before, been together in this very spot at the edge of the woods.

He still had the card for Sam's old therapist buried in his wallet. It was the second time in two days he'd thought about it. Maybe he *should* see someone, sort out the weirdness going on.

They passed the spot where the old shed was nearly invisible in the growing dusk, sagging against the gloom. No sign of wasps. *Of course not*, he thought, with a pang of irritation, *they followed you home and moved into your chimney*. Sam and Vanessa never looked in that direction, too enraptured in their discussion of how Vanessa once got a table at the craft fair at Saint Malachy's, how much jewelry she'd sold and to whom. Abby was quiet beside Corey, looking nervously around her.

Vanessa left them at the end of the path with a final set of foliage-scented hugs. By the time they reached the porch and looked back towards the woods, she was gone.

Vanessa

The room was silent. No insect sounds, no light breeze coming through the window. As if nature had withdrawn its head in expectation of a storm. Vanessa pushed herself up, then forward, settling down on top of Corey. He was full inside her, hard, even though at this hour the man was lost in sleep. He would wake in a moment, just prior to his own release and she would let him, stare into the glint of his eyes in the dark, join him in spirit as well as body. She moved with a frenzied urgency now, head spinning from the fullness of him, faster. The new mattress was silent, with no risk its rhythmic motion would wake anyone else. Everything was in her control, for the moment. Corey's breath in sleep became a gasp; then her body was filled with his sudden heat as he climaxed inside the condom. She shuddered, forced herself to leave her eyes open and meet his, which had blinked to alertness. She tightened her body's grip around him, moving faster and faster, always looking at him, and he at her. She ground herself lower, making him gasp, before leaning forward, hesitating, kissing him, wildly, passionately. In this moment of lucidity and confusion, he returned the kiss. They were one, perfect, complete. His kisses became less wanting, more reflexive, and he softened inside her. Vanessa leaned forward, holding the condom in place until he was out of her. She kissed his forehead, his nose, whispered, "Go back to sleep," which he did. *Spent.* From the side table, she lifted the warm facecloth she'd brought with her, cleaned him up, wrapped the condom in a tissue, then carefully dropped it into the pocket of her robe as she slid it on. She quietly opened the bedroom door and peered cautiously out.

Empty. Once in the bathroom, she made no further attempt at being quiet, though she kept the facecloth in the robe's pocket beside the tissue, just in case. When she emerged back into the hallway, it remained deserted. Vanessa returned to the master bedroom.

Everyone remained deeply asleep. She smiled a little, kissed his cheek before leaving the room for the last time.

Back in the hall, she leaned against the wall, feeling guilt's inevitable return. This was against *The Rules*, not just a few but every single one. She forced her smile to remain locked on her face though it was without any meaning, invisible in the dark in any case, and reminded herself that sometimes you broke the rules for a good reason. She laid a hand below her belly, feeling the lingering memory of him still inside her. Her smile faded. There was a reason for what she'd done. A good one. None of this was selfish. If she got a little pleasure from it, so what? She'd done nothing wrong. This would work. It *had* to work.

Vanessa tried in vain to keep Hank Cowles from returning to her thoughts. The *Destroyer of Worlds* as he was known by so many. The name was appropriate enough. She would beat him this time. She would *win*. She had the advantage. *She* was real. *He* was not, at least not the man currently haunting Corey's family.

Why was she so obsessed with him? Leave him to the purgatory he'd been cast into. He had no power over anyone.

She stepped lightly down the hall, trying not to think. It wasn't healthy. She was getting too deep into Corey's world, had to remain objective though this had begun to feel impossible. Vanessa was quickly becoming as lost as the man she'd just, effectively, raped.

Hank Cowles would laugh at the idea. Maybe he was laughing now, he and his stupid little dog.

She let out a breath. *Stop it!* Stepping outside into the cool night air, it was easier to follow such a command. A *little* easier, at least. And tomorrow she would meet the man himself, face the demon chewing apart Corey Union's soul.

Corey
Thursday

I

Corey woke from a stone dead sleep so abruptly his first waking breath was a prolonged gasp. He waited, heard only Sam's steady, nasally breathing beside him, still asleep. He rolled over, draped his arm across her. She felt good against him, more so as she reflexively snuggled closer. Why did he feel like such a piece of shit? He hadn't done anything wrong. Just a stupid, *stupid* dream. The second one where he'd had sex with their neighbor, no snippet or fragment this time but a drawn out, vivid play. A long way from seeing clowns rolling past on the back of a caboose like he'd long suffered as a child. He craved for that nonsensical but nightmarish image of his youth over this. Less a suggestion he might be attracted to another woman. Corey reached down, felt himself. Warm, but dry. *Good.*

He lay beside his wife for a long time, her arm wrapped around his in sleep, but eventually being this close became too hot. He pulled free, kissed her shoulder before rolling over. His head felt thick, hovering on the edge of sleep but never sinking under the surface. He waited.

Sleep would not come.

Corey finally gave in and glanced at the clock. Two-thirty-seven. Three and a half hours until he was supposed to wake up and get ready for another day. What day *was* it? Thursday, he thought. His brain began the mental planning reserved for the drive into the city. He tried to stop thinking, let his mind empty and drift, *like a balloon loosed from a child's tentative grip.* He was getting pretty good at that.

G. Daniel Gunn

Focus on the balloon, he told himself; *watch it drift*. He imagined himself rocking back and forth between the clouds, pushed by unseen hands.

All around him, imaginary birds sang, bees hummed, buzzed louder – *shit*! That wasn't his imagination. Though faint, the buzzing was coming from down the hall.

They're back. He could pretend they weren't, pretend he was a balloon again but knew the truth - he was going to lay here listening to them until...

Corey slid out of the covers smoothly, not wanting to wake Samantha. He'd wander down the hall to see how bad it was (he'd closed the flue, of course he had...), get a drink of water, swallow some Tylenol. Not that Tylenol had any way of helping him sleep without a good dose of Codeine, but until he broke down and bought some sleeping pills, taking *anything* was better than nothing at all.

Corey stepped barefoot into the hall. He smelled it immediately. Wet stink of garbage, rotting food, back of the throat tang of vinegar. He laid a hand over his nose and mouth. For a few seconds, all he smelled was his own, sweating skin, then the reek found a path between the creases of his palm and back into his head. *What the hell is this?*

Flashing images fought for attention in his imagination. Food gone bad, dead animal outside. He leaned into Abby's closed door, breathed in. The smell was not coming from in there. Best not to check on her, risk letting the odor into her room.

When Warren had walked them through the finished construction, he'd suggested a cap for the flue top, to keep squirrels from falling inside. Corey thought it would be too ugly up there, and the house was built far enough from the trees to keep critters off the roof. *Obviously not.* Something had crawled inside, then died. Maybe it disturbed the nest

120

and now he'd be paying more money to clean out its corpse *and* end up installing one of those stupid caps.

He stepped quietly to the end of the hall, hand back over his face and reached for the light switch. *Wait.* Corey listened, heard nothing but the usual serenade of nature outside the windows. Had the buzzing been his imagination?

But the *stink*... he lowered his hand. Still there, somewhere. The kitchen maybe. He turned in that direction. The back door was closed. Night glowed blue through the four-square window behind the curtain.

He reached around the corner and turned on the overhead light.

He stared, fumbling to make sense of what he saw. Corey looked around the room for Abby. He stepped further in. No one here. Of course not. The light had been out.

Scattered around the kitchen table were dozens of sandwiches. Peanut butter and jelly if his guess was right, bread stained purple from long soaked through with jelly. Each rotted on a separate paper towel. Five, no *six* glasses of milk, most half full below thin film of ghostly white as if the milk had leaked through a pinhole in the bottom. Drained, evaporated.

That was the smell. Sour milk, stale bread. All along the edges – crust cut off, the way she liked it – more stains, maybe mold.

Nothing clicked in his mind, no sense to it. Corey took a second step into the room. At the far corner of the table – Samantha's secret book of poetry, open, pen resting on top with the exposed pages stained with coffee circles and other unidentifiable markings. He couldn't move any further, only stared at the sandwiches, the book, finally forcing his head to turn away towards the counter. A jar of peanut butter beside the sink, another of jelly, covers askew on top as if something had escaped and –

Corey turned off the light, pressed both palms against his face. Nausea churned inside him, mixing, readying itself for release. He had no balance, finally leaned on the corner of the wall at the boundary of kitchen and living room, the border of madness and sanity. Nothing made sense, so it *must* be him. He was crazy.

And his throat was dry. Even with a tight, worried stomach Corey forced himself to swallow. He was sleepwalking. Hands still on his face, smell of his own skin, a real sensation.

If he was asleep a second ago, he was awake now. No bees, nothing wrong in the kitchen. He would turn on the light, prove everything was normal. He tried to move a hand that way, could not. He *would* not.

Back to bed, yes. *Go back to bed and forget all of this. Hurry.*

Everything, every day, everywhere the world was twisting inside out, going wrong. *He* was wrong.

Something buzzed beside his ear. Corey used one hand to swat at it, connected with nothing. The whine of small wings, joined by a second, and a third. They were back. The bees were back.

Corey stayed where he was, one hand hovering beside his head, the other pressed against his face, against the smell he refused to acknowledge. He would not move until he knew for certain he was awake.

Another sound, now. Ticking, like the clock, but coming from outside, on the front porch. Corey pivoted sideways, toes moving from the cool linoleum to the hallway carpet. He lowered the other hand to stare at the same nighttime glow outside the windows beside the front door. Nothing moved outside, not that he could see. It was so dark, though.

Tickety, tickety, went the sound again. *Click, click, click.*

Claws. When the word came he knew it was true. Claws on the porch.

Corey whimpered, sensing the walls beginning to melt around him, heated rubber sagging, his world no longer solid. *Sam,* he thought, *and Abby. They need you. Fight this!*

Thinking of them helped. The walls righted to solid masses again. *What would Abby do if her father went crazy? I have to stay strong.*

He had to *protect* them.

So many little phobias, fears, twitches he'd allowed himself lately. It wasn't fair to them. It was selfish. If he focused only on Sam, on Abby....

Something bumped against the front door; then the ticking resumed. It wasn't a large porch. What the hell was out there?

Go down and see. Turn on the outside light and see. Be a man!

He straightened, pushed himself deliberately towards the one of the narrow windows beside the door. If there was an intruder, or a stupid raccoon which was probably all it was....

He flipped on the outside light, turned his head against the window.

The porch glowed a dull yellow. Nothing. No animal, no fleeing man in black ski mask, no pile of dog shit left outside the door by some kids.

He couldn't see much of anything past the steps. The front yard looked empty. Whatever it was had probably slinked back into the thin patch of woods between the house and road.

Go back to bed.
Open the door.
Go back....

Corey tightened the bathrobe and opened the inside door, stood in front of the screen door and checked the porch one more time. Still empty. Until a white dog emerged from the cover of the rhododendron bush Sam had planted last week. Corey knew this dog, had seen it walking with Hank Cowles.

Its stump of a tail began to wag, a vague blur in the murk outside the circle of the light. The little dog opened its mouth as if in to yawn. It hissed instead. Not a bark or growl, just a steady hiss like escaping steam. Corey expected to see it collapse into itself, deflate like a balloon...

...floating above the trees now, think of the balloon, sailing away...

Headlights up the driveway, bright square eyes. He prayed it was a police cruiser. They'd tell him of a trespasser in the neighborhood, explain he wasn't mad, wasn't losing his mind. The car pulled to a stop in front of his Honda, engine idling.

A growl made Corey look back down. Nurse Charles's mouth had closed, lips raised, tiny white teeth. *No, no this is wrong.* He looked back towards the police car, but that wasn't what it was. A white *In Service* sign flashed from the roof. The yellow cab's back door opened.

Corey closed his eyes, thought of the balloon, but the sky in his mind was filled with burning clouds, roiling black with red zips of lightning. Was this how the mind went away, how it died, in a mental firestorm?

The cab's horn began to honk in a protracted *beeeeeeeeeeep.* Corey kept his eyes shut tight, even as the dog started barking. He would not look at the cab, which was not real anyway, nor the dog, nor the clouds or storm building in his mind. None of it was real.

He finally covered his ears and screamed, trying to block out the noise. Eyes still closed, he turned and stumbled back into the house, tripped on the leg of the recliner and dropped his hands to catch himself. Behind him, the screen door had closed, but he knew the dog had followed him inside. Corey could hear its tiny claws on the squares of tile in the foyer. He would not look. Instead, he crawled further into the living room, around the chair, surrounded now by the renewed buzzing of the wasps and stench of the house. He reached up, found the recliner's arm and climbed up onto it, pushing to the floor a pile of newspapers, only absently noting their unexpected presence, and curled into a ball with his feet pulled up.

Something small landed on his head. More bees. They *were* bees, had to be, and if he did not bother them, he would be safe. More landed on his arms, crawled along his neck. He curled tighter and began to scream again, and again and again, and would continue until everything went away.

It did not. Beside his chair, the dog renewed its barking, stirring up the bees. The patter of wasps on his head and arms, in his hair - not stinging, they weren't stinging, not yet at least – overpowered by the pounding of a fist against the side of the screen door. Why didn't he just come in?

Try as he might, Corey could not focus on Abby, or Samantha, could not help them anymore. The end had come and he was too afraid to do anything but force himself into stillness and hope the bees did not sting and the dog not bite and he kept on screaming as the night dragged on and on and on....

II

A touch on his shoulder. "Corey?"

Corey opened his eyes, confused. The living room was filled with bright sunlight. He'd been asleep, in the chair, curled up, hiding. Samantha leaned over with a look of tentative amusement, changing as she got a better look at him. "Corey, why are you – " Her eyes drifted over him; her mouth tightened. "I thought you'd managed to get out this morning without waking me, but – "Again, she didn't finished the sentence, only waved a hand at him.

"Daddy, are you staying home today?" Abby had a box of Pop tarts in her hand, waiting for Sam to get one into the toaster.

Corey uncurled his legs. They were stiff and his back hurt. "I…" What was he going to say?

As he leaned back into the chair, stretching his legs free of the robe, Sam's wonderful, cool hand pressed his forehead as it had done last night. Could she feel how fast his mind was racing, trying to rework what had happened, to rationalize it? How could he explain that her husband could no longer protect her, care for her, that he'd gone completely *ga-ga* last night?

"You're a little warm, but not too bad. How are you feeling?"

Maybe he wasn't crazy. He could think, appreciate the feel of his wife's touch, miss it as she moved her hand away. He could never tell her what he'd seen. A lie was all he could come up with. "Sorry," he said, forcing his breath out in a casual stream of air – *like the dog last night, leaking, deflating before it began to growl, don't -* "couldn't sleep last night... Did I wake you at all?"

Sam looked sideways, considering, then shook her head. Her expression, Corey was delighted to see, had softened from fear to, maybe if he was lucky, a touch of appreciation. *Just keep lying and that look will always be yours*, he thought. His gut hardened. He wanted to cry.

Corey forced himself not to look where his feet were, afraid of seeing dead wasps littering the carpet. "Anyway, sorry. Figured I'd let you sleep and curled up on the chair, read for a while. Finally fell back to sleep." *Liar, liar, pants on fire*....

Sam did a cursory glance around, perhaps looking for some corroboration to his story. There was, of course, no book. Regardless, she leaned in and embraced him. "My knight in terrycloth armor," she said, rubbing her hands along his robed back. "You don't look like you've slept much. Maybe you *are* sick. Why not call work then sleep in a little?"

He grunted, already thinking that was a good idea. He stood up, pulled her close and glanced at Abby still waiting at the edge of the kitchen spinning the box of Pop tarts between her hands. Corey kissed his wife's ear, whispered, "Maybe I will."

She pushed him away, gently, adjusted his robe. "Sounds like you haven't slept much the past few days." Her hands lingered on the folds, eyes down. "Maybe it's just the new house." She didn't sound convinced. No more than he was. She must have decided to leave it alone, looked up – she had beautiful blue eyes speckled with brown – and kissed his cheek before walking into the kitchen, plucking the Pop tarts from Abby on the way. Corey looked around the living room. Hadn't he knocked some newspapers off the chair? The floor was clean except for a couple of naked Barbie dolls under the side table. Another illusion of the night. Newspapers had no place in this house. They only fed the fire of his madness.

Sam called from the kitchen, "Abby and I are going to visit the library today. They're having a story time."

He nodded, knowing she wouldn't see it. *Story time...* the thing Vanessa had suggested. So much happening in one week. How much more would come to push him further down the rabbit hole before it was over? Corey stopped at the door to the bathroom. He needed to brush his teeth, get back into bed, sleep away the night so he could wake up new, *better*. He doubled back and leaned into the kitchen. The room was clean, orderly. *Safe* as always. Samantha was pulling the Pop tart from the toaster – hardly more than warmed, the way Abby liked it. His daughter was at the table tracing the Formica patterns with a fingertip, completely lost in the exercise.

All was well with the world. Corey faded back down the hall before Sam caught him spying. In the bathroom, his reflection refused to meet his eyes as he brushed his teeth. He didn't blame it.

III

The Hillcrest Public Library was an impressive blend of two worlds, the modern and the historic. Large stone blocks had been arranged with a symmetry only masons of two hundred years past could have achieved with minimal tools save a desire to build something functional and pleasing to the eye. Rising two stories from this stone foundation, the library shone with recently-restored brickwork, according to the sign on the wall of the reading room where Samantha waited. Through the arched doorway, Abby and seven other children fidgeted before a narrow faced old woman who read from *The Lorax*. Of all the Dr. Seuss' stories, Sam thought this one might be too heavy-handed for such a young crowd. Still, the children listened to her hushed reading, worrying in their own ways about the *Truffala Trees*. Sam tried to avoid the searching gaze of another mother sitting across the alcove. The woman was tall and lean, a mass of blonde hair rising from her head in a tsunami. Since they were seated in facing chairs – the remaining mothers having slipped away to their cars or the bookshelves – Sam felt bad for avoiding her unspoken plea for company.

She turned away from the children and whispered, "I'm Samantha. That's my daughter, Abby, in the pink t-shirt." She nodded into the main room. The woman's expression brightened with relief.

"Fran," she said, offering her hand. Sam took it. It was warm and damp, unlike the dry, confident feel of Vanessa. She chided herself for the thought. Fran added, "That's my Honey sitting next to – was her name Abby, you said?" Sam assumed she meant the red-haired girl with whom Abby was whispering in a miniature rendition of their conversation.

"Yes. Honey? Is that her name?"

Fran put long painted nails to her face to cover a smirk. "Yes, seriously. One of those family names we *had* to use else risk excommunication from the family. Honey, like the bees."

Sam tensed, couldn't believe that was a coincidence. She fought to believe it anyway, even as the sun coming though the tall, stained-glass dimmed to yellow. *Yellow, like the bees.*

"Are you OK? Samantha, was it?"

She would roll with it, *swim with the tide until it carried you home.*

"You said bees, that's all. We've been having some wasp problems in the new house. Caught me a little off guard."

Fran clapped her hands together – her hands were always in motion, like a baker kneading dough. "Are you the family that built on the Cowles property?"

Sam leaned forward. "You know Hank Cowles?"

"No."

The woman said nothing else, eyes clear but hardly blinking. No *real* expression to gain any meaning. She was simply done talking. Sam wondered if everyone in this town was crazy. Maybe that would be a good thing. She'd fit in better.

"Oh," Samantha said, then looked around for something to inspire a conversation. "This is a nice building."

"Yes, we come here every Thursday for Story Time…"

Stepford, Sam decided, *that's what this woman reminded her of, one of the wives from that movie.*

"…since there really aren't too many children Honey's age on our street." She glanced into the room. "Our daughters seem to be hitting it off."

The two girls were now listening attentively to the old woman as she reached the part where the *gloppity-glop* was muddying up the river. Sam shrugged. It would be good for Abby to make a friend. Even if the kid's name was Honey and her mother a robot. "They seem to, yes. Have you lived in Hillcrest long?"

Fran nodded, the wave of hair coming in, drifting out. "Cab and I moved into town after we were married. It seemed like such a nice town - "

Cab. Honey. Bees. Yellow.

Please, God, everyone in town has a screwed up name but that doesn't mean anything....

Samantha cleared her throat, but was spared having to find a comprehensible reply. Fran added, "Like I said, there are simply no girls her age on our street. It would be wonderful if maybe – Abby was it? – could come to our house for a play date. Tomorrow maybe? Honey would be so thrilled!"

Sam smiled, pushing up her cheeks with some effort, feeling like a clown. Where had she left her notebook? On the table, maybe. *God, no...* Corey was home. *It's under the mattress where your husband sleeps, where he lay lost in his own world.* What did it matter, anyway? He told her in no uncertain terms he didn't care if she kept her poetry from him, and he'd always known where she hid it. Maybe that's what was bothering her, the secret. No longer hers. Never had been.

"Or another day is fine. I'm sorry. I can be so pushy sometimes."

"No, I'm sorry. Tomorrow would be nice." She'd said this out of reflex, before fully understanding what the question had been. *Play date, that was it.* "If it's not an inconvenience."

The hands rose and fell, waving away the smoke of doubt, *the fog curling about our wrists and trying to pull us all into its undertow.*

She liked that line. Hopefully, she'd remember it.

"No, none at all. Does she still nap?" Sam shook her head. "Good, good. They're getting older now, aren't they? Honey still goes down in the morning for an hour, gives me a chance to try my Pilates routine. Have you tried Pilates?" Sam shook her head again. New recipes intimidated her. "Oh, it's wonderful. You'll have to try it. How about one o'clock? Just after lunch? Honey will be so thrilled."

"That would be fine. I should check with Abby. Sometimes she can be shy."

"Of course. We have to let them make *some* decisions, don't we?" Flutter, wave.

The conversation wilted into silence. Before it could collapse entirely, the old woman closed *The Lorax* and thanked the girls "so much" for their attention. Abby and Honey were chatting, like the friends Fran *so hoped* they would be, as they found their mothers. Seeing them like this, Samantha didn't think her daughter would object to a play date. It would be good. Give her some time alone while Abby made some friends.

Would Vanessa would be home? A warm feeling accompanied the thought. She didn't curse herself for it. Not this time.

Vanessa

Vanessa stared at her own reflection in the mirror. As usual, she didn't like what she saw. A hypocrite, a cheat, a lonely pathetic woman lost in others' illusions. She spit, rinsed, worked on brushing her hair. Last week cutting it short had seemed like a good idea, but she continued to feel the presence of the lost braid, a phantom limb reminding her every day how much uglier she was without it. It taunted her like the world itself had always done.

She put the brush down. *Good enough.* She'd see how it looked once it had dried completely. She wished Robert would leave so she could walk out of the bathroom naked, as she liked to do most mornings, most *usual* mornings, and let the cool air dry the remnants of the shower from her skin. It was a sensation she loved almost as much as she hated everything else about herself. A *Yin* to the *Yang* of her own self loathing. Especially today.

She'd broken *The Rule*. Not just last night-- she wasn't going to pretend this was the first -- but she'd gone farther, beyond any reasonable line. She spent a long hour afterward rationalizing everything from as many angles as her tired mind could create but she, more than anyone, knew the danger of building illusions. The eyes glaring back at her this morning in the mirror were tinged red. *Not enough sleep, Vanny? Maybe if you stayed in bed with your cocoa and book instead of sneaking into Mister Union's, you'd be feeling more chipper this morning.*

She lifted the robe hanging on the back of the bathroom door and wrapped it reluctantly around herself; stepped into the bedroom and dressed. Robert called through the door, "I'm going to head home, Vanessa.

You've got your *other man* coming over in a few minutes, don't you?" He laughed, never one to hide an innuendo if he could help it. But he knew she was a professional. Vanessa almost laughed at the irony.

Dressed, she could have gone out into the hall and spoken to him face to face. Instead she shouted through the closed door, "That's fine."

A pause. "OK. See you again tonight, then?"

"I'll be counting the hours." She hoped he noticed the sarcasm. Robert only laughed, the sound fading as he headed for the door. He was an on OK guy, she supposed. Kept things business-like most of the time. Unlike Andrew. She shouldn't look forward to his arrival as much as she did, or smile at the thought of him. He was nice, but she couldn't afford to let anyone get too close. Not now.

Robert's car started outside, crunch of tires on gravel. After fidgeting with her drying hair in the mirror over the dresser for another few minutes Vanessa finally left the bedroom, wandered into the kitchen. The coffee was on. Robert earned some brownie points for that. She took one of the oversized ceramic mugs from the cabinet, filled it and wandered outside to the porch. She closed her eyes and let the morning sun burn away any sleep lingering behind her lids, losing herself in the coffee steam, the aroma.

Movement in the yard. Vanessa looked up through the steam. Hank Cowles stood by the tree line, staring back at her. She gasped, almost spilled coffee across her new white blouse. Wiping her steam-damp face with her hand, she stood and peered over the railing. The old man wasn't there, of course. Just the twisted arms of an oddly shaped clump of mountain laurel.

She sat back down. Did *he* know how she'd broken so many rules, that she'd physically intervened against him? Did Cowles understand, watching from his own private prison cell, that *she* was the one who would finally break the hold he had on the Unions?

She laughed, tried to at least, wasn't very successful, took a sip of coffee. It burned her awake a little more. *Don't head down that path.* Hank Cowles did not know. How *could* he?

Didn't matter. The need to step inside Corey's world, become the wedge between him and his wife and child, between him and Cowles, was growing dangerously towards desperation. Time was running out. The clock was ticking and she had to try anything, *everything*, before –

Before what? The end of the world? Union's fantasies, his *phobias* as he himself called them, had no basis in reality and if she ever forgot that important fact, she'd be as lost as he already was. Corey didn't understand what was happening, not consciously, but was beginning to recognize what she was doing, removing Samantha from his life permanently, along with his daughter. It was surreal how he had misinterpreted her love for *him* as some forbidden love for his wife.

Vanessa wasn't in love with Corey. That was ridiculous.

Just lonely. Very lonely, and afraid.

The clock is ticking.

That theme kept coming back.

Nurse Charles stepped from the shadows of a narrow cluster of trees, near the place she'd imagined Hank Cowles. Vanessa stared down the mirage until it became a white cat. It noticed her stare, returned it with a belligerent flick of its tail before running across the yard and disappearing into the woods again.

There had been the expected barrage of objections from Jim Chen in response to her request. He didn't like what she was doing and took every opportunity to tell her. Vanessa didn't lie to him, though her explanation was a watered down rendition of how she actually felt. Hank Cowles was the catalyst. He had set the clock ticking towards the end of Corey's world – both real and imagined. He was both figuratively and literally the *Destroyer of Worlds* and she couldn't touch him, could only coax Corey Union from the old man's grip and towards... (*towards* what*, Vanny, your own waiting arms? Grow up...*).

Confronting the man face-to-face would be risky, on some level she wouldn't fully grasp the extent of the risk until the meeting occurred. She'd never been anywhere near him physically. No words had ever passed between them. Ironic, really, the idea of two people in the universe who had the most influence on what was happening never once laying eyes on each other.

Until today. If for no other reason than to dispel any illusions about the man – *the demon, the monster* – that had taken root in her sleep-deprived brain thanks to Corey. Hank Cowles couldn't hurt *her*. Both of them knew that. Or they would, soon enough - she needed to believe that fact if she ever hoped to make it back from this surreal week in one piece. Already, she felt herself coming undone, losing her true purpose. Vanessa only had a couple more days to finish the destruction of Corey's world, of everything he pretended to love, in order to save him.

She was doing it for *him*.

No one else.

She took another sip of coffee when the distant whine of a motorcycle reached her from up the road. She smiled again and got up, slowly, walked around the house to meet Andrew Booth as he killed the engine and swung off the seat. Her knight in shining armor riding on his steed, coming to her rescue. He'd appreciate the image. That would send the wrong signal, however. Still, seeing his large, dark face emerge from under the helmet, she didn't care. *Maybe*, she thought. *Maybe when this is all over....*

Corey

Corey sat cross-legged on the living room floor, wearing only a pair of boxers long past their prime. Everything he owned was old, worn out. Including the clock in front of him. He watched the second hand count out the moments of the day in quick jerks while the minute hand crawled towards another hour. He'd not been sitting here more than ten minutes, but his body felt heavy, weighted into the rug as if inexorably sinking into the fibers, melting like the walls had done last night – *just a dream. Just a bad dream.*

The house was quiet without the girls. He'd managed to fall into a rough sleep after calling work. *Was* he sick? Not physically. Now that he was aake again, and staring at the old clock, he wondered what he was waiting for. The bees to return? Was the swarm going to return every time he didn't wind this stupid piece of junk? He hadn't wound it this morning. Corey stared at the ugly finish, gaudy design. Everything about the clock was awkward and poorly made. Just because something was old didn't make it worth keeping. He would defy it, wait for whatever entity, God or the devil or the *Ghost in the Machine* to demand he do his duty. And for what? So the stupid thing could *still* lose five minutes a day?

Corey sighed, feeling stupid, then got up and wandered back into the bedroom. He didn't consciously know what he intended to do, not really, until he'd lifted a discarded pair of chinos from the floor and pulled out his wallet. His fingers found the compartment behind the credit card where he kept random papers. Movie rental ID, AAA card. He thumbed through the small stack, pulled out the tattered business card of the woman who had treated Samantha after the miscarriage. The business card for someone whom Corey found himself thinking about a lot lately, though Sam had never thought too fondly of her. Looking at the card, he realized Doctor Reilly was more than a simple therapist. The name had the suffix of "MD." Psychiatrist, then? A professional, someone who might be able....

Don't. You're just tired, a lot on your mind. The house, a million details and decisions during construction, the world burning and curling up like a piece of paper on fire.

He'd bent the card between his fingers. *You need help*, a new voice, distant in his head, told him. A woman's voice. Maybe the person printed on the card, speaking to him through the talisman he held between his thumb and finger.

Corey walked slowly down the hall, glanced at the clock and decided *Story Time* would probably last a while longer.

The phone hung on the wall just inside the kitchen. It was suddenly in his hand, though he didn't remember picking it up. Nothing was in his control anymore.

That thought pushed him to dial the number. As it rang, Corey prayed she wouldn't answer. If he got a machine, he wouldn't leave a message, lie to himself that he'd tried.

A woman answered after three rings.

He could hang up. What if she had Caller-ID?

"Hello?" she said a second time.

"Doctor Reilly?" This was wrong. He was fine. *For Abby*. He was doing this for Abby, and Samantha.

"Yes, who is this?"

He could still turn back. The phone was slippery. He said, "Corey Union. You treated my wife once. Samantha?"

"Samantha? Samantha Union. Yes, I remember. You said your name is Corey? Is Samantha all right?"

"She's fine." *Jump right in or hang up.* "I'm calling for another reason."

Silence. The woman was waiting, as only a psychiatrist-therapist-whatever could do, and there was comfort in that fact. "I - " he swallowed, licked his lips. Every word had to be pushed like a reluctant mule. "I seem to be… having problems. Relaxing. I'm afraid of things. I have a clock. And there are bees. And…" He wanted to say, *and an old man named Hank Cowles stares at me from imaginary cabs or from sidewalks with his little monster dog.* But it wasn't true. None of it was true.

None of it is real.

"Yes," she said, confirming his thought. "And… what?"

He pulled the phone cord to its breaking point in order to keep an eye out the living room window, making sure Sam and Abby weren't coming up the driveway.

He pushed more words loose. "I don't know what is going on. Nothing is normal, not anymore. I'm seeing things. They can't be real." *Rotting peanut butter sandwiches and stained notebooks and cabs and dogs and bees.* "The bees are real. At least, they *look* real." He sobbed, swallowed it down, squinted, looked outside again. He was becoming confused as to what he was actually saying aloud and what had only been thoughts.

"Corey, where are you now?"

In my living room.

"In Hillcrest?"

"Yes."

His heart rate picked up. Something wasn't right. "How did you know…"

After a pause, "How did I know what? Corey?"

How did she know they'd moved to Hillcrest?

"You must have told me," the voice said.

The bees announced themselves from inside the fireplace. Corey heard their angry whine, a thousand small planes diving down the flue, hitting the trap.

The woman answered a question *he never asked.*

"Mister Union, wait."

"What the hell is going on? Who is this?"

"You called *me*, remember?"

He looked out the window again. Hank Cowles was standing in the driveway. The old man raised his long-sleeved arm in a slow greeting. He was laughing. Nurse Charles, *what a stupid fucking name*, wagged her tail beside his ankle. Corey could just make out her horrible pink tongue.

Reilly's voice was a tinny whine, bees trapped in the earpiece. The buzzing inside the flue was getting louder, tapping against the vent hood, trying to get inside.

The clock. Wind the clock.

"No!"

He pressed the disconnect button and tossed the phone onto the couch. The cord tried to curl back in on itself, pulling the handset to the carpet. Corey walked slowly – *show no fear* – into the kitchen, away from the front of the house where the terrible old man, *none of this is real;* he *is not real*, was watching and waving and laughing.

When he reached the kitchen table, Corey froze. Vanessa was on the porch, staring at him though the picture window. Her beautiful face was stone, expressionless. She wore the same neck-buttoned dress, long black hair loose and blowing in the breeze.

The sound of the bees faded, then was gone. Only the ticking of the clock remained. He shouldn't be able to hear it, not from here. Corey dared not break eye contact with his neighbor, even when the rotted smell returned. The stench filled the room until he covered his face as he'd done last night and squeezed his eyes shut. Blinded, wandering sideways along the kitchen, his hip collided with the kitchen counter. He slid down, the cabinet handle pressing into his back.

Bird song through the window. Corey opened his eyes, the dream sinking away. Morning air blew into the kitchen like Sam's kisses over his skin, bringing him back to reality. To *here*. The real world. Not any safer than the nightmare, but normal, sometimes even happy. For the moment, perhaps for the last time, he was safe again.

Vanessa

I

After lingering for a few minutes with the air conditioning on high, Vanessa killed the ignition and got out of the car. Summer heat poured over her in a wave, but that was good. Woke her up. She had to stay focused.

Corey had come *so close*! He'd made the call; had actually gotten up, lifted the handset and returned with it to the couch, though he'd never actually dialed a number. Not that it would have made a difference; the house's phone service had been long disconnected. Vanessa had played along with the scene, and in the process managed to ruin everything. All this time, to confuse actual dialogue with his thoughts. *Such an idiot*!

She closed her eyes. It was a success, no matter how brief. What too many people in her profession would call a "breakthrough."

She took a deep breath outside the front doors, let it out. The people inside, not the least of whom was the man waiting to introduce her to Hank Cowles, were protective of their residents, loathsome and vile as most might be. Vanessa straightened her blouse, brushed non-existent lint off the black skirt before stepping into the lobby. The air inside was bitter cold, helped to mask the myriad of scents, of emotions, lingering in every corner.

Bad sign. She was starting to think like Samantha Union.

The security officer looked up from the desk. His gray hair sharply contrasted his deep black skin. Aside from this single piece of furniture, the oversized foyer was stark save a series of cameras mounted in the corners of the ceiling.

"May I help you?"

143

Vanessa handed him one of her business cards. "Hi. I'm Doctor Reilly. I have an appointment with your Deputy Director, John Soames."

II

Judging by the tang of disinfectant and wet streaks along the floor, the hallway had been recently mopped. The walls, however, hadn't been painted in over a generation. They were beige, faded and stained. Voices drifted out from behind each door as they passed. Some sang; others shouted unintelligible words, sermons offered blindly through the thick walls, begging for attention. Centered above Vanessa and Soames, the wire-meshed lights were caked in dust, casting the depressing atmosphere with a garish, yellow glow. One bulb flickered in a silent death throe as they passed beneath it.

John Soames was a thin man in a suit that did not fit. He walked with arms at his sides, fingers flicking and curling over themselves like snakes.

"We'll wait for Martin before opening the door. I wouldn't say he's dangerous - not here I mean. *Out there*, well," the snakes ceased their dance for a moment, then resumed. Soames let his sentence die under the dusty light. Vanessa didn't need him to finish. The man whose cell they were approaching had been, for the past two years, Venning Memorial's most famous, or infamous, patient.

She fought the urge to whisper. Instead, she said, as casually as possible, "If he's not dangerous, why is he in solitary?"

Soames did not answer immediately. They rounded a corner into a hallway much like the previous, dimly lighted, in need of paint. The odor was stronger here, air stale. The passage ended at a reinforced, electronically locked door after only two cells on each side.

A large Latino man with fat arms waited by the first door on the left.

"Oh, Martin, you're already here. Good; that's good." This served as their only introduction. Soames turned back to Vanessa. "We keep the patient in here because he was causing *undue hardship*," he italicized the words by forming flaccid quotation marks with his fingers, "among the other residents when we let him mingle for very long."

"Undue hardship?" she said. "You mean violence?"

Martin laughed. "No, Ma'am. Just freaky." He shrugged. "Wasn't him, anyway. It was Nurse Charles."

Vanessa tightened her mouth, tried not to show surprise. "You let him keep the dog?" If they had, they were as insane as Hank Cowles.

Soames said, "Martin, please. No, Doctor. We didn't. They never found the animal, to be honest."

"Probably ate it for lunch," Martin said, chuckling. At the director's glare, he moved to the second door.

Soames said, "Everything will be clear when you meet him." He nodded to Martin, who pulled a set of keys from a retractable wire attached to his belt. After spending a few seconds looking for the right one, he inserted it into the lock but did not turn it. He said to Vanessa, "The guy's not known for violence, but I'm going inside with you, anyway."

"No argument," Soames added before she could reply, fingers resuming their dance at his side.

Martin continued, "If I sense anything wrong, or you give me a nod, I'll get you out of there before the old man can blink twice. Got it?"

Vanessa tried to smile, gave it up and said, "Got it."

He looked at his boss. "You going in, Doctor Soames?"

"I'll wait out here if that's OK." He turned to Vanessa, eyebrows raised. "Doctor?"

"That's fine." Vanessa couldn't take her eyes off the door.

Martin nodded. "OK. Show time!" He turned the key, but before opening the door slid aside a small panel at the top and said, "Mister Cowles? We're coming in, sir. You have a visitor."

He glanced inside, shook his head with some unspoken irritation, then slid the panel close and opened the door, leaning back into the hall to wave her inside. "After you."

Vanessa stepped in. The room was known in most circles as a Quiet Room. It had once been solitary for the more violent patients, as evidenced by the markings on the wall where padding had once been fastened. The padding was now gone, no *rubber room* here, but apparently no one felt the need to scrape the walls clean of old adhesive nor add paint. A unsheltered toilet had been installed in the corner with a fixed seat, no lid. Hank Cowles had forgone the room's only chair and sat on the floor beside the bed, opposite the door. Clad in the institution's standard gray pajamas, he leaned against the wall with both legs straight out in front of him.

His left arm was limp, hand resting on the floor, palm up. His right, however, moved steadily back and forth a few inches above the floor. The pantomime was obvious. He was petting an imaginary dog, over and over from the head (Vanessa assumed) down the back, returning to the head, down again. Gently, steadily. A small dog, *Shih-Tzu* if she remembered the reports in the papers and, of course, what she'd learned from Corey during their sessions.

Hank Cowles didn't look as old as she'd imagined, though his records pegged him at eighty-three. He was balding. Whatever white tufted hair remained on his scalp was wild from neglect. His face, however, was alive and bright. After so much time in his situation, most people would have the characteristic sunken eyes, lost look or blank stare. Some clear sign of defeat.

The old man was very alert. And smiling.

"Mister Cowles, this is Doctor Reilly. She'd like a few words with you. I trust you'll give her the same courtesy and respect that we offer you. OK?"

For such a large man, working in one of the toughest wings of the institution, Martin was a regular gentleman.

Hank nodded, said nothing.

Vanessa knelt, then sat back on her calves. She had not moved much past the door, which Martin now closed behind her.

She said, "Mister Cowles," keeping with Martin's etiquette. "I promise I won't take too long. I just - "

She just *what*? All she wanted was to look at him, preferably through a two-way mirror, prove to herself that he was real, harmless. She did not like to admit the latter. But it was there, the need to see and to know that he was harmless to everyone, including Corey.

She swallowed. Hank watched her. His smile dropped a little but still held an amused smirk. Perhaps he was pleased to have company. The right hand continued patting the non-existent dog. Up, down, perfectly matching what she assumed was his old pet's contours. It was disconcerting, the exactness of the movements. Vanessa was beginning to understand what Soames had meant, why he chose not to spend much time here. She sniffed, considering her options.

Honesty was the best approach. What the hell did she care what this monster thought? Vanessa broke eye contact for only a moment, realizing this was the wrong thing to do, forced herself to look up. His eyes, blue and clear, had not shifted except to blink. "Actually, I'm not entirely sure why I came. I suppose you might say I have a professional interest in your case."

Hank's hand stopped, resting on the dog's back. He laughed, the sound half human, half growl. He looked down suddenly, whispered, "Stay. Good girl." The dog growled one more time. He resumed his petting.

The dog growled?

"Hank," Martin said, his voice so loud and sudden Vanessa flinched from it. "I think the lady would appreciate you not doing the doggy noises. For now at least. I forgot to warn her about that."

Hank glared at him, any humor lost in that one slow turn of his head. It returned again when he focused on Vanessa. "Some fear dogs," he said, his voice dry but with an underlying strength that matched his eyes, "fear *Cerberus*'s multiple heads rising over the horizon to devour the world."

He was quoting some poet Vanessa remembered reading – recently, in fact. *Where?*

The air around her became very cold. Her skin responded, tensing. Then came an empty, hollow feeling in her gut. She remembered who'd written that line of verse. A woman who had been dead for almost two years. He'd just quoted from Samantha Union's journal.

Corey

Abby and Honey had each settled on a book after a half hour of whispers and giggles among the bookshelves. Abby chose a gentler Dr. Seuss, *Green Eggs and Ham*. They had no books by that particular author in the house. He'd always seemed too surreal for Samantha's tastes. Honey clutched two Early Reader books, part of a series with magical woodland animals helping a kindly old veterinarian solve mysteries. Honey gave a quick, book-bending explanation to Fran, who stretched out her face with false excitement – *so* false Sam guessed not even her daughter would be fooled into believing the woman was interested.

Samantha was filling out a library card application as the girls waited impatiently by the counter. Fran said, in a half whisper, "So, your property has quite a history, you know."

Sam's hand twitched as she wrote her address – had Fran been following her progress along the form? *Quite a history* had enough of an ominous tone she did not respond. Instead she asked, "What's our zip code again?"

Fran told her. Sam wrote the number with fervor, hoping such an absorption in the task would dissuade –

"Two people over the past hundred years have," she leaned in, "died there."

Sam stopped writing, closed her eyes. Of course, nothing hopeful like Washington camping on his way to Lexington. Two people dead.

Still trying to ignore the woman, not take her bait, Sam handed the form to a ghostly thin girl behind the counter who only held it in front of her and stared at Fran, nodding. She then turned to Sam and said in a similar conspiratorial

149

tone, "It'th true." The words carried a heavy lisp. Pierced tongue, probably, to match her nostril, eyebrow, lower lip and other, less visible places.

Thrilled to have a larger audience, Fran said, "One was stung to death. A hiker, was it? Twenty, thirty years ago. Ran into a nest in the middle of the woods. The property's been all woods forever as far as I know." The ghost girl nodded. Fran added, "I guess he was allergic."

"The other one wuth way back, what, nineteen-fifteen, nineteen-thickteen. A boy, only thirteen yearth old, mauled by wolvth, or thomething like that."

Fran straightened, struggled to regain control of the conversation with a mad wriggling of her fingers. "Coyotes," she said, "and I have a hard time believing your mother gave you permission to mutilate your body like that, Susan." *Susan*, Sam thought. *Two s's. Thuthan, now.*

The girl rolled her eyes and looked to Sam as if to say, *Can you believe thith bitch?*

"Well," Sam said, not meeting the eyes of either, "at least it was a long time ago." She gestured to the application still captive in the pierced Susan's hands. "Are we all set with that? Abby wants to take a book out, but I still have my card from Worcester if that'll work." Susan looked down, scanned the sheet, nodded her head.

"Lookth good, Mittheth Union. Let me jutht type it in...."

She bent over the keyboard, stared down through a clear plastic section of the counter at an old CRT computer monitor. The plastic was so scuffed Sam wondered how she could see anything.

In the meantime, a second librarian, the same older woman who'd read *The Lorax*, took up post behind the counter and began to check out Honey's book. Abby looked worried, but Sam pointed to the girl and mouthed "one second" while raising a finger. Abby got the message and brightened.

"Still," Fran said, "best not let your daughter play in the yard alone. Do you have a dog?"

Sam shook her head.

"Well, if you're cat people, best not let the poor creature wander outside. Outdoor cats don't live long in Hillcrest. "

"No cat, either." She spoke quietly, not wanting Abby to pick up on the conversation. Of course, if she was going on a play-date, and Honey had a dog, they would hear about it.

The younger librarian finished typing, scanned the barcode on a key-chain tab, handed it to Sam. "All thet, whenever you want to uthe it."

"Thanks." Sam walked around to the front of the counter and handed the small card to her daughter. "Here you go, Sweetie. Hand it to the nice lady when it's your turn and they'll let you borrow the book." Abby held the plastic tab between two fingers. When Honey moved aside, Abby handed it to the older woman.

"And what have you got today, Sugar?"

Abby handed her the book. Not *Green Eggs and Ham* after all, Sam realized. The book's cover depicted a hand-drawn city street. A pig-tailed girl with a white dog in her arms stood before the open back door of a taxi. The door, adorned with a sunny bumble bee logo, was held open by a kindly old driver, hat held in his other hand. *Celia Takes A Cab*, the title read.

The colors were varied and in Sam's opinion too bright. Just right for getting a child's attention. As the woman scanned the library card, Sam shifted the book to see the cover better. The driver's smile looked like a snarl, his grip on the door too tight, ready to slam it closed behind the girl when she climbed in. The bright yellow door, laughing bumble bee, colors faded on the old cover. She didn't like it. The book was suddenly whisked up by the librarian who scanned its bar code then handed it back to Abby.

"I thought you were getting Dr. Seuss," Sam said.

"Honey said this one was really good. I've never been in a taxi cab before. Have I?"

Have I? Have I?

"No," she said. She took the library card back with damp fingers. Trickles of sweat rolled down her sides. She wanted to go home, let Abby read her frightening new book while she lay in her own bed and wrote, put some order to her jumbled thoughts about this strange day. See it in words and poetry, organize, arrange. Make right again.

Corey was home. Maybe he would read the book to Abby. Somehow, though, Samantha thought he might not want to, either.

Vanessa

Vanessa focused on her breathing, slowing her system down, careful not to break the stare of the old man sitting opposite her on the floor. A technique she'd mastered long ago, a way of collecting her wits after a disturbing statement from a patient. But this...

"How do you know that particular line of poetry?"

Hank Cowles smiled, resumed patting the invisible Nurse Charles. "How do you think, *Doctor* Reilly?"

She shook her head. "I don't know, *Mister* Cowles. Why don't you tell me?" This man enjoyed playing games with people. The best reaction was to ratchet up the aggression. Just a little, see how he responded.

"I enjoy writing poetry," he said, "don't you?"

"Not particularly. Are you saying you wrote it?"

His smiled widened. "Wrote what?"

"Don't screw with me, sir. Where did you read that line?" It occurred to her suddenly that maybe he'd gotten it from Samantha Union herself. She must have had the notebook with her, one of them at least. The thought sent gooseflesh up her arms.

"Why do you care?"

"Why do you always answer a question with a question? Let's say I have a professional interest in your answer."

"It's not my place to help you with your job."

Vanessa decided to change the topic, maybe throw him off. "Why do you pretend to be patting your dog?"

His hand hesitated, just a little. When he resumed, each motion perfectly matched the one before. He managed to squeeze out another growl, and Sam could see no movement in his throat to reveal he'd done it. He *was* good.

"Steady, girl," he said, "she meant nothing by it. What makes you think Charlie is not here?"

Charlie.... his use of the nickname bothered her. Corey had used it often as he spoke Hank's lines, calling the dog *Charlie.* An obvious nickname, but Vanessa had checked, found no reference in any story that Cowles called the dog by this name; assumed it was simply Corey's imagination at play.

Hank's eyes widened, his mouth opening in silent laughter. He leaned sideways, tilted his head, though always looking at her. His position gave the impression he was trying to see past her. Or *through* her. More gooseflesh. *Stop it. Focus.*

Behind her, Martin's voice was as much a growl as Hank's impersonation, "Steady there, Hank. No sudden moves."

Hank glared but straightened and returned his smile to Vanessa. "I apologize, Doctor. You have a fascinating way of thinking. I enjoy being with psychiatrists, watching how they search for patterns in everything, uncover meaning in the most obscure statements."

Not knowing what else to say, she said, "Thank you."

"It's been quite fun playing our little game."

"You consider this a game, Mister Cowles?"

He pursed his lips, looked down at Nurse Charles, gave the imaginary dog a scratch behind her ears. "Today," he said, before looking up, "no. More an intermission."

"An intermission."

He laughed. "Doing the echo trick. Fine. Yes, an intermission. But the game continues on its own. Let's call it the calm before the final storm, or," he pursed his lips, "the setup for the Big Finish. I thought I would give our mutual friend one last moment of happiness." Hank leaned forward, just a little, so as not to draw Martin's attention again. "It will make losing everything again so sweet. Are you sure you wish to leave your patient alone for so long? Not that I mind a little break from your meddling. Still," he leaned back and shrugged, "your involvement has added quite a refreshing dimension to it all. You've been a formidable, if mostly *ineffective,* adversary. Let me see, how did Charlie put it to me last night?" He looked up at the ceiling, hand sliding down the dog's back, rising up, sliding back, "Ah, yes. *This one's a hoot.* A hoot! Can you believe she said a thing like that?" Big smile.

Vanessa shifted, wanting to close her eyes and gather her wits. It wasn't possible, not without admitting he was winning. He was searching her out, listening for clues as to what her goal was in visiting him, finding enough to twist around and mess with her head. It was working.

She shook her head. "I don't believe any of that."

Another growl. Vanessa surprised herself by laughing.

"Charlie doesn't appreciate your scorn, Vanessa."

He knew her name. Martin had introduced her only as Doctor Reilly. No first names, always a rule. *Someone* had slipped. He'd probably heard their conversation from the hall. No matter. The patient was controlling the moment. Time to leave.

She held his gaze without speaking, longer than was necessary, trying to build some semblance of dominance, said, "Thank you for your time, Hank." No formalities. He hadn't earned it.

Destroyer of Worlds.

Stop it; just go.

She uncurled her legs and got up stiffly. Hank watched her, still smiling. "Good, good," he said. "I look forward to tomorrow. Personally, I think what you're doing is a bit risky, but I admit it's a rather unique method of treatment.

Everything you're doing, I mean. " His broken smile had become a leer.

How could he – no! He does not know! He's fishing, nothing more.

Or he did know everything and was worried it might work? The fact that she thought this proved the old monster had won, pushed her mind too close to his.

"Good day," she said, nodded to Martin who opened the door, keeping his eye on the old man all the while.

Hank's right hand dropped to the floor, as if tired of the pantomime now that his audience was leaving. "Good day, Doctor," he said. "We're a lot alike, you and I."

Vanessa stepped through the door, felt something brush past her ankle. Nothing there. She did not turn, even as Hank added, "We're both trying to destroy his world, but for different reasons, I sup-"

Martin closed the door.

In the hall, Vanessa took a half step sideways and leaned against the wall, trying very hard to breathe, focused on her heart rate and willed it to slow down, slow... down. Soames waited beside her. Obviously, she was not the first to need decompression after a conversation with that man.

Corey

Corey had fallen back into a dreamless sleep. He awoke to daylight and someone's lips touching his own, wet, pressing. Hands across his bare chest, pulling on the waistband of his boxers. He opened his eyes, slowly, aroused yet dreading who he would see. Samantha's face drifted over his, then was lost when she sank against his neck, kissing, both her hands slowly, but insistently, touching every part of him. He arched his back to kick the shorts loose under the sheets, whispered, "What about Abby?"

Sam came up for air long enough to whisper, "Nap. I locked our door just in case." The warmth of her voice mixed with a cool breeze washing through the window. He let himself be lost in her touch, her urgency for him. She added, "I missed you," before dropping back down to kiss his shoulder, bicep.

Corey's eyes rolled in sensory overload, a stretching physical need, reaching out for her. They never separated for more than a breath, pressed into each other, rolled across the bed, climaxed together. Finally, exhausted, they settled together on top of the bed.

She lay on his chest, as spent as he was, and ran a couple of languid fingers over his sparse chest hair as if afraid of losing the moment if she did not constantly touch. Every connection sent a small jolt through him, thrilling and relaxing, paradoxical moments only possible after love-making. The air cooled as the pressure outside dropped. The sun was still out but the coming storm was unmistakable, pressing the curtains into the room one moment, sucking them against the screen the next. He loved these moments, the charged air, distant rumble of a storm which had not yet made itself known.

A small thump on the bedroom door. "Mommy?"

Sam stretched across his body, said loud enough for Abby to hear, "I'll be right there, Sweetie."

"Were you taking a nap with Daddy?"

Corey laughed. Sam bit him on the arm. "Ouch!"

She giggled, took the sheet and flipped it over his body, pulled on a robe for herself. When the door was open Abby did not enter. "I'm hungry. Is it suppertime?"

She bent down and kissed the girl on the forehead. "In a minute, Cutie. Let me get dressed."

Abby turned toward Corey after Sam disappeared into the bathroom. "You feel better, Daddy?"

He stretched, holding the end of the sheet so it didn't slide off him. "Much better, Sweetie. Why don't you head into the kitchen and I'll be right out to get you something to eat."

"It's macaroni and cheese day."

"Of course it is. With ketchup?"

She nodded. "With ketchup!"

He listened to her soft footfalls down the hall, stayed on the bed a while longer, enjoying the lingering feel of Sam on his body, the sound of his wife puttering around in the bathroom. Another cool breeze danced through the window. Perfection. He didn't want it to end.

Vanessa

John Soames' office was a chaotic jumble of papers, books and manila folders. One bookshelf-lined wall was crammed with medical texts and periodicals stuffed into every available space. A couple of trophies, as well, racquetball or tennis, hard to tell from what she could see of them amid the clutter. Soames carefully pushed aside a stack of folders, then lifted one in particular. He opened it, scanned a few pages, closed it and handed it across the desk to Vanessa.

She flipped it open, inwardly cringing at Hank Cowles' face staring at her from the first page. An expressionless photo, not much better than a mug shot. She decided his time in this place had not yet erased whatever humanity remained, but sharpened it if the mentally dangerous man she'd just spoken with was any indication.

The other sheets offered nothing of interest, a few attempts at medication, notes in Soames' own barely discernable handwriting of failed group therapy attempts. The final note struck her as appropriate.

After review with attending physicians in units 16 and 17, Board agrees no further attempts at insinuating subject into patient community will be attempted. Patient's odd statements, constant mental games, especially but not exclusive to pretext that dog is real, have been cause of excessive anxiety in population. Not worth pursing at this time. Confinement, with two (2) one (1)-hour walks outside until such time as a complaint is lodged by patient or his attorney.

Vanessa closed the folder, handed it back to Soames who said, "I apologize, not letting you make copies. HIPAA policy."

"Don't apologize."

He tapped the folder against the desk top. "I assume you were reading the isolation decision?" Soames looked at something on the floor behind her, a brief flit of his eyes before focusing on her again.

Vanessa nodded.

He continued, "I don't suppose it was much of a surprise considering how you looked coming out of his cell just now." Another flit of his eyes past her chair. She resisted the urge to look. During their walk to the administrative wing, what had been an initial suspicion had blossomed into anger that she hadn't considered the possibility immediately. Cowles had spoken as if he knew everything that was going on back in Hillcrest, more than even her own chief of staff, Jim Chen probably knew. She forced herself to relax, tempered her anger to a more reasonable assertiveness which needed a rational voice. *A voice crying in the wilderness of her heart*, Samantha Union might have said.

"Doctor Soames, I need to ask you something. Please don't take it personally, but I insist you be as honest as possible."

"Of course." Quick distraction in his gaze behind her again, then, "I'll do my best."

"Had Mister Cowles been informed of any details about my patient, any form of treatment he may be undergoing prior to my arrival?"

Soames leaned back, not as startled as she'd expected he would be by the question. The folder in his hand stopped its constant tapping against the desk. He looked down at it, shook his head, then looked her in the eyes when he spoke.

"Not that I know of. You only explained what you were doing with Corey Union yesterday. I've told no one else. I have not seen Mister Cowles since then, save a quick glimpse through the door as you entered." He tapped the folder twice and smiled. "That was enough for me, thank you."

"You're not his attending?"

A raised eyebrow. "On the contrary, access to the patient is limited to Martin, the other orderlies in that wing, and myself." He shrugged, gestured in her direction with the fingers of his free hand. "There are exceptions, always are, but I promise you, Doctor, I have not had a word with him since our conversation. To my knowledge, no one else who might be familiar with your... *experiment*.. has either."

Experiment. It was as good a term as any. When she'd proposed the idea to Jim Chen last month, she'd referred to it as *radical therapy*. In the end, same thing.

"Could Martin have known?"

Soames shook his head. He leaned forward. "Cowles is a sharp cookie, Vanessa. Obvious signs of megalomania, delusions of grandeur. A strong sense of power." He leaned back and opened a drawer in the desk. "All the same thing, really. With an added possibility of schizophrenia, localized as the delusion of his dog," another quick glance behind her, then a blink, "but very, very clever."

He slipped the folder – *shoved* it, actually – inside the drawer. "Very clever, and dangerous because of it." The drawer slammed.

She watched him for a moment, unconvinced that anyone was clever enough to know so much from just a few words. He *had* to have inside information. She had one other theory, which troubled her simply because she hadn't completely ruled it out. She touched two fingers to her temple. "He has a way of getting in here."

When Soames glanced behind her again, she turned around. Closed office door, green-stained brass umbrella stand, currently empty, a few magazines stacked on the floor under a table. "What's back there that's so interesting, John?"

Soames didn't answer. Vanessa turned around and settled back in her chair. Soames' face was pale; he was licking his lips. Was he heading for a burn-out? Happened a lot in their profession. "Nothing. Just... just have a hard time keeping eye contact sometimes." His smile was disarming, dishonest as it was. She let it slide, tried to bring the subject back on track by tapping her temple again. "About this. Talking with Cowles, he knew a lot about me and my work. Appeared to, at least. More than he should have without someone providing him with information."

Soames was fighting the urge to look away again. He folded his hands against his stomach. "I'll wager he said nothing specific. No names, no concrete details?"

She stared at her lap, tried to replay the conversation. "No. Nothing specific. It felt like he was phishing, I'll grant you that much. Just...." She shrugged. What could she say without giving away what she really wanted to ask. That Cowles had been phishing for things he appeared to already know?

Soames nodded. "*Phishing*. An interesting new word, that. Fits with his pattern. The patient knows how to manipulate a conversation. No different than how professional psychics work. Feeding generalities to the customer, getting specifics in return only to spit these back into their astonished faces."

Vanessa folded her own arms across her chest, tried to look skeptical.

"You don't *believe* in psychics, I assume?"

He shook his head, laughed. "No. Absolutely, no."

"People can't read minds, then?"

"People can *infer* a great deal from one another, some better than others. A few of my patients and many successful psychiatrists exhibit a strong sense of empathy. It's how you and I do our jobs, reading another's feelings. But mind-reading in the popular sense? That's a load of crap, if you'll pardon the language."

Vanessa smiled. He was a sweet man. She found herself looking at his folded hands. A dull gold band on one finger. Edge of a photo frame posing from behind the stack of folders.

"I've said worse," she said. "But to keep on the topic for a moment longer. What about the opposite? A man like Cowles, he'd be good at putting thoughts into other people's heads, wouldn't he?"

Soames looked stunned for a moment, lost the struggle and turned his head directly at the umbrella stand, or whatever kept his attention so distracted. When he looked back, he said, "Thoughts? Are you serious?"

"Not thoughts, per se." Yes, *thoughts, per se.* "I mean… *suggestions.* As terrible a person as Cowles might be, he's loaded with charisma. He knows this, too, and uses it effectively."

"Most successful serial killers do, Doctor Reilly." Soames' tone was now hard, professional. A wall had gone up. "And as distasteful as the statement may sound, in regards to using that charisma to commit his crimes, Hank Cowles was, unfortunately, very successful."

She nodded. The statement was distasteful, but just as true. Over the course of seven months, the old man had lured four entire families into his unregistered taxi and carried them away from the world forever. There had been only one exception. Corey Union had escaped, by virtue of never actually climbing into the cab with the rest of his family.

Soames glanced casually at his watch. She'd overstayed her welcome. It was time to go, anyway. Her pager had vibrated on the walk to the office. Jim Chen's number. She'd ignored it, wanting this opportunity to speak with Soames in private, but her boss did not like to be kept waiting. "I apologize for taking up so much of your time." Vanessa stood, as did her host. He reached across the desk and they shook hands.

"Please," he said, amiable again, "it's no trouble at all."

Rather than follow her to the door, he sat back down.

She held the door open but turned back to face him. "John, mind if I ask why you keep Hank Cowles' folder in your desk?"

Soames pursed his lips, looked down. "Well," he said, "I guess it just feels safer that way."

"Safer?"

He shrugged. "The media buzz has died a little, but leaving medical records belonging to the," he made his flaccid quotation marks again, "*Destroyer of Worlds* where the press might be able to get to it, seems a bit of a risk. Don't you think?"

Her stomach tightened, hearing the term which had so long been echoing in her mind. *Destroyer of Worlds* – a name shouted in despair by the wailing sister of one of Hank Cowles' first victims. Afterwards, every media outlet repeated it with gleeful solemnity.

"I suppose it's the safest thing," she said, then turned away, letting the office door close behind her. She needed to get out to the world of normalcy for a while. Maybe buy herself an ice cream before calling Chen.

Of course, she had no time for such a luxury. She knew the reason behind the page. A reminder. Tomorrow was the final day. Her last shot. What had Cowles called it? *The Big Finish*. He had no idea what was going on outside his boxed world, was in no rational way going after Corey Union to finish what he had started. In this regard, however, he was right. One way or another, tomorrow was the end of the road.

In his office, John Soames let out a long, hitching breath, then leaned back in his chair. He willed himself to relax, now that he was finally alone. The dog's growling continued from the corner of the room. He tried to ignore it. It wasn't real. What had Reilly said? *Good at putting thoughts into other people's heads....* crazy statement, impossible.

He looked in the direction of the umbrella stand, squinted, as if looking too closely at the little white dog might blind him. It was there, teeth bared around a small menacing growl. *Not real*, he thought. *Not real.*

Corey

The sky over the porch is dark gray, swirled in black. Night presents itself not as a sweeping blanket but a hundred black snakes insinuating themselves into the sky. In the distance, thunder rumbles like a panther's hunger, giving up the hunt, wandering southward for its meal. No flashes of lightning, only frustration and anger drifting by, drifting away.

Samantha scowled, finding the metaphor forced, true as the sky's description was. Time felt vague, slow in the gloom. The edge of the thunderstorm which had apparently decided to stay on its own side of Wachusett Mountain, drifted south towards better game. She leaned back in the wicker chair, glanced into the kitchen through the picture window but could not see the microwave. It was probably close to eight-thirty by now. Corey had read to Abby then tucked her in before coming onto the porch for a little while to sit with Sam. He could barely keep his eyes open, so she'd sent him to bed.

He'd noticed but never commented on the open spiral notebook on the table beside her. Just a quick glance before focusing only on her. She loved him for that. He'd gone to bed without argument, leaned over her and kissed her cheek, the connection an electric feather touch. He'd whispered that he loved her, would protect her forever.

At the time, Samantha only heard the tones, the deep affection in his words. She looked up at the sky, the delineation between gray and black blurring in the coming of true night. No stars.

I'll protect you, he'd whispered, *forever.*

It was a nice sentiment. Recently, they were both trying to protect each other. But his pledge had an underlying urgency to it, some imminent danger close by, *soon*. Had he listened to the news, maybe caught a whiff of it accidentally during the day? On the drive back from the library a song had been interrupted for an *important news brief* - uncharacteristic for an Oldies station which normally abhorred living in the present. A state of emergency had been declared in a fifty-nine-mile radius around the nation's capital and other major cities across the country – but she'd turned it off, not wanting any details which might be accidentally repeated by Abby when they got home. Abby hadn't complained, only glanced at her mother with a quick, indifferent stare before looking out the passenger window at the town passing by.

Sam held the notebook with one hand, pen in the other, the only light spilling onto the porch from the kitchen. She crossed her legs and let the book flop lifeless into her lap. Her tea was over-steeped at this point and cooled. Not much of a tea drinker, she'd brewed some tonight, thinking of Vanessa. They'd gone an entire day without talking. The absence was noticeable in a week themed by their neighbor's presence. Strange to miss someone other than Corey. She hadn't had a close woman friend for a long time, maybe not since high school. *That* had been the attraction she'd felt the other day. Not physical, but a mental one.

She missed having a friend.

Now wasn't exactly the best time to go looking for one. Corey was having a hard time. His phobia that the world was coming to an end was getting worse. *Growing like a lone weed, inexorably overtaking the garden...* These words, Sam was startled to see, had just been written in the notebook. She didn't remember doing it, but then writing was like that sometimes. Automatic, like breathing.

She flipped it closed again and tossed it onto the table, just missing the mug of tea. Maybe the world *was* coming to an end. Right or wrong, Corey needed her and she couldn't spend her days writing dreamy lines which no one would ever read, when she should be focusing on her family.

Samantha got up, walked to the edge of the porch, pulled in a deep breath of green mixed with humid, distant electricity. Dark green, moist and rich like soil, a soft, beautiful smell. Trees swayed in the wind, slight tinge of rain somewhere far off. Behind these, the sky flashed. Ten seconds later (*One one-thousand, two one-thousand...*) a distant rumble, the panther stalking off.

Her eyes scanned the dark wall of woods. What was Vanessa doing now? Was she home? It occurred to Sam to invite her over tomorrow for lunch, a visit while Abby was on her play date. But, no. Corey might go to work, but he might not, in which case they could spend the time together, alone. Best not to have visitors. If he went into work, she could unpack more boxes, vacuum, get laundry going. Keep the house in order, occupy herself with the mundane until her husband came home.

They needed more stability, routine. The world might want their attention, wedge itself between them and shout, *look at me*! She wouldn't look, wouldn't let anything come between them. Even Vanessa. Their beautiful, free-spirited neighbor may not be doing it intentionally, but she was rising between her and Corey, if in no other way at least emotionally. Samantha couldn't let that happen.

She went inside, notebook in hand. She'd tuck it back under the mattress and leave it there for a while. The clock on the microwave read *four thirty-nine*. Still early. She –

Sam looked back at the clock.

Nine thirty-nine.

Nine thirty-nine. That was better. A little later than she'd thought, but more realistic than four in the afternoon. She shook her head, drifted out of the kitchen and down the hall. She was falling into her own mind too much, wasn't seeing the world clearly enough. After checking on Corey she might watch some television until she felt tired enough to sleep. Catch the news. Quietly, so as not to wake anyone. If the world was really going to end, she'd best learn how it was going to happen.

Vanessa

Pine Glen Mental Health and Rehabilitation Hospital sat prominently atop one of Worcester's seven hills, a bulky, efficient hive dominating the Zawalich Square neighborhood. Ignored by most residents, it was the largest and oldest institution of its kind in central Massachusetts, desperately clinging to an affiliation with the Commonwealth's jail system by way of the Venning Memorial Building, a high security prison for the criminally insane, hidden twenty miles west in the quiet town of Barre. Because of this association, Vanessa had been able to arrange today's visit with Hank Cowles. Jim Chen pulled the necessary strings, as he'd done to arrange her current *experiment* with Corey Union.

It was well past four-thirty before Chen called her name through the open door of his office. Vanessa rose slowly from the plastic chair. This forced casualness was her only way of striking back for being made to wait nearly twenty minutes, ineffectual as the gesture might be.

Unlike Soames' office, Chen's was wide and spacious with a western view overlooking Worcester. The man behind the desk was stiff and short, a Korean-American who'd come with his family to this country as an infant. Thirty-nine years later, he was Chief Resident in the long-term care wing, and Vanessa's director. She sat in a comfortable leather chair after Chen had risen from behind the desk and waved her into it, taking the one facing her. One sock sagged slightly under the cuff of his slacks. Jim Chen was known among the staff as a hard-ass, even a bully, but most of his employees begrudgingly admitted he never openly shoved his power in their faces. Never a conversation over a desk.

Most of them didn't know Chen the way Vanessa had been forced to recently, the way his stare sometimes lingered a little too long after he spoke, glancing down her body while fiddling with his glasses. Subtle comments made which might imply nothing more than an interest in his employee's well-being: how she was sleeping, was she getting out and having enough fun? Stupid remarks, never quite meshing with the professional air he so liked to carry about himself. They probably meant nothing, *certainly* meant nothing. She was being paranoid.

Chen did remove his glasses now, deliberately rubbing a small cloth across each lens. Two fingers doing a slow circle, one on each side.

"Did your jaunt to Venning produce any fruit, Doctor Reilly?"

Vanessa had worked out the answer on the drive here. Hesitation offered too much meaning to this man, most of it wrong. "Yes, in fact it was very helpful. Thank you."

Chen stopped cleaning his glasses, fingers frozen midswirl. He stared at her long enough to make her worried – which was, of course, the intent.

"Why?" he asked.

She had an answer for him, but needed to be cautious. Like Cowles, Chen was good at extracting information you weren't planning to give. "Excuse me?"

He returned the glasses to his face. "*Why* was your visit with Mister Cowles helpful?"

No hidden agenda, then, simply curious. For now. Nevertheless, behind the round lenses, Vanessa tried not to see a smoldering, expectant gaze. Her stomach tightened. She had to go to the bathroom. She was being foolish.

"I felt that in order to fully understand Corey Union's mind, how to get around the obstacles he throws in the way during therapy, it would be good to meet, face to face, the man who murdered his family."

Chen snorted. He wasn't fooled. "Doctor Reilly, that was *why* you went. I heard this already. What I want to know is, in retrospect, why you feel the visit was beneficial to your treatment?" Before she could answer, he leaned forward, resting his elbows on his legs and putting himself closer to her. She swallowed. He said, "After all, I'm not wrong in assuming Mister Union has never had any interaction with the old man, save a brief passing comment on that unfortunate day. The rest he has completely fabricated, or gleaned from the newspapers and news coverage?"

News coverage. Even those simple terms did not come close to the media circus surrounding Cowles' arrest, the discovery of thirteen bodies in his basement and in the woods behind his house, including Corey's family.

The loss of everyone he loved in such a horrific manner was enough to shatter any man's mind. The constant hammering for interviews, flash photos of the devastated survivor assured he was never going to come back from the shock in any sane form. He was devoured by the public's appetite for others' misery. He drowned under their weight, all the while grasping for hope. But, truly, there was no hope. Corey Union had withdrawn into a fantasy world, bringing his family home to Hillcrest – most of them, at least. Always Abby, but never their second. Never the baby. In the new world, Samantha had miscarried.

At least now, two years later, the world had moved on to whatever new sorrow was offered upon the news outlets' teat, leaving Corey alone with the morsels that remained of his soul.

Honesty was the only way to answer Chen now. "I've been living, so to speak, in Corey's mind for the past year, Doctor Chen," careful to keep everything formal, not giving any opening. "He's haunted by a man whom, as you've pointed out, he barely knows except by consequence. In a way, Corey's fantasy version is the only Hank Cowles I know. If I'm to help Corey, I needed to understand the real, flesh and blood monster."

Chen leaned back, an uncharacteristic – in her presence, at least – professionalism taking over. "Did you?"

"Yes." She wouldn't be able to avoid answering the next question. She'd allowed herself to be backed into a corner.

"And how does he compare to the magical monster?" Chen reached out to the table beside him as he spoke, lifting Corey's folder. He did not open it, only raised it up for dramatic effect. "How does the dream compare with reality?"

She swallowed. "Perfectly."

There, she'd thrown him. Chen looked stunned, maybe a little concerned. "Perf... are you telling me that Hank Cowles is," he flipped open the folder, turned pages looking for something, finally pointed at the fourth page. He paraphrased her own notes, "that Hank Cowles is most likely the angel of death, intent on using Corey to destroy the world? Is that what you are saying, Doctor Reilly?"

She nodded her head, enjoying how this flustered the little man. "Yes. His personality, his voice, matches the one Corey imitates. If I didn't know better – and of course, Doctor, I do, please don't worry about that – I'd swear the Hank Cowles knew exactly who I was and why I was there, perhaps even what was going on in my patient's mind back in Hillcrest."

Chen said, "I'm canceling your little experiment, Doctor Reilly, and having Mister Union returned to the hospital as soon as our meeting is done." He tossed the folder onto the small table beside him and stood. "Which, I'm afraid, it is."

His statement was so sudden Vanessa could only stare at him from her chair. "I – excuse me?"

He whirled, removing those damn glasses of his and pointed with them. "You're much too close, both to your patient and his delusions. I've had enough patience with -"

Vanessa practically leaped from her chair. "You promised me!" She was sick of the pretense, of this man pretending to be concerned about anyone but himself. "One week! What more do you want..." She stopped, not wanting to go there, wondering suddenly if she'd just been, in fact, *led* there.

Chen straightened, displaying a tremor of a smile which he quickly suppressed. "You've spent nearly a week living in Union's old house and aside from some brief lapses into reality, I don't see - "

"One week. You promised. Saturday he can come back to the Glen. We had a deal. Don't you *dare* go back on that now."

"We can't afford a full-time orderly staying with you any longer. And you have other patients."

"I'll do this alone, then. He's not violent. And you know damn well the rest of my patients are covered for the week."

Chen crossed his arms, the spectacles dangling from his right hand. He began to speak, closed his mouth, looked towards the ceiling. Considering... *something*. He sighed, gestured to her chair. "Sit."

"I'd rather not." Vanessa was trembling. Chen took a step closer. She didn't want to notice his breathing had changed, was deeper now. The smile barely hidden under the mask of seriousness he was so adept at maintaining.

"Fine. Perhaps. With a slight revision."

"What kind of revision?"

Another sweep of his hand, slight. "You're sure you won't sit?" When she didn't answer, he nodded and said, "You can finish out your precious week, but you do it alone. I will notify Robert Schard that he's not to report to you tonight, but return for his normal shift at the hospital. When you arrive at the Union house, you will tell," he turned, wandered to his desk, ran his finger over the planning blotter he kept in the center, "Andrew Booth before he leaves that he is to do the same tomorrow." He paused. Vanessa tried to maintain her angry stare, not let on how much she actually preferred this.

"From the time you return there tonight until I send the van Saturday morning to collect the patient and return him to Pine Glen, you have him all to yourself."

She blushed, cursed herself for it.

Chen *did* smile this time, and that damned breathing of his was getting worse. There had to be a price to pay. But assuming the man was looking at her in any way but professional was childish musing on her part, nothing else. She couldn't imagine any of it was true. She looked away from him. For his part, he remained a little too close, watching her. What if it was true? What if she only needed to —

He continued, "If I agree to this, I would require an email status sent every two hours. You are responsible, and if anyone asks about this new set-up, it was your idea, done at your insistence." He stepped close enough for her to catch the barest whiff of cologne, faded from the day. "I could lose my job for letting you do this, you understand."

She clenched her fists, wanting to turn from the lust which now wafted off the man. It had to be that. But to vocalize such a thought and be wrong, would end everything, maybe her career. Still with her back to him, needing to be sure, Vanessa whispered, "If I agree to this, what do you get in return?" *Don't answer that,* she thought; *don't say anything. Just let me take care of Corey and don't make me choose.*

She sensed him approach, close enough to touch her, though he did not. He was being careful, as careful as she. *He's not going to say it. You're being a fool.* "I think I've communicated clearly enough what it is I would like, Doctor Reilly." Closer, his breath gently stroking her hair. "And if I did not believe you would be willing to pay, I would not have given you such a lucrative deal. If you wish to finish this experiment of yours," her shoulders tightened, her entire body trying to curl away from him, from the truth, "if you truly want this one final chance to help Corey Union...."

Bastard, she thought. *Fucking bastard. Damn you damn you damn you!*

She'd already gone too far, though, stepped over too many lines in the sand with Corey. Chen must have known this. Maybe Schard reported her going into Corey's room, and Chen held onto the information. His Ace. Not that it mattered. In the end, it was just one final line to cross, if it helped Corey. She could be alone with him, all night, all day tomorrow.

You're no better than Chen, she thought. *Maybe you're worse.*

Vanessa nodded, hardly moving her head. It was enough. While he wandered to the office door and turned the lock, she slowly began to unbutton her blouse. She turned her back to him and let the shirt drop to the floor to the sound of his belt coming undone behind her. Vanessa closed her eyes while she finished undressing.

Corey

In the distance, thunder rumbled, each time startling Abby awake. She pulled the blanket close to her chin and waited. No flashes, yet. The room glowed in the night light, but there were shadows in the corners. None of them moved, not yet. She waited for the flash so she could count until the boom. Daddy had taught her the trick to see how far away the storm was. He knew things like that. Abby curled tighter under the blankets. It was hot. She was sweating, but the layers offered comfort. Helped her feel safe.

No new flashes, but another distant rumble. Was the storm coming towards them, or going away? If it came, it would be loud and scary. Abby waited for the next boom, trying to fall back asleep but anxious, certain it would come. If it was louder, it was coming towards their house. Then the flashes, the lightning, would return. The more she thought of this, the more frightened she became. Tossing the sheets and blanket aside she slipped out of bed, bare feet on the warm floor, and tiptoed into the hall.

The door to her parents' bedroom was open. She looked behind her. The lamp in the living room was still on. That meant Mom and Dad were awake. A rush of joy. She could sit with them on the couch for a while. She turned back, stopped at the edge of the hallway. The kitchen was dark. In the living room, her mother knelt on the floor in front of the ugly old clock with the shiny boy who looked like a girl with so much pink skin. In the glow of the lamp beside the couch, the figure seemed to move, dance. She didn't like the clock. It scared her sometimes, though she didn't know why.

Her mother was staring at it, sometimes looking up at the fireplace. Abby took a tentative step into the room, looked around to see if Daddy was there. No. Maybe he was asleep. He'd been sick today.

"Mommy?"

Her mother looked up quickly, turned her head and smiled when she saw Abby. That smile said everything was all right. Her mother reached out a hand. "Come here, Baby." Abby walked to her, knelt in the same manner as her mother in front of the clock. Samantha put an arm around her in a short, pulling hug. "How come you're awake, Sweetie? Have a bad dream?"

Abby leaned in. "I heard thunder."

A gentle shake. "It's OK. Far, far away. It won't bother us."

"Maybe it's coming towards us. Maybe it's going to get loud."

Another rumble, not *really* louder, but exposed in the room like this it sounded scarier. Abby climbed onto Samantha's lap. That was when she noticed the time on the clock. Two hands, straight up. That meant midnight. "How come you're awake, Mommy?"

Both arms around her now, chin resting atop Abby's head. She could feel her mother's mouth moving when she spoke. "I don't know. Couldn't sleep, I guess."

The girl leaned back, wanting to feel as much of her mother against her as possible, get far from the creepy boy-girl statue. "I don't like that clock," she said, warm in the embrace.

"I don't much like it either, but it's special."

"Why is it special?"

A shrug. "I'm not sure. It's your father's, so that makes it pretty special. Do you hear it ticking?"

Abby did. The sound was quiet, steady. She nodded.

"It hasn't worked in a long, long time," Sam said. "Daddy's excited to have it going again."

"With the key he found?"

"Yes." Her mother sounded like she did when she was writing in her book, dreamy. "He found a key, wound the clock."

Another rumble, not closer, not further away. Just the same.

"Daddy's scared of the news."

"I know. He's had some bad things happen a long time ago. Doesn't think the world is a very nice place anymore."

"Is it bad? The world?"

"No," she whispered. "Not always. Daddy thinks so. But we're here to help make him better."

Abby managed a quiet giggle. "We live here."

The hug tightened, pulling her closer. She liked that. "Yes," her mother said, "we do."

"I don't ever want to leave. It's nice. And I get to play with Honey tomorrow, right?"

A long silence, long enough that Abby began to worry that she'd changed her mind, wouldn't let her go. She said again, "Right?"

A kiss atop her head. "Right. You get to play with Honey."

"Are you going to be there, too?"

"No, I'll stay here. But I'll pick you up, any time you want."

"Will you be lonely?"

"I'll definitely miss you, my cute, darling little girl." Another squeeze.

"Maybe the lady that lives in the woods can visit."

Another hesitation, then, "Maybe."

"Miss Charles, too."

The hug tightened, softened again. "We'll see."

Abby wanted to talk some more, squeeze the moment, enjoy this special time. She was sleepy, though, leaning more and more against her mother. Samantha was silent, holding her daughter, looking at the ugly clock, listening to the time ticking away. Not understanding why she was up so late, not remembering how she came to be here in the first place. She'd gone to bed after the weather report, must have fallen asleep. Now she was on the floor in the living room, in a nightgown she didn't remember putting on, holding her daughter in the middle of the night.

Thunder rumbled, keeping its distance, circling like a shark.

"Come on; let's get you back to bed."

Abby was already half asleep. "Can I sleep with you and Daddy?"

She almost said no, then decided against it. Samantha wanted Abby with her, with *them*. Tonight, at least. She got up, lifted her daughter, carried her into the bed. Abby wriggled to the center of the mattress. Sam was relieved to notice her own pillow had an indentation where her head had rested recently. She hadn't imagined going to bed, at least. She left her nightgown on and joined her daughter under the sheet.

Thunder growled like a panther in the brush, waiting to pounce.

She ignored the image, rolled over, draped her arm across her daughter and sleeping husband. Abby gently laid her own hand on top of Sam's. It was warm; three bodies joined, the most wonderful place to be. As she drifted into sleep, Sam thought that something, some*one*, was missing. But no, just the three of them. Warm and loved and together in the night as the rumbling continued far away, where it could do no harm.

Vanessa

I

Andrew Booth sat in the chair, quiet as a mouse, listening to Samantha and Abby talk, the words barely audible from Corey's lips. Conflicting emotions, watching the scene play out from the corner of the bedroom. It broke his heart to see a man so completely lost, whose world had been so horrifically destroyed. At the same time, it was oddly warming to see how much comfort Union's wife and oldest child brought to him. They were real to him, so much so that he curled up in the bed and held close to his side an arm which was not there, yet which embraced him, kept him safe, reminded him he was loved.

Andrew leaned forward, prayed silently – he'd already made the mistake once of speaking out loud in Corey's presence. Since then, he'd become a part of his world, a co-worker. Best not speak aloud now, even in prayer, and risk having the fictitious Andrew Booth appear in the bedroom in the middle of the night. He thought, *Lord, help this poor man, your wounded child. Lead him back to us from his darkness. Amen.*

He repeated this prayer at the end of every shift, for every patient he'd seen that day. This week, that meant only Corey Union. He and Robert had been assigned split shifts at the house as Vanessa surrounded the man with his old, familiar world. Andrew sat back in the chair in the corner of this bedroom which Corey and Samantha had once shared. The chair creaked, but Corey did not stir. The room was big, bright with sunshine slanting in at a steep angle through many windows. He could imagine they'd been very happy here.

He got up from the chair, thinking how desolate it must have felt in the house after the murders. Thank God they hadn't been killed *here*. How much worse would it have been if... no. It couldn't be any worse.

He wandered down the hall in his stocking feet, into the kitchen and glanced at the clock on the microwave. Six-thirty. Vanessa was a half-hour late. She'd called his cell to say Chen wanted to meet her before she returned to Hillcrest.

He didn't like where that took his thoughts. Had Robert told the chief about his suspicions? That was ridiculous. Schard could be a loudmouth sometimes but even *that* would be too much for him. Besides, if he *had* said anything, the call Andrew had received on his cell phone ten minutes earlier would have been much different. The nursing supervisor, Betsy, said Chen wanted Andrew back at Pine Glen tomorrow. Robert wasn't coming in tonight, either. No one was. But they *were* allowing Vanessa to finish up the week solo. That didn't make sense, but at least the experiment wasn't canceled. That said *something*, he supposed.

Andrew opened the fridge and took out a Coke. He pressed the can against his belly to muffle the sound of the air escaping when he pulled the tab. It was too good of a buffer. He needed to start hitting the gym again, get back the shape he'd had ten years ago. Always more time when you're young. Now... now he was sinking under thirty-two years' worth of gravity.

No wonder Vanessa didn't seem interested in his offer.

Don't be a dick, he thought. *She's a little* preoccupied *at the moment.*

Preoccupied with... stop it! Just speculation, nothing more. Andrew had tried to keep his anger in check when Schard had called him earlier, filled him in on a couple of events he hadn't put in the official log-- specifically how Vanessa had gotten up in the middle of the night and wandered into Corey's room. She'd come out later than she should have, had it been a simple night check. She must have assumed Robert was sleeping in the other room and not noticed.

Robert Schard was a dickhead for even mentioning it. Andrew closed his eyes and took a swig of Coke. It was cold, gave him a twinge of a headache. *Sorry, Lord,* he thought. He was thinking this way a lot. Pissed off at everyone, overprotective of a doctor who was friendlier than most, close enough to consider a friend. She probably never gave him a second thought in any other way.

Still, the idea of him and Vanessa someday, maybe being a couple, wasn't impossible. It felt right when they were together. She talked to him, smiled when she saw him and seemed to enjoy his company.

Andrew took another swig. Everyone was getting a little batty this week, cooped up in a house filled with ghosts, getting pulled into a man's narrated delusions. *All for the good,* he reminded himself, *all for the good.* Just grating on the nerves sometimes.

Andrew didn't like the new arrangement. Didn't matter that Corey Union wasn't dangerous. Half the time he was one blink away from vegetation. But this whole affair, this last ditch immersion therapy of Vanessa's to draw him out – *that* felt dangerous in a hard-to-pinpoint way. Especially when the man spoke Hank Cowles' lines, or growled like that stupid dog.

He could change his voice in so many ways, keep them consistent day to day. More than that, sometimes Andrew wondered if Corey might not be in complete control of his strange, imaginary world. Like he was playing a part in someone else's dream, a puppet whose strings were pulled from off-stage. Stupid thought, of course, but it wasn't a theory he'd come up with himself.

Vanessa had.

A quietly mumbled statement meant only to vent her frustration. Every time she got close, the scene would change. Corey would become resistant, or disoriented. He'd pull back like a turtle into its shell or, more often, change persona. Sometimes Hank Cowles, more often he'd take on the role he'd created for Vanessa. *Bad Vanessa*, as Andrew referred to her, only half-joking. Bad Vanessa was, of course, Corey's way of letting them know he understood what they were up to, if only unconsciously. Trying to destroy a family which had already been ripped away from him two years earlier.

Andrew leaned against the counter, soda can in hand, wondering if they had Tylenol somewhere in the house. Vanessa had probably given Chen the same line she gave Andrew this morning for why she had to see Cowles in person. Understanding the man who had affected Corey so dramatically, glean some insight. Andrew wondered whether the Chen believed her any more than he had. In truth, Vanessa had gone to face Corey's demon in person, prove to herself that the idea he was in any way involved in what was happening was pure lunacy. She was exhausted, and it was beginning to show in some of her decisions.

Maybe that was why Chen had wanted to see her.

As soon as he stepped outside, Vanessa's car pulled up the long driveway. As much as he tried to hide his pleasure, Andrew's heart sped up when he saw her through the windshield. He chided himself for even *imagining* the possibility. Not that she was a model of beauty. She could be, if she got herself into shape and had a better self-image.

Like him. He never once considered the differences in their skin color as having any bearing. Vanessa didn't have a bigoted bone in her body.

Maybe when this was over. When she was able to let Corey go.

Andrew moved around the corner of the house and waited on the front walkway as Vanessa gathered her bag and travel mug. She smiled, rather sadly it looked to him. The grass around them was mostly dead, long overgrown and collapsed in on itself.

Vanessa dropped any pretense of a smile as she approached. In fact, she looked like she'd been crying.

"You OK, Van?" A nickname he'd come up with recently and had risked using only once before.

She shook her head and walking directly into him, let the bag and mug drop to the dead grass beside the flagstones and pressed her face and hands against his chest. Andrew froze in surprise, arms raised on either side of him. She began sobbing against his shirt. He wrapped his arms around her, unsure what was going on but taking a guess Chen had pulled the plug on her, too. He rubbed her back, whispered that it was OK, not sure if it was, but in a selfish way enjoying how good she felt, how much she trusted him.

Vanessa finally pushed herself away and wiped her eyes, sniffed once. "Sorry. Had a rough day."

He wanted to keep holding her, touching her. He chose not to press and lowered his arms.

"Chen canning our vacation early, then?"

She looked confused for a second, then understood. "Oh, no. No. Not exactly. Did Betsy call you?"

He nodded. "Pulled the plug on me and Robert."

"Yes. Sorry. I enjoyed having you around." She caught his gaze, blushed and looked down quickly. "Both of you."

He wouldn't read anything into that, much as he wanted to. "I can come tomorrow anyway, on my off shift."

"No," she said, quickly. "No. That would piss him off too much."

"Chen?"

She nodded.

"He give you a hard time?"

She laughed, covered her mouth, removed her hand and waved the question away. "How's the patient?" She bent down and retrieved her stuff from the ground.

"He's fine." Andrew stared at her sad, puffy face, silently pleading for her to look at him. She fidgeted her bag back over her shoulder, moved the travel mug from one hand to the other. He added, "I wrote the transcript in the book, as close as I could to what I heard. Abby and Sam just had an interesting chat, you should take a look at it as soon as you can. Corey thinks it's midnight, by the way. Abby and Sam are in the bed with him. Abby was scared by the thunder."

She looked up. "Thunder?"

In many ways, listening to Corey was like being a storyteller's audience. Corey spoke to his wife; she spoke back; but always it was Corey talking, changing his inflection enough to distinguish each speaker. He often lapsed into a dreamy narrative to describe the scene, talking of the weather, physical qualities of the characters. *Especially* the weather. Always hot, sunny and clear; day and night generally following real time, until today. Distant thunder, sometimes, like now.

Sometimes Corey punctuated his story by walking around the house, aware of his surroundings but seeing more than was really there, pantomiming mundane acts like cleaning dishes, or winding the clock. Things got rough when Corey imagined himself alone with his wife. Then, he would do things which Andrew was obligated to observe, detail in the log book while doing his best not to watch too closely the man masturbating in his bed or on the porch. Vanessa had been around for that latter episode, saving Andrew from having to play voyeur.

He pulled the over-laden bag from Vanessa's shoulder and looped his arm through the strap, reached for the door. She did not object. As they stepped inside, he lowered his voice. "There's been thunder in the distance, in *his* world I mean. Hasn't gotten any closer, though."

She didn't reply, but from the way she narrowed her eyes, the storm's presence bothered her. He added, "Mean anything?"

"I don't know. *The calm before the storm?*" Her voice had a tremor when she spoke. He put the bag down beside the chair but before she could step past him, Andrew took her arm.

"Vanessa."

She stopped, looked back with an expression that almost made him let go. Was that fear?

"What?"

He lightened his grip until only a couple of fingers were hooked under her arm. "Did you get any sleep last night?"

She paled. "Why?"

"Why? Because you look like death on toast, that's why."

She smiled. "I think you're mixing your metaphors."

"Seriously," he let her go but stayed close, "you're not doing yourself or Corey any favors by driving yourself into the ground."

"I know," the words coming out as a sigh. "I know. I'll sleep better tonight, I promise. I *did* sleep last night, a little but...." She looked as if Andrew believing her was the most important thing in the world. "Just not enough. Miss my own bed, I guess."

He grunted, nonverbally telling her he thought she was full of shit, and followed her into the living room. She added, "Just leave my bag there by the couch. I'll take it into the room later."

She'd been staying in Abby Union's old room. For the overnight shift, Robert Schard had been using the spare bedroom, a room significantly non-existent in Corey's world.

Vanessa continued into the kitchen and poured water into a *Hot Shot* to make tea. She'd brought this from home, a small dispenser that heated a mug's worth water in less than a minute. She wanted to avoid any sounds in the house that might interfere, or worse, become indoctrinated into Corey's fantasy. *Muddy the waters*, she'd said once, something like that.

Andrew leaned on the wall at the entrance to the kitchen, keeping his voice low. "His sense of time is pretty whacked today. After his little adventure last night, wandering out front." He looked back into the living room. "Not that I don't want you comfortable, but maybe you should camp out on the couch tonight in case he decides to sleepwalk again."

The water was hot already. She poured it into the mug, dropped in a tea bag. Without looking at him, she said, "He wasn't sleepwalking. It was all part of the play. Leading to some kind of *Big Finish*, or something."

"You think something's going to break?"

She looked up. "What? Oh, no, just repeating something Hank Cowles said."

Andrew straightened. "Van," second time in a half hour and she didn't flinch at the nickname, "I thought you'd be over that once you'd met the guy."

"I never really believed he had any influence. At least..."

"At least what?"

"Until I met him."

"And now?"

She dabbed the tea bag a few times, finally let it sink to the bottom of the cup. "No. Honestly. He's just an ultra-freaky guy."

Andrew sang out on impulse, "He's super freakaayy...."

She laughed for real; covered her mouth, looked at him sideways. The gaze between them lingered. It was a very nice look. Andrew would do anything to see that again and again.

"Hey," he said, "I'm all packed up, but I can swing out and get you some food before I go. Pizza or something."

"I'm fine. Thanks." She played with the tea bag string.

It was time to go. *Never overstay your welcome*, his Pop always said. "OK, well, I'll go, then. You think any more about my offer this morning? It wouldn't really be a date, not *really*, but it might be nice to get around more people who live in *this* world."

Her brow furrowed again. *Bad sign.* He raised his hand, "Hey, I love Corey as much as anyone. I'm just... I'm just worried about you. I'm allowed to care about *you*, too."

He thought she was going to cry again. Vanessa let go of the tea bag, walked up and stretched on tip toes then kissed him lightly on the cheek. Touched the other with her fingertips. She was down and back at the counter before he could react.

"OK," she whispered. She was blushing again.

He thought, *OK what? OK* what?

"OK, you'll go?"

"Saturday. Right?"

He nodded, trying to rein in his excitement. *Be calm, man; be cool.* "Right. Well, great! I'll see you on Saturday morning, anyway. Betsy knows I want to be one of the guys who brings Corey back. But *you will call me*, I mean it, if you need *anything* tonight. Or tomorrow. I wrote my cell number in the book. Promise me you will, if something comes up. Anything."

"I promise."

He nodded, looked away so he wouldn't be tempted to return her kiss. "OK, well, be careful." He wandered into the spare room, grabbed the backpack loaded with his toothbrush, deodorant and a mystery novel and slung it over his back.

Vanessa was still in the kitchen, leaning on the counter and finally sipping her tea. She wiggled her fingers *bye*, still blushing (*a* very *good sign*, he thought). Andrew waved back, went out the front door. When he closed it, a new emotion, one he hadn't felt since this week had begun, crept into his chest. Maybe it was that he'd finally gotten a chance for an actual date with Vanessa, but things had been getting weirder with Union.

He touched the door, one last connection to the woman before stepping from the porch and walking, reluctantly, to his motorcycle. He did his best to ignore the fear rooting though his gut.

II

Watching Andrew navigating the orange-striped Kawasaki down the driveway and out of sight along the road, Vanessa wanted to run outside and scream for him to come back, tell him *everything*. The sound of the bike's engine muffled through the trees, faded, was gone.

She was alone. Vanessa wandered into the hallway and stared at the master bedroom's closed door. Apparently, Andrew had closed it so they could talk.

Bad day, she'd told him, after breaking down in his arms. Strong arms. He was in love with her. If not love, then a pretty deep crush. Andrew wore it on his sleeve, though he probably thought he'd successfully hidden his feelings. She liked him, more than most men she knew. But today in Chen's office, Vanessa had decided she could never love anyone. She didn't deserve it. On her hands and knees in front of the desk, throwing away what was left of her pride to a man who was no less a monster than Cowles. Chen was one of many destroyers of her own, sad little world.

She closed her eyes and leaned against the wall. No sense lying to herself. She could have said no to him. Chen had offered his price, and she paid it. Yes, he'd obviously planned it out carefully, dangling what might be Corey's last chance over the abyss and asking, in so many words, how much his salvation was worth to her. A couple more days and he would have lost his leverage.

She could have said no, could have reported him. Could have. Should have. Didn't.

The door at the end of the hall blurred out of focus. Her life was a wasted landscape, but Corey had a chance to be saved from.... *from himself.* Hank Cowles was insane and could do no more than he'd already done.

After he'd finished this afternoon, Jim Chen whispered, wet and satisfied into her ear, *Tomorrow's your last chance, Doctor. If anything is going to come of your little experiment, it has to be by then. We're taking him back Saturday, no debate.*

Leave it to him to have sex with a subordinate then act as if it had been no more than a business meeting. Vanessa pressed her hand across her midsection, pushed, as if forcing out the physical memory of him inside her. At least she'd insisted Chen use protection.

She moved into the kitchen, sat for a time drinking tea from the same oversized mug in which she'd had her morning coffee. Andrew had taken the time to clean the dishes while she was out. Vanessa pictured him over the sink and smiled. It wouldn't surprise her to find her bed made with a chocolate on the pillow.

She took another sip and stared at the painting of lonely MooMoo hanging above the table. After Corey's older brother Eric found him living in such squalor, peanut butter sandwiches made every day for a daughter who would never eat them, stale and molding, newspapers scattered about, the worst of their stories clipped out and burned in the fireplace, he'd brought his brother to Pine Glen. Eric Union got power of attorney over Corey's affairs and used what was left of the insurance to pay down the mortgage and refinance so he could continue payments on the house. He never took ownership, always assuming Corey would come back someday. That was two years ago. Corey's condition never improved. Eric's little brother never came home, until now.

Vanessa finished off her tea, stared blankly out the picture window towards the back woods. Before she left for her visit with Hank Cowles today, Andrew had surprised her by asking her on a date. Saturday night. Quick to point out it wasn't *actually* a date. Not really. *Singles Night* at his church – something they did every week "since forever," suggesting it would do her good to get around other people for a while.

He was right. She hadn't been on a real date in years. She'd come to Pine Glen from the Pendergrass Clinic, a small outpatient center in Providence. A small clique of friends would drag her to bars, an occasional movie and even a couple of blind dates. None panned out. *You're too gloomy*, Amanda told her once. *You've got to lighten up if you want to make any sort of impression.*

She'd tried, moved to Massachusetts and got her practice up and running under Chen. *Literally,* as it now turned out.

Don't think of that.

Instead, she thought of Andrew. Big, sweet Andrew inviting her to a church function as if she wasn't a morose, self-obsessed slut, but instead someone worthy of his affection.

Vanessa slowly got up from the chair, lifted the mug, only to realize there was nothing left inside but a shriveled tea bag. She drew the lingering scent of peach tea into her nostrils, laid the cup on the counter and walked down the hall towards the master bedroom.

She'd said yes to Andrew. Fine, that was fine. He'd discover the real Vanessa on Saturday night and realize his mistake. Until that happened, for the first time in a long, long time, she was looking forward to something unrelated to the hospital or her patients. A chance for a normal life.

The inspiration was brief. Vanessa opened the bedroom door and saw Corey thrashing under the sheets. His eyes were closed, mouth moving, saying nothing. He was probably awake, but in his mind he might be sleeping, having another nightmare. She rounded the foot of the bed, slipped onto the sheets and lay next to him, ran her fingertips lightly over his forehead.

"Shhhhhh, it's ok." Always a whisper, when she spoke to him this close.

His skin was hot, sweating. She pulled back the sheets a little. Andrew or Robert had dressed him in clean pajamas, still standard hospital grays. Probably Andrew. He was good that way, able to manipulate Corey's dream-like movements to bathe and dress him without Corey fighting against the intrusion or incorporating it into his fantasy.

Vanessa leaned forward, kissed his forehead twice. Corey calmed. Her stomach ached with shame. "I did it for you," she said, scooted down and laid her head on his chest. His arm wrapped around her, warm arms, loving like Andrew's. It felt so good to be like this.

"Sam," he whispered. She closed her eyes, tried to pretend he'd said her name and not to be jealous of a woman long dead.

She'd insinuated herself into his world, felt an unwanted thrill at how he'd molded her into such a mysterious, strong-willed character. A villain, true, though that made sense considering her objective. Vanessa whispered his name, ran her nails along his belly. She couldn't stay like this, not now. Maybe later. She had to make her report to Chen. Maybe she could lie and say her cell battery was dead and she couldn't connect the laptop to the internet. Reception was bad enough out here.

He wouldn't believe her. But what did she care?

Corey's hand moved up her arm, caressed her with sleepy fingertips. In a whisper, she told him everything that had happened with Chen, but nothing about Hank Cowles. The old man would be making an appearance in Corey's world soon enough. No need to expedite his arrival.

She dreaded what would happen next. Something would, and soon, if his imaginary thunder storm was any indication. She got up carefully, read Andrew's notes over the next few minutes, trying to anticipate what kind of scenario might be playing out. Andrew was right, the conversation between Samantha and Abby in front of the clock was hopeful. Through them, if only for a brief time, Corey admitted why he'd recreated them. She had to get into his head and bring him further out, before Hank

Cowles destroyed his world again, as he'd appeared to have done at least a dozen times in this man's mind since he was admitted to the hospital. Each time through some end of the world scenario, as if Corey needed to punish himself for not dying with his family, working out more elaborate ways of being killed alongside them.

Timing was important. Too forceful, stepping too far too quickly and he'd run, at least mentally.

Again, the idea that Hank Cowles was somehow pulling the levers in Corey's mind, finishing what he'd started, itched in her imagination like a scab. And, again, she reminded herself that this path led to her own madness. She was beginning to think it might already be too late for such consideration.

Vanessa put down the notebook and returned to the bed for a few more minutes, wrapped her arms around Corey's body, played with the waistband of his pants, enjoying the moment without worrying about being exposed, and hating herself for it.

Corey
Friday

I

On the last day of his life, Corey Union opened his eyes to a beautiful, sun-filled morning. He turned in the large bed, listened for a while to Samantha's rhythmic breathing. No Abby, however. Sam must have brought her back to her own bed at some point. He stretched, careful not to wake his wife and glanced at the clock. Five minutes before the alarm was set to go off. No sense closing his eyes again. He reached out, turned it off. At least Sam won't be awakened by the static voices. Let her sleep. God knew, he'd done enough of that himself yesterday.

No dreams last night, not that he could remember. No monster forks from the sky, no burning mushroom clouds. Nothing. The sleep of the dead. All of the strangeness and stress of the past few days had sweated out under the sheets. Today would be better. Today would be normal. He'd make sure of it.

Corey slipped out of bed, brushed his teeth, stepped into the shower. Maybe he'd allow himself to get to work a little later this morning and get Abby up himself. Let Samantha sleep. Their morning ritual of embracing and tender goodbyes was a pleasure he looked forward to on waking, but they would see each other tonight. Showered and shaved, he stepped into the hall and waited, head tilted. No foul stench, nothing but green summer smells, a hint of roses opening to the sun outside the living room windows. What if he called in sick again, took the day with Abby? She

197

had a play date with some girl named Honey. Who was he to stand in the way of her first friendship in town?

Corey bypassed the kitchen and squatted in front of the clock on the hearth. It occurred to him that all the strangeness of the week began *not* when Vanessa had first introduced herself, but when he'd found the key and wound this ugly thing up for the first time. As foolishly superstitious as this connection sounded to him, there *had* been the incident with the bees and the clock the other night. Again, stupid, but hard to shake. The real world crowded his mind with enough thorns. He didn't need to invent any more.

His ankles ached from hunkering, but Corey continued to stare at the shiny boy presenting the clock with a mighty *ta-da!* Antique or not, it was becoming a source of stress.

His next decision was the obvious conclusion, if not a little irrational even to him. He would *not* wind the clock. Let it wind down and once it died and life got back to normal, superstition or not, Corey would tuck the thing back into its *Misc.* box, new key included, and toss it in the attic. Maybe someday, when he found the nerve, and his sanity again, he might take it down.

Probably not.

In some far back room in his mind, he heard their strange new neighbor say, *That's good, Corey. Very good.*

He should add one more item to his *Hundred Things* list. Spend as little time around that woman as possible. Keeping Sam away from her new friend might prove more daunting. He stood up finally, ankles straining, never taking his eyes from the boy and his Amazing Clock. *First thing's first.* When the haunted clock went night-night, his neighbor might magically change into someone normal. *Back to a pumpkin at the stroke of midnight, falling asleep in the garden.*

Writing Sam's poetry again. The temptation to sneak into her notebook and write it down was dangerously tempting. After the other night, they'd not spoken about it again. Any interference by him with her hobby now would prove she'd been right about not sharing her secret with him.

II

"Put this in your pocket. There, good girl. That's our phone number. If you want to call me, you just give this to Mrs. –" Samantha mentally searched back to the conversation with Fran in the library. Abby stared at her, waiting. "Abby, what's Honey's last name?"

She shrugged. "I dunno. She didn't tell me."

Sam tucked the slip of paper into the pocket of her daughter's jeans skirt. "Well, no matter. I'll ask her mother when I drop you off."

Abby took out the slip of paper and began reciting the numbers. When she was done, she gave her mother a narrow look and said, "Do I *have* to call you?"

Sam felt a piece of her heart fold into itself. *No, Sweetie,* she thought, *you don't. You're growing up so fast, but you still need me. I need you.* "No, Sweetie," she said, "only if you need to. I'll pick you up before dinner, how's that?"

"Sounds like a plan," Abby said with a nod, so much like her father.

With her two favorite Barbie dolls, one adorned with a wedding dress, the other in dancer's leggings and fluorescent leotard, Abby climbed into the mini-van. With hastily scribbled directions from Fran between her own hand and the steering wheel, Samantha drove north through streets she hadn't yet explored. Now and then they passed homes situated close to the road on small lots, but the majority of driveways were spaced far apart, houses invisible through the thick foliage. Hillcrest was a marriage of unspoiled nature and cultivated lawns, exhaling calm into Sam's open car window. So wrapped up was she in the perfection around her she noticed too late the rusted, dented street sign and passed Fran's road. She did a three-point turn and pulled into the street, never once meeting another car coming in either direction. Over the next hill, Fran's short driveway led to a sweeping semi-circle in front of a brown French Tudor. Samantha half-expected a valet to rush out and take her keys, but the only people in sight were Fran and her bouncy daughter with the strange name. A name, however, which fit the world they now lived in.

Vanessa

"Oh, I think they'll get along just fine," Corey said, his voice taking on the throaty rasp he'd used for Honey's mother in the library. He was slumped in the recliner opposite the couch, fireplace on his left, a sagging cardboard box which once contained a six-pack of Sterno fire starter logs perched at the edge of the raised granite hearth. To Corey, this box was an ugly, frightening heirloom, one which he'd decided to hide away in the attic this morning after it wound down for good.

Vanessa leaned back on the couch, open notebook beside her, watching the story unfold like the children had done in the library in this man's mind yesterday.

In a pale, neutral voice, void of emotion, he said, "Sam nods and takes the woman's hand, wanting to step fully into the house, sit at the kitchen table, tell the Stepford wife that she'll be fine right here, just ignore her. I want to be ready in case my daughter gets frightened. She didn't. Instead, Sam smiled, trying to emulate the easy, concealing grin the woman before her had perfected, and said, 'I'm sure you're right. In case you need to reach me sooner than five, our number is on a piece of paper in Abby's pocket.'"

Corey stopped, blank face staring at Vanessa, never seeing her.

Part of the pattern. His imagination recharging. Vanessa had never tried writing fiction, but imagined this was how a novelist might work, cover as much ground as the muse allowed then stop, think, imagine, build another corner of her world.

Then, when ready, continue.

"A fear suddenly gripped her," he said suddenly, "so much so that she almost asked for the slip of paper back. She'd torn the sheet from her notebook." As he said this, Vanessa unconsciously moved her hand over her log book, caught herself and stopped. As far as she could glean from Corey's brother and two long-distance conversations with Samantha Union's only relative, an elderly aunt living in Minnesota, Samantha had never written poetry, was never much of a writer at all. The old woman had apologized, though, as she'd been, in her words, a bit of a "distant relation." Still, as he spoke, Corey registered everything going on around him, and sometimes used what he saw in his own world. The spiral notebook had been a constant presence here.

"What if a line from her poetry had been scribbled on the other side," he continued. "Had she checked?"

He stopped again. Vanessa remembered Hank Cowles, how he'd quoted the line of Samantha's poetry. It *was* written down, somewhere in the log beside her. Unless Andrew or Robert was secretly spying for the man, the only other possibility was that Sam's poetry was, in fact, lifted from somewhere else, buried memories of an old high school composition class. Maybe Corey himself was the writer. Though nothing in his records indicated as much, it would explain his ability to paint such vivid worlds with only his voice. What it did not explain, however, was how Cowles knew to use the line in the first place.

There was another possibility, of course, but Vanessa ignored it.

"She did not," Corey said, "but played the dutiful role of neighbor and trusted this stranger with her child's life."

His narrator's voice had sharpened, deepened. Vanessa leaned forward. A tremor, a memory intruding on his narrative. ...*trusted this stranger with her child's life.* She waited for these moments.

Corey swallowed, then shut down, eyes still closed. If his posture in the soft chair hadn't suddenly become straighter, more rigid, Vanessa would think he'd fallen asleep. He wasn't, but he was definitely done for now, having drifted too close to what he'd spent so long avoiding. Corey would stay like this, coming back to life enough to eat (depending on what time it was in his world), go to the bathroom or, if Vanessa was lucky, continue the story.

She had to go to the bathroom, herself, anyway.

"Corey, I'm going to the bathroom. Please stay where you are. Do you promise?"

Of course he didn't answer. Vanessa went into the bathroom but left the door open. When she'd finished, and walked back into the room, he was still there. She returned to the couch and curled up, made some notes in the book. Reaching over to the end table, she picked up the dog-eared paperback she'd been reading and settled in for the wait.

Corey

I

The heated political debate between Andrew Booth and Robert Schard on the walk back from their project status meeting was tempered, to the point where Corey had to suppress the urge to ask what was wrong. Everyone in the group understood the need for subtlety, at least when Corey was around. They probably made remarks when he wasn't with them, but in his company, they respected his desire, his *need*, to stay buried as deep in the sand as possible. That never stopped them from competing for the most jabs and puns while they gave their summaries of the past week to the project leader, Jacob Harris. Today was different. Jacob's half-smile, the mask he wore when enduring the usual childishness wasn't needed this afternoon. Facts were given, estimates offered for completion. First Andrew, then Robert, finally looking down the table to Corey who stammered out his inadequacies. Their manager nodded, never smiling, never writing anything down.

The meeting ended quickly with Jacob saying, "Amanda Wails has issued a statement I need to pass on. Given what's happened in D.C. and San Diego, all off-site training and business travel has been suspended indefinitely. She's issuing a formal memo before the end of the day. Check your email. I don't suppose I need to elaborate?"

He'd looked pointedly at Corey, who had no clue what Jacob, or the company's chief executive officer for that matter, was talking about. He shook his head and that was it. Jacob stood and muttered, "Try to have a good weekend, guys," before leaving the room.

Now, as the threesome returned to their aisle, all Corey wanted to do was go home. Maybe call Sam so she could find out what was happening, wrap it in words he might be able to swallow. She probably knew already, would know the best way to tell him. How bad could it be? She hadn't called; it was a beautiful day. Most people had come into work even though it was Friday.

Turning into the first cubical, Robert said, "OK, back to work." Andrew Booth nodded without replying, moved into his space and disappeared below the half wall. Corey stopped before entering his own at the sight of an old man sitting in the guest chair.

Hank Cowles smiled and waved a pale, spotted hand towards the desk chair. Corey did not move. He grabbed the top of the wall, unsure what to do or say. How had that psycho gotten in here?

"I told them I was your father," Hank said. "You weren't at your desk, but the nice security woman let me in so I could wait."

Corey shook his head. "She wouldn't do that. You're not an employee."

Hank laughed, laid his hands flat on the legs of his tan chinos. "Dem dere's the rules, boyo." He swiped his hands across his thighs, raised them up, liver spotted planes taking flight. "But you must understand by now. If you don't, you will soon enough. I get whatever I want, at whatever cost. Please, sit."

Corey didn't want to sit. He glanced over the top of the half-wall. Andrew was turned in his direction. The big man raised an eyebrow, gestured a hand towards his phone and mouthed, *Call Security?* Corey looked at Hank, back over the wall and shook his head. Why bother? He stepped into his cubical and sat, turned his chair towards his guest. Hank craned his neck and said loud enough to be heard over the wall, "Thank you for your concern, Mister Booth. I trust you won't interfere any further in my affairs?"

Andrew rose over the wall like a dark moon. The skin around his clenched jaw was splotched gray. He stared at Hank but said to Corey, "You call me if you need me, Corey, OK?"

Corey thought, *What the hell is going on?* "Do you two know each other?"

His cubical neighbor's jaw loosened a little. He mumbled, "No, no. Just a lot on my mind, I suppose. Sorry."

Then he was gone.

Corey closed his eyes, did not want to –

"Look at me, young man," Hank said.

Vanessa

"I said, 'Look at me.'" Corey's voice had taken on the thin, papery quality of Hank's voice. Corey's rendition was quite different from the way the man actually sounded, Vanessa now knew. She was curled up on the couch, paperback closed beside her. It had been over three hours since Corey's story had paused. Three hours, lunch for both – Corey had moved to the table under her gentle guidance, ate the sandwich she'd put in front of him without speaking, drank the milk, moved back to the couch, same posture – and another bathroom break for Vanessa.

Now things had resumed. She found it interesting that the character of Andrew Booth had taken such a sudden, active role. He usually only made an appearance in his world when the real Andrew was physically in the room. Corey had delegated him to the role of co-worker as an excuse for his existence. But the players in his world needed to be consistent, to be in their place when required. She supposed –

Corey shook his head, eyes still closed but tighter than usual, fighting. "Don't want to look," he whispered, "don't want to."

Vanessa spoke up. "Corey, you don't need to look at him. He's a bad man. He's not real. Hank Cowles cannot hurt you or make you do anything you -"

"Shut up, bitch!" His eyes opened, paper voice tighter, just as dry and aged, but now sharp with hate. "You've had your time with him; now shut the fuck up!"

Vanessa leaned against the back of the couch. What the hell was that? This was the first time one of his characters spoke to her directly. The *real* her. Maybe this was a good thing. Corey was staring. She nodded at him to go on, took up her notebook, wrote down the dialogue so far.

Corey's eyes closed. He cleared his throat, opened them. He stared at Vanessa but did not see her, not any longer. "Where's your dog?" he asked. No fear in his voice. In fact, he sounded annoyed.

Very good, Corey. Fight him. Beat *him.*

Corey

I

"She's keeping an eye on other matters," Hank said, and again did the twin plane take-off movement against his pant legs. The gesture reminded Corey of a pouting child, bored with having to sit still for too long. He was not looking at Corey, only his own spotted hands as they rose up, sailed back down. Any fat in the old man's body had long ago evaporated. All that was left was skin and bones.

"What – " Corey began, then glanced at his monitor. He'd been timed out, would now have to enter his password to get back in. He continued looking at the screen when he said, "What do you want, Mister Cowles?"

"You didn't wind the clock last night, or this morning. That troubles me. Thought I would come by, see if there was something wrong, something you might need. We can all use a friend to keep us motivated."

How could he have known? Corey pictured the clock's round face, the slowing of the hands. Maybe Hank Cowles was not really here. Maybe Corey was hallucinating, going crazy. What was that thing... *schizophrenia*? Hearing and seeing things –

"Are you done?" Hank sighed. "I'm really very busy. Places to go, people to see, worlds to destroy. Oh, wait, " he snapped two twig fingers, "that's right. Destroying the world is your job, isn't it?"

Corey's shoulders shook, like tremors in the earth, as he turned the chair slowly back to the old man. "Please go away. I'm sorry for whatever is wrong with you, but I've done nothing. I don't even know you. You need to leave me and my family alone. You've been spying on us, maybe even looking through our windows. Stalkers get arrested. You don't want to spend the next few years in jail, do you?" He'd been able to maintain a steady, calm voice, never yelling but not sounding soft either. *Never show fear.* "You need to leave me, now, or I will have Andrew call security. If I even see you walking down my street, I'll call the police. Do you understand me, Mister Cowles? I need to know if you understand me."

Hank's bottom lip began to quiver. *Oh, this is great*, Corey thought. *The guy's going to start crying in my cubical. He's nuttier than a peanut and you're telling him he's going to jail!*

But the old man did not start crying. He nodded, said, "Yes, yes I suppose you're right." Then, as if remembering something, he looked up, face bright, no sign of fear. He snapped his fingers again and said, "I know, why don't you," he pointed at Corey's face, "go home, right now, and wind that fucking clock before I kill every member of your pretty little family." He leaned forward suddenly and grabbed Corey's shirt in two thin fists, moving so quickly Corey didn't know how to react except crane his head back and stare, chin tucked in, recoiling as if from a punch.

Hank continued, "You wound the clock. You set this damned thing going, set *everything* in motion. You wonder what everyone's so upset about around here because all of a sudden pretending the world is soup spoons and monkey shit isn't working anymore. It's not. *It's not.* You wound it and began the End of the Ages. Now you're the only one who can see it to its conclusion."

...wound the clock and began the end of what? What the hell was he talking about? Cowles' words were jumbled and confusing, so much so that Corey only now realized the guy had just threatened to kill Samantha and Abby.

No, he thought. *You won't touch them.* "Not this time," he hissed, and leaned forward, or tried to. Overpowering the man should have been easy; grab his shirt and push him back, scream at him to go to hell, *touch my family and I'll kill you first.*

He couldn't move. Cowles' grip was iron-hard. The old man leaned further towards him, half raised from his seat, pressing his knuckles into Corey's collarbone. Where was Andrew? He must be hearing all of this! The knuckles were hurting, pressing into muscle, maybe even cutting him.

"Yes, yes," Hank hissed. "I'll cut, and do worse." His breath was sour, as if he hadn't brushed his teeth in weeks. "You're afraid of the world crashing around you, think you can control it by ignoring it. Now, Boy, I'll tell you a secret. Ducking for cover in your little hidey-hole of a home is the very reason for what is going on out there," he nodded towards the window. "It's your fault. The clock is ticking, but now it's winding down. It's winding down and so is the world. You need to go home, wind it, get the world ticking again. If you don't, if the clock stops, the world goes *boom!*" He shook him for effect, bony knuckles pressing harder. "Do you understand me, Corey Union? I need to know *you* understand *me*. You have what you wanted. Control, over everything and everyone. Wind the clock and save the world. Let it die and so does everything else."

Cowles shoved him once, let go and leaned back in the guest chair. He resumed sliding his hands across his pant legs, sailing them up, up, down. "Pretty straight forward if you think about it." Eyes cast down, already elsewhere in his thoughts.

Corey curled up, lifting his feet from the floor. He tried to straighten, tried to say something *defiant*, but his brain was spinning, catching and dropping the contradictions in what Hank Cowles just said. He couldn't believe that nonsense, could he?

Of course not. Of course not. It was B-movie fodder -- fantasy.

Hank stopped mid-flight, turned to him. "Fantasy?" He laughed, yellow teeth, a few missing. "You're one to talk about fantasy, Corey. *I'm* the one who's here this time, but Charlie is waiting back in Hillcrest. Charlie and my little army."

"Army?" His voice was so weak, wanting to be left alone. Where the hell was Andrew?

Hank got up, lips opening and closing, "buzz, buzz, buzz...." and giggled.

Wanting to cry, wanting to lash out if there wasn't a chance of falling under such inhuman strength again, Corey merely watched him wander into the aisle beside the windows. Hank looked out over Main Street, hands on hips.

"Go home, my sad little friend, and do your duty." He twisted around, turning his body while the brown shoes still faced the wall. His face twisted into a smile. "Unless, of course," *giggle*, "you need a ride, Mister?"

Corey's heart melted like plastic, then hardened into a painful new shape. Before he could leap to his feet and throw himself at him, Hank had turned around and walked away.

Corey was suddenly standing, without remembering doing so, understanding that if he *had* leapt towards the old man he'd have sailed through the window. He stumbled into the aisle, but Hank Cowles was gone. Andrew was gone, too. The floor was quiet. A few steps at a time, checking every workstation, every chair, up his aisle and down the next.

Need a ride, Mister? Playing over and over in his head. Why were those words gutting him hollow like this?

He stopped after the third aisle. Everyone was gone. *Home?* Corey wandered back to his desk, tapped the mouse and reentered his password to get into the network. Clicked on email. A message from Jacob to the team,

In light of what is happening, everyone, except for service-critical personnel is authorized to leave. Head out whenever you want, and go home. Be with your families. You're all in my prayers, especially that we'll see each other on Monday. Don't enter the time as vacation - personal time is fine. Go home soon.

Jacob.

Corey read the email over and over, knowing if he stopped, he'd be tempted to look for other emails or go online and check out what everyone was so upset about. It was bad, really, really bad. Breathing fast, he closed his eyes, tried to calm down. Hank Cowles hadn't really been here. He couldn't have disappeared that quickly.

Corey got up, wandered over to the bank of windows. Traffic must be bad outside if everyone was being let go. Four flights down, the street was deserted. A couple of empty cups rolled along the sidewalk. A single section of newspaper fluttered against the traffic light a block south.

Where were the cars? Cowles' visit hadn't been more than a few minutes. A cloud passed overhead. Corey looked up, blue sky, occasional weak tuft of cloud, but nothing – then they came into view, dropping in front of him and curling like smoke before dashing north, pulled along by a vacuum left in the wake of all the missing people. Bees, some long-bodied yellow, others sleek black wasps, fat bumble bees, swirling and mixing like a tornado past his window. All migrated north, towards Hillcrest. Towards home.

So many. Impossible. The smoke of their mass thinned until the last few stragglers passed between the buildings; then Corey was alone again, fingertips pressing on the glass, heat outside trying to squeeze through.

Home. He turned back towards his desk, picked up the phone and hit the speed-dial, got the *bleep-bleep* of a broken connection. No lines out. He pressed flash, tried again. Same alert. Phone lines were either too crowded, or non-existent.

The clock is ticking, but it's winding down, like the world.

He'd said something like that. Corey stared at his monitor, at the open email. *Go home to die*, it may as well have said. Corey couldn't stop it. Didn't matter if a crazy person said he could. A clock. Nothing but a stupid, ugly clock.

The screen saver flashed on, WG Industries logo, bouncing around a field of black. Beautiful summer day reflecting on the glass from the window behind him.

He tried the phone again, slammed the receiver down as soon as the alert bleated in his ear. Corey grabbed his briefcase, checked his pocket for the keys, the usual end of the day routine. Barely two o'clock in the afternoon and the building, the whole city, was empty. He walked towards the elevators, slowly, calmly, waiting for people to reappear, for this mad hallucination to end. All the way down to the Parking Garage Level 2, doors opened to an empty span of concrete, save one lone car. *His* car. Waiting to take him home to die with his family.

II

The house was too quiet without Abby puttering around. No television, no small voice asking what she was doing, if she wanted to play a game. No singing songs or moments of startled warmth as her daughter hugged her legs in a sudden urge to show how much she loved her Mommy.

Peaceful, as well, a breath of quiet to be Samantha. Answering to no one. Sam tapped the open notebook with the pen, scrawled random lines around the page. She'd written two short verses, on the paradox of wanting time and missing the lack of it, missing her daughter. Worrying. Two small moments of thought in words and lines and stanzas.

At the moment, however, she felt no inclination to do anything but run the pen across the freshly turned page, draw random shapes and find hidden pictures in her mind. Something moved at the edge of her vision. She looked up, expecting to see a rabbit or squirrel across the yard. Vanessa emerged from the wooded path. Even without the usual summer humidity it was hot, near ninety but Vanessa wore the same black dress. It swayed with her motion. Perhaps as a small acknowledgement to the weather, she had the top button of the dress undone, exposing a long, slender throat. The dress had no sleeves this time. Sam was surprised Vanessa would simply wander onto her property like this, uninvited, but acknowledged a thrill at seeing her. She was lonely, and bored, not knowing what else to do with her time but write, even as laundry and yard work needed her attention. Today was a respite from the mundane. A new, wonderful excuse to do nothing practical was now walking towards the porch, waving.

Samantha laid the notebook on the table and dropped the pen on top of it, rose to meet her neighbor as she stepped onto the porch. Vanessa didn't slow in her approach, simply closed the distance and wrapped Sam in a long, soft embrace. Leaves and cut grass, cool nights overhead as their bodies pressed together. One day Sam would ask about that, how such a wonderful scent flowed around this woman, but did not get the chance. Everything happened too suddenly.

Vanessa pulled back, laid a gentle hand on Samantha's cheek. Sam waited, expectant, unsure what it *was* she expected and pretended she did not know. The woman's free right hand reached back, pulled something loose from around her waist. Sam's breath caught as her imagination traveled faster than the reality of what was happening. Vanessa's arm swung back.

The long knife glinted in the sun, then was lost from view. A sudden sharp prick under Sam's chin, in the soft place between jaw and throat. She took in a quick breath but did not move, her brain focusing only on the steady, feather-light pressure of the blade.

Vanessa smiled, a warm, caring expression. The point of the knife pressed harder. Sam tilted her head back, hoping to forestall the inevitable breaking of skin, the knife pushing into her brain.

The woman's other hand lingered on her cheek then touched her own face, as if transferring the feel of one to the other. She said, "I'm sorry, Samantha, but it has to be done. You'll understand later. Right now, you have to do exactly what I say or I'll have no choice but to kill you. Nothing personal, I promise. Corey's coming back and I need to be with him, alone, for a little while. "

"Please," Sam said, but stopped speaking when the point pressed though her skin, just a little. No pain, but something wet ran down her throat. *Please*, she thought, hoping to convey the word with her eyes.

Vanessa leaned forward, kissed her cheek on the very spot her fingertips had brushed. "I'm sorry," she said, "we have to go."

She shifted, moved out of sight behind her. The blade swiveled and curved across her neck but never lost contact. Sam whimpered, closed her eyes, waited for the slash, the cutting open of her throat. "Open your eyes, Samantha," she said, "and begin walking towards the stairs, then down, back the way I came. The path."

Was she taking her to her own house? *Why, why, why?* She wanted to scream, but every step down, across the grass, was a new chance for the blade to slice her open, spill her life down her t-shirt. Abby needed to be picked up. She would do whatever Vanessa wanted, so she could be free to bring Abby home. Pick up her daughter then *run, run, run.*

The pressure of the blade lessened, had turned so the sharp edge was aimed away from her when she moved into the trees. Still, the contact was there, never broken. "Watch where you're going. Look down." Samantha did, slowly stepped around the roots and shallow impressions in the path, moving her head only enough to scan the terrain a few feet ahead of them. She didn't dare trip, end up sliding along the blade.

She couldn't die. Abby needed her. Corey needed her.

Vanessa said Corey was coming home. How could she know that? He would have called. Sam walked and thought, *Stay away, Corey. Go get Abby and go far away from here.*

Thunder rumbled again in the distance. The sound was out of place. No rain was in the forecast; the air was dry with no taste of a storm. Another rumble, still far off. *A plane, only a plane.*

Why was Corey coming home?

In unison, the tops of the trees bent in a wind she did not feel here, sheltered by their presence.

"Here," Vanessa said. Her left hand pressed on Sam's shoulder, directing her off the path, towards a tall, collapsing structure half-buried in a copse of trees. Corey's hidden shack, Sam guessed, where he'd found the key.

"Watch your step. Please don't try to run." Vanessa pressed the dull side of the knife harder against her jugular to emphasize the request, moved it around until it rested against her right collarbone. "We're almost there. But we have to hurry, before your husband gets home."

Sam risked, "Why? Why do you care if he comes home?"

They stopped in front of the cockeyed door, open and leaning on one hinge. Inside was dark. Trapped heat drifted out from this darkness like settling steam.

Thunder again.

"He's going to wind the clock, and I have to stop him. As you can hear, the world is coming apart. If he winds it, it's over. The clock must continue until the end. He has to let it wind down. It has to stop."

She spoke these words matter-of-factly, but what she actually said tore apart any hope that Vanessa could be reasoned with. She was insane. Her new friend was crazy and was going to kill Corey over a clock. "Inside, quick."

Sam hesitated, understanding now that doing what she said was only going to hurt Corey, not help him. *One more time, try and talk to her.* "Please, take me back. I'll move the clock. You can take it with you, even. I promise. Take it, smash it, just leave us alone."

The fingers of Vanessa's hand squeezed around her left shoulder, pulling a bit of Sam's tee shirt and skin. Samantha moaned but was too focused on which way to break free, where to hit Vanessa first to avoid getting cut too badly. "I don't have time to explain, Samantha. I wish I could. He's the only one. I can't touch it and you can't do anything, either. He's the one who wound it." She pushed Sam towards the door.

Now, do something now!

As soon as Sam thought this, a sharp pain ripped into her right shoulder, heavy pressure following, harder, insistent. She cried out. The pain worsened. The blade was inside her. She screamed, "Stop!" when it twisted, tearing her muscles. Out, then in again, an inch from the first spot, so deep! Sam screamed again, losing focus on her thoughts, fell forward. All sense of time and place were jumbled in the jagged pain racing through her body, washing down from her shoulder. How badly was her shirt ruined? Were any fibers inside her body? Sam was barely aware how bizarre these questions were, but held them close as she stumbled into the shed, trying to get away from the knife and the pain.

A foot kicked her behind the knees. Sam fell, her right arm ineffectual when she landed and rolled over onto it, wondering if dirt was getting into the cuts. When she was on her back, Vanessa pressed her knee into Sam's stomach. The blade drifted between them when she said, "I'm so sorry, Samantha, but you were going to do something stupid and I don't have time to fight you. Please do what I say or I'll find Abby and kill her. I'm sorry, I really like her, but I'm out of time and you have to do what I say. Please just do what I say."

Staring past the knife, coated with blood that also dripped down the handle and over Vanessa's fingers, focusing on her face at last, Sam forgot the pain. Abby's name filled her with cold, killed whatever fight was left.

Vanessa continued, "I will, not that I want to, but you need roll over right now and put your hands behind your back. If you do what I say, you'll be fine and so will Abby. I'll come back and set you free. I promise. That's a bad cut on your shoulder and you'll bleed out if I don't come back soon. But I have to go now or you *will* die. So will Abby and everyone else. Do you understand? I have to know you understand."

Outside the shed, the trees bent under another boom of thunder. *It's not thunder*, Sam thought, then could think no more as she was rolled onto her stomach. Her arms were pulled back, the right tingling into numbness. Vanessa pulled her wrists together. Samantha dropped her face into the dirt floor, crying against the dust. She coughed, choking, turned her head and spit. The pressure on her back lessened but her arms remained behind her, locked in the vice of Vanessa's hands.

"I promise," Vanessa said again, moving but always keeping contact, picking something up beside her the same color as the floor. An old rope. A long coil of it pulled out of sight then wound around her wrists so quickly Sam fought only in reflex, forced herself to calm, wait, wait for Vanessa to leave. There were other things in the shed, further back, small lumps of shadow. Sam was pushed sideways again and screamed at the jagged twist in her shoulders. Clouds of dry earth rose up but settled again over everything, her shirt and face, Vanessa's black hair. Sam coughed, closed her mouth and eyes, breathed shallowly through her nose. Her ankles were bound. Again she was rolled over and did not fight, felt no pain. A moment later, her legs were bent back and she was hog-tied with her face turned away from the dirt and the dark unmoving shapes in the far corner of the room, lost in a shed in the middle of the woods and she was going to die and who was going to pick up Abby? Who was going to save her daughter?

The pain in her shoulder simmered, then ignited again, a slow fire, worsening as she focused on it. Too much, all of it, too much. She turned her face into the dirt and cried, feeling the ground muddy from the tears. She could hardly breath, looked away from the shape of her captor, knowing everything was over and wishing she'd been stronger.

Another rumble, further off in the distance. She waited for the knife to jam into her back, burst her heart.

All was silent, except the constant rustle of the trees outside, the wind, her own breathing. She *was* breathing, still alive. No talking. No voice. Sam jerked sideways, trying to reposition herself. Her shoulder twisted, the muscles not responding the way she wanted. But no pain. Just a spreading numbness across her back, like blood. Not a good sign. Vanessa was not coming back. Sam rolled onto her belly again, twisted until the doorway was visible. Her right eye was caked in the mud, useless. No Vanessa. Sam was alone. Maybe forever.

A fly buzzed in the corner of the small room. She looked up with her clear eye. The ceiling looked so far away, a single beam with strands of webbing drifting down like old party decorations. What had this place been? She wriggled her arms and legs, trying to find a weak point in the knots, but the rope had been wrapped around and around, no knots except maybe one between her hands and feet. She stopped struggling.

The fly buzzed again. She wished she could clear her right eye enough to open it. Instead, she rolled, adjusting her body's position to offer a better view of the shed's interior. Vision slowly adjusted to this new lack of depth perception. She saw the nest. A massive, oblong mass of gray dominating the front corner near the door. It was covered in black and white wasps. A drone flew off, disappearing through the door to be replaced by another coming in. Samantha stared at the unthinkable mass of them. She sucked in a dry breath, held it, afraid if she let the air out too quickly it would hit the nest, anger the wasps.

She could not look away from the writhing monster in the corner. She finally stopped thinking, closed her clear eye. Someone would come for her, if she stayed perfectly still, if she did what she was told. Someone would come.

III

Corey didn't encounter another car until he'd turned off the highway. It moved across his path at the first intersection. Not long after, a second passed in the opposite direction. By the time he reached the *Welcome to Hillcrest* sign, he'd begun to see people along the road - a man in overalls walking with a cell phone pressed to his ear, two children playing on a swing in the town's small park. Whatever was going on, news hadn't traveled this far.

That was crazy. The city had been *emptied*. Maybe the phone lines were down here. Corey hadn't been able to get through to Sam during the drive. No phone lines meant no Internet. It made sense, in a day where nothing else did.

As he passed the town common, following the main road west, two men, one dressed in suit and tie and the other in a dirty white t-shirt and jeans, ran across the square in front of the library. Corey lost sight of them a moment later. Thunder rumbled in the distance. He had begun to think it was not thunder, but didn't have the time or inclination to find a high ground to see the source, see what was coming up behind him.

His own road finally appeared, shaded under a dark green canopy. The air was cooler here. A mosquito landed on his arm through the open window as he turned into the driveway. Corey pulled the arm in and crushed the bug against the inside of the door. A smear of his blood between vinyl and flesh. He'd have to remember to come back out with a wet rag before it dried.

The mini-van was in the driveway. Was Abby visiting her friend in the morning or afternoon? He could head back out to bring her home, especially if what was happening was bad enough that...well, was bad enough.

More thunder accompanied his walk to the front door. The sun slanted west but remained high, still bathing the house and yard in bright daylight. No fear here, no worries. The day was beautiful, their home a dream. He opened the door and stepped inside. They would gather up Abby if need be, entrench themselves in the house or the yard, be together.

"Sam?"

No answer.

They'd work together in the garden planting seeds, giving life a chance to grow, to be something. No television, but they could watch a movie, something to ride out the storm.

Sam's notebook was on the back porch, pages fluttering in the growing breeze, pen at rest halfway across the table. Corey leaned over the porch railing. No one in the garden. "Sam?"

Two hands on his shoulders, long fingers sliding over his collar. He moaned in surprised pleasure, leaned into her, saw the hands on his shirt, slender, painted nails. Sam didn't paint her nails. Lips on his neck. Corey turned his head, stiffened when his lips brushed Vanessa's cheek. She kissed the corner of his mouth.

He spun around and stepped back, pulling her free while at the same time holding her wrists. The railing pressed against his back. Vanessa laughed, stepped closer, bending her arms between them. "I thought you'd be happy to see me. I know Samantha was." She pressed against him, pinning their hands between them. Her lips on his, smell of forest walk, leaf cover, green canopy flashing, pine needles underfoot.

He shoved her away. She did not resist, moved with it, almost floating like a child's balloon. Vanessa shook her head, smiled and walked towards the kitchen door. He stayed at the railing, needing the distance between them.

"Wh-where's Sam?"

She did not answer, only reached out with one sleeveless arm and crooked her finger. Slender arms, freckles and thin wisps of hair along the skin, twin braided pigtails down her back. Corey struggled to concentrate. "Where is she?"

Another rumble in the sunny, blue sky. He pushed away from the railing, followed her into the kitchen but not before casting a quick glance at the notebook discarded on the porch table. Sam was here, somewhere. They were swallowed by the cool dark of the house. Already Vanessa had drifted around the corner into the living room.

More forceful now, his patience thinning but beneath it, a growing terror. "I said, where is Samantha? Where is my wife? I want to know where she is *now*."

Vanessa sat on the couch, patting the cushion beside her. Another rumble rolled past the house. This time, Corey felt it in the floor. He stood at the kitchen boundary, staring at her, uncertain what to do. He should go down the hall, into the bedroom. That's where his wife was, had to be. In bed, sleeping or... or what?

"Come, sit," Vanessa said. "We have a lot to talk about and, to be honest, we have very little time."

He shook his head. He wasn't going anywhere, especially nowhere close to her. He glanced down at the clock. The foot high man in blue pants screamed silently at him, *laughed* at him. With an undercurrent of impatience Vanessa said, "Corey, sit down here and I'll tell you everything."

He stepped towards the clock instead. Two steps, three. "Do *not* go near that clock, Corey, or your wife will die." He stopped, eyes on the blue and pink man that smiled like a lunatic. Everyone wanted to kill his family. They'd done nothing. They were perfect, innocent. Vanessa continued, "She will die alone, knowing you abandoned her. She'll die of starvation or thirst or more likely blood loss. Killed by an animal wandering by and catching her scent. Do you want that to happen, Corey?"

Two explosions. *Boom! Boom!* Someone pounding out the finale to some tuneless symphony. The sound had texture, splintering behind the trees, reaching through the open windows all around them. Somewhere, an army of giants was stomping their way into town.

Corey turned fully towards Vanessa. She carried herself so easily, even while saying such horrible things to him. She shifted on the couch but an after image remained, one that was softer, less angled but still intense.

The shadow Vanessa said, "Corey."

The harder version laughed, looked sideways at him, "I'm over here." She slid back, merging with the ghost.

Her cell phone rang. Vanessa said, "Shit!"

Vanessa

"Yes, what is it?"

Corey's face melted into its usual, slack expression and he stopped talking. He stared, confused by the interruption. Vanessa had only a few minutes before he righted his world and began speaking again.

Andrew Booth's deep voice on the cell phone. "Van, sorry if I'm interrupting. Wanted to check in, see how things were since no one's heard from you all morning. Chen's pretty pissed. I assume Corey must have - "

"Listen, Andrew, first off it's Vanessa, and yes, we *were* shit deep into things and now it's all stopped because the phone rang."

Silence on the line. She'd hurt his feelings. Damn it, why hadn't she turned off the ringer? Andrew surely must have thought this himself, but rather than remind her, he only said, "I apologize. I'll leave my phone on if you need anything. I just know what it's like being alone when he's going full tilt. Just make sure you don't get too pulled in - "

"I appreciate your concern, Andrew," she said, whispering, not wanting his alter ego to make an unexpected appearance in Corey's world, not during what most certainly was the *Big Finish.*

Silence lingered on the other end. Finally, "OK, good luck, Vanessa. I'll be right here if you need me."

She privately wished he'd continued with the Van nickname, but this was not the time for backtracking. She was close, sensing the time approaching to interject herself more forcefully into the scene, before it was too late to do anything but watch Corey fall apart completely, die with his family in this fantasy world. She wondered where Andrew was now. Hopefully close, in case she really *did* need him.

"Thanks. I'm sorry for snapping."

"No problem. Turn off the ringer, but make sure you leave it on vibrate. I promise not to call unless it's an emergency."

She nodded, not caring if he missed the gesture. "Will do. Talk to you tomorrow."

"Bright and early. Bye."

"Bye." She pressed the disconnect button, immediately opened the menu and changed the ringer to vibrate, tossed the phone onto the couch cushion behind her. While Corey was describing the events on the porch Vanessa had moved to sit beside him, an act which the man had seamlessly incorporated into his world, putting his own version of her, the *bad* Vanessa, in the same spot.

Corey remained quiet. Vanessa waited. He'd been speaking slowly all day, mouth moving like a puppet with someone's hand up his back, reaching into his mind, controlling his thoughts, building up his world so it could be torn back down. It was impossible for the crazy old man in the hospital cell to make Corey Union think or do anything. Nevertheless, the idea wouldn't be shaken. She'd let it settle in her mind. Of course it wasn't true, but it gave her focus, gave her something – some*one* – to fight.

And fight him, fight *it*, she would begin to do. It hurt her to hear how she was represented in Corey's world, this *dream in yellow* as the man's late wife might say. Vanessa was not the villain. She was trying to be the hero, his knight in shining armor scaling the castle wall to rescue him from the dragon before it could –

Shit! She ran both hands across her face. Andrew was right. She was falling too much into this. If she was going to accomplish anything in the next twelve hours, she had to be professional. Had to be objective. Had to be detached. But like it or not, she had feelings for this sad, pathetic man, far beyond what was healthy or helpful.

She watched him sitting, blank, occasionally licking his lips, frozen in a house, a world, vastly different than reality. A world where the most important people in his life still had a chance for salvation. Vanessa curled her legs further underneath her. Maybe Hank Cowles was right, in his own psychotic way. This was the end. Corey's family would die all over again, and when that happened, his mind would, in effect, reboot, and start all over again.

No more. She had to step inside his world now. It was the only way to pull him from the fire before it swallowed him again.

Corey licked his lips, blinked three times in quick succession, and whispered, "Sam. Oh, Sam...."

Corey

I

Samantha had rolled onto her back again, wishing her inured shoulder protested more than it was doing, wanting to feel pain to know that it was still there. Enough dirt had dried over one eye that the constant flow of wasps overhead seemed without distance. The beam above her looked so old she wondered how it had managed to hold up the roof all these years. One section of the ceiling *had* cracked apart to expose a dull gray sky. No more blue. It had washed away in whatever violence was happening outside. The wasps passed to and fro above her. Sam wriggled herself closer to the open door knowing at the same time she was closer to the paper monster beside it, a monster with a thousand burning stingers in its belly.

She craned her neck, watched the nest. Wasps swarmed over its surface, pouring out of a dozen holes. They never came too close, but they knew she was there. Their constant recon flights were a warning, or a preparation.

Sam whispered, "Corey," then dared no more. The entire population of the nest was crawling out for a glimpse of the intruder. Spectators for whatever was about to happen. *Romans in a coliseum.*

The next crash of thunder – so close now – sent a cloud of them into the air, but they settled back. A few drifted towards her. One alighted on her cheek; another wandered through her hair. She tried not to think about

Fran's story, the person stung to death so long ago, most likely in this very shed. She did not want to become that person. The wasp on her cheek stepped towards her open eye. It's alien face was huge and out of focus. She stopped breathing. The black monster lifted away from her face. The one in her hair remained as an itch she couldn't scratch.

She dared not move now. Wanted to become a stone on the floor. No threat. She turned her eye towards the door as the next boom rolled overhead. The world outside, from this perspective, was upside down. Hank Cowles hung a few feet back from the door, staring in at her. His skinny hands gripped the splintery handle of an old, rusted pitchfork, fingers twisting tighter, coiling over themselves like snakes. His smile was upside down, hands curling tighter on the handle. The tines of the fork glistened in the fading daylight. Samantha willed herself not to see him. Just an illusion. The finger snakes continued twisting. He stepped closer, eyes burning into hers, telling her his plan without needing words.

He stopped at the threshold suddenly and looked left, towards the thin path from which he'd obviously come.

Samantha closed her eye, focusing on the wasp's tiny footfalls along her scalp. When she opened it again, the doorway was empty, save the nearby trees waving goodbye in the growing wind.

II

"I don't like thunder," Honey said, leaning forward, sharing this secret. "Do you want to trade?" She held up a brown-skinned doll wearing a silver spacesuit. "Astronaut

Barbie for..." she considered, probably deciding the one with the wedding dress was off-limits then picked up Aerobic Barbie, "This one."

"Honey? Sweetie where are you?" Abby wondered if Honey's mother was calling *her* Sweetie. Maybe Sweetie was Honey's middle name. That was funny enough to elicit a giggle.

"We're in the bedroom, Mommy!" Then in a whisper, added, "What?"

Abby told her, and Honey shook her head. "No, no. My middle name is Samantha."

Before she could tell the girl that was her mother's name Fran called again, "Honey, why don't you and your new friend come play here, near me. OK?" Another crack of thunder, still far off. Abby wanted to count the seconds between flashes, but it was too bright outside to see any. Honey gathered up her dolls, Abby hers and they left the bedroom, wandering down the curving staircase into the foyer. Honey's house was so *huge*. Abby didn't like it much. It was old and creaky like a haunted house.

She followed the girl through the open kitchen into a wide, sunny family room. The mother was sitting forward on a plush white chair and stared at the TV. She motioned absently with one hand. "Go play behind the couch, Sweetie. Mommy wants to watch the news. Maybe we can have some dinner soon." There was a wide carpeted area between the tall windows and the couch. As they headed that way, the woman looked up. "It's Abby, right?"

She nodded.

"What time is your Mommy coming?"

"I don't know. I think I'm supposed to go home for supper."

Honey said, "Can she stay with us? Can she have supper with us?"

The woman looked back at the television, watched for a while. The two girls stood beside the couch, waiting. A pretty Chinese woman on the screen was saying, "...current estimations close to ten thousand within the strike zone...." Finally, Honey's mother looked at her. The tears falling down her face gave Abby a bellyache. Grown ups weren't supposed to cry. Her Daddy sometimes looked like he was going to, mostly when he watched the news like this lady. Why did they watch it if it made them sad?

"No, Honey, I'm sorry. Not today. There's a lot going on." She wiped her cheeks with the ball of her palm, tried to focus on Abby. On the television there was a man sitting at a desk. The picture fizzed and blurred. He said, "Mixed news coming from the west coast. In the Middle East..."

Honey's mother spoke over him. "You can come back again real soon, and we'll have macaroni and cheese. How's that?"

"Sure!" both girls said, and on that note they moved to the space behind the couch. The sun faded outside.

III

Vanessa slid closer on the couch. Corey didn't remember sitting down. Now he was too damned close to this woman and her autumn-scented madness. "Where's Sam?" His arms were shaking. Vanessa reached out, ran her hands up and down them. Rather than pull away, Corey found an odd comfort in her touch, forgetting for the moment she'd just threatened to kill his wife. He probably had misheard her. *Had* to have.

Abby!

"She's fine, and so is your wife."

He tried to pull away but her hands tightened around him. The grip hurt his arms. She leaned in, drew Autumn around his face and heart. "Listen to me very carefully, Corey Union. Your wife, and your daughter, are gone. They've been gone for two years." Vanessa doubled again. He tried to blink away one of the images, focus only on one but the figures fought for the same space. The illusion flittered away, leaving only the one, softly-smiling woman.

"What are you talking about?" His vision blurred again, but this time it was his doing. He tried not to cry, wanted to be strong, defiant. "Where are they?"

Something exploded outside the house, rattling the windows. One of the removable sashes fell loose, tilted in with a soft thud on the back of the couch. The shaking subsided but the rumble continued, fading but never completely dissipating. Outside, the sky darkened, lightened again. Corey wondered if the sun had exploded and was fighting to hold itself together. Stupid thought, but... When the thunder – *it's not thunder you know it's not thunder where is Abby where is Sam* – moved on a new one took its place. Sound of a weed whacker outside, someone cutting along the house. Then tap-tap-tap against the metal flue behind him. The bees had come back.

"I have to wind the clock," he said, not meaning to say it out loud, knowing he'd just stepped over some line. Hank Cowles was right. He had to stop whatever was happening. He could do it.

The hands squeezed his arms again. "Don't pay attention to that sound, my love." *Pay no attention to that man behind the curtain.* "You have to let the clock wind down. The only way to save the ones you love is to stop what the old man has started. You have to - "

"– remember, Corey." The ghost head broke off, separated, *this* woman's face less distinct and less menacing.

Corey muttered, "Hank Cowles said, he said...."

"He murdered your family, Corey." A monstrous crash outside; something slammed into the side of the fireplace. The brickwork cracked. The man trimming the weeds outside might be hurt. "Focus, for God's sake! The cab, remember? They got into the cab and he - "

Corey screamed, threw himself forward -- a desperate surge exploding out of him like the storm outside. Rage and fear so hot his face felt like it would melt. His forehead slammed into Vanessa's, both versions of her. She tumbled backwards off the couch.

Corey shouted, "Shut up! Shut up! Shut up!"

IV

"I want to go home," Abby said, standing alone in the middle of the room. Her new friend was currently wrapped in her mother's arms. She'd run there after the last, terrible thunder clap. Everything was getting dark. She'd stayed too late; now it was night and she was trapped. Honey's mother was crying, pulling her daughter against her breast. Were they afraid of Abby? Strange and confusing pictures danced on the television, sometimes overlaid with bursts of frightening static. More people came into focus, news people, only to be lost again when the screen glowed white, whiter still, then dark. Nothing showed now. Not even static.

The world went *boom!*

Abby held her fists against her ears in the growing dark and screamed, "I want to go home!"

Honey's mother looked up, remembering she was there. "What? Oh God, I'm sorry, Sweetie. Get me the phone." She looked towards a small table beside her chair. She could have reached for it herself, but both arms were busy around Honey, wrapping her up. It wasn't fair! They were supposed to be playing. Abby ran over, picked up the phone and held it out. It took another few seconds for the woman to untangle herself and take it. She sniffed, wiped her face, said, "What's the number, Dear?"

Abby couldn't remember. She stared at the woman, couldn't remember the number. "In your pocket, girl. Hurry."

My name is Abby, she wanted to scream, but reached into her pockets until she found the paper in the right front. After staring at the slip of paper for an eternity, Honey's mother *finally* pushed the numbers.

The house began to shake.

V

Corey paced the room, unsure what to do, always coming back to the clock, the ugly fucking clock that had been hiding with his family for years and never worked. And now the world was breaking apart and he was supposed to do something about it, but what? He took a step towards it, then another. *Wind it; wind it.* From the chimney. the tapping of the bees continued. Trying to get in, to make him wind the doomsday clock one more time.

On the floor, Vanessa curled her legs under her like a snake, eyes intense when he finally turned his attention back to her. At least now there was only one of her, though her outline was vague, as if that other ghost waited just under the surface. He *wanted* her to stop him, needed her to make sense of all of this. "Leave it alone, Corey. If you wind it, then there's nothing more I can do for you; do you understand? Think of your wife." Which one was speaking? Which one was real?

The phone rang from the kitchen wall, its shrill scream battling for attention with a new explosion outside. The living room darkened further. Were the clouds burning through the sky overhead? He did not want to look out to see.

The rumbling faded. The world held together for another minute. He stared at the phone, wondering if he'd only imagined it when it rang again. A tall man stepped into view from the kitchen. Hank Cowles still wore his long plaid sleeves buttoned to the wrist. He lifted the handset from the wall, said without expression, "Hello?"

"Give me that!" Corey stepped forward, though his feet seemed to want to stay behind. Hank raised his hand, palm out. The air solidified. Corey pushed forward, could not move any closer. The old man tilted his head into the phone, said, "Yes, that's fine. I'll let Mister Union know you called. Die well." He giggled and hung up.

The air thinned. Corey stumbled forward and landed on one knee.

"Your daughter is at her little friend's house. She's about to die, unless you wind that clock as I've instructed."

"He's lying, Corey! He wants you dead, wants to finish what he started two years ago. Don't you see? None of this is real!" Vanessa's hair was short again. She knelt beside the couch, looking up at him with eyes full of tears, eyes that no longer mocked but cared about him. Loved him.

The tapping from the fireplace stopped, replaced by a droning whine that surrounded the house. No sign of them, yet. Maybe they were flying off, giving up.

Vanessa screamed, "Corey, focus! Look at me!"

"Charlie, shut this bitch up, please."

With a yip of delight, Nurse Charles padded into view from the kitchen, ran towards Vanessa on its little legs. Vanessa shook her head. "There is no dog, Corey. It's just you and me. Hank is not here! He can't hurt you any more than he already has. That day. Remember that day?"

The white dog stopped beside her, raised its lips. Small white teeth Corey thought would look more menacing if the damn dog wasn't so small. But it *was* dangerous! Old man and dog were terrible things, destroyers of worlds.

Vanessa said, more quietly, "Yes. Yes, they are."

"Time's wasting, Charlie," Hank said. "Hurry along."

The dog lashed out. It sank its teeth into Vanessa's arm, shook back and forth with a growl. Vanessa became indistinct again, fuzzy around the edges. She lashed out with the arm, her own face a snarl. The dog couldn't hold on, tumbled across the rug and stopped against the chair. It righted itself, growing a little larger in its rage as it moved towards her again.

An explosion outside slammed hard onto the roof, twisting the house against its frame. Corey stumbled sideways, heading into the kitchen. "And where are you going, young man?" But Hank did not move, merely folded his arms across his chest and followed Corey's progress. "The clock is that way!"

Corey didn't answer, too intent on a single purpose now that he'd gotten past. The back door was propped open to the world outside but he ignored what he saw, trees bending towards the ground, the red glow in the sky. Vanessa screamed in pain from the living room. Corey reached for one of the white-marbled handles emerging from the butcher block. The blade was long and wide. He turned back, ready to shove it though Hank's chest if he tried to stop him.

The old man did not, merely lowered his arms to his side as if offering himself. Corey ran past him, back into the living room.

The dog's white fur splashed in red from Vanessa's torn and bloody arm. She thrashed at it, trying to shake it off but it would not let up. It released the arm only to close over the other. A piece of flesh the size of a dinner roll hung from her left bicep and blood poured from a hundred thin gashes in both arms and one leg, blood running like paint. Nurse Charles kept at her, trying to find a way past her flailing and mangled arms looking for her throat. Vanessa saw Corey approaching and shouted, "The dog can't hurt us, Corey! Look at me! It's not real."

He did look, saw the kindness in her and knew he needed to save her.

"Stop!"

Corey focused only on the dog, slammed the blade of the knife through the Shih-Tzu's back. It yelped in surprise and pain, little legs flailing against the blade which pinned it flat against the carpet. Vanessa crawled back, left a red path in her wake. Corey pulled the knife free but as soon as he did the dog wriggled back to its feet. He slammed the blade down again. This time the point embedded into the floor. "There!" he screamed. "It's dead. It can't hurt you!"

Nurse Charles did not yelp this time, nor show any sign of pain. She thrashed under the knife, snarling and nipping towards Vanessa's ankle and Corey's bloodstained hand.

Hank stood by the phone and laughed, holding his hands to his sides, leaning back like a melodramatic stage actor.

As the dog thrashed, the knife sank deeper. White curly fur soaked red with blood. *No,* Corey realized, *the knife isn't sinking.* The dog was growing. Two fleshy bubbles pressed outward along its neck, on either side of the snapping head.

The dog curled its long legs, too large now to be pinned to the floor. It rose up, the new twin growths taking form and opening their own mouths. When the monster shook itself, the knife flew free, landing harmlessly against the far wall. Nurse Charles was the size of a Saint Bernard, still growing. Its three heads dripped saliva and loomed over Vanessa as she crawled backwards towards the door, bleeding from dozens of small violent bites. The hem of her dress had risen up her legs, twisted around her. She screamed, "Stop it, Corey! The yellow! Remember the yellow! The cab! They got into the cab!" One of the heads closed over her calf, pulling her back into the room. She screamed. The second head bit into her belly, ripping the dress to tatters then chewing into the soft skin beneath. The third closed around her throat. Her head fell back, a strange noise escaping between her lips, half choke, half laugh. Corey stood motionless, seeing it all as a dream which he could wake from if he only rode it out. Vanessa's bare, free leg kicked against the couch.

She gurgled something.

Hank Cowles finally stepped forward – *the smiling old man trots from the driver's side to open the rear passenger door, waving Corey's family into its depths with a dramatic flourish. Abby points at the passenger side window,* Look, Mommy, he has a little dog. *Small pink tongue, stub of a wagging tail. Sam laughs at the sight and Abby scrambles into the back seat, the girl no longer wary of the fat yellow car with the large bee on the door. Samantha kisses Corey on the lips.* See you in a couple of days, Honey. *Corey kisses her back as the old man waits beside the open rear door, his smile dropping a little. Corey leans towards the squirming bundle in his wife's arms, touching the... kissing the... and Abby in the back waving* Bye, Daddy! *and Corey waving,* Say hi to Mickey and don't have any fun until I get there, *and Abby nods in mock seriousness as if to say* Of course not, Father, *and the old man is now confused.* Aren't you coming, too, sir, *aren't you coming, too, sir, aren't you –*

The dog, or *dogs*, were hunched over the twitching remains of his neighbor. Her free arm gripped one of the heads only to have another curl towards it, take it by the elbow and bite down, crushing the bones. Her fingers splayed, swelling, fingernails bursting loose in a spray of blood.

Smoke poured into the room from the kitchen, smell of burning wood and curling paint. For a moment, Corey thought the swarm had found its way in. The buzzing of the wasps outside was louder, only to be drowned by another explosion. His house was burning. He didn't know what to do. A new sound joined the chorus – too many sounds, too many things happening – the ticking of the clock behind him, once, twice, each like a gasp. It was dying. The world was dying and it was his fault. The floor shook constantly now. Smoke rolled across the ceiling and filled the room.

"Time's up, Mister Union. I cannot force you, but you need to wind it. Now or never. If you want to save them, you have to hurry!"

A scream caught in Corey's throat like a tumor. He wanted to curl into the corner and let someone else stop it all. But if he gave up, everyone would die. Everything would be gone. He turned around and lifted the clock. It weighed nothing. The ticking grew louder as it slowed down, no longer keeping time, merely struggling to stay alive. Each *tick* was like a small explosion, a child to the thunder of the world's death. Vanessa's wet gurgles and the growling and gnashing of the dog's three heads. The key still protruded from the back. All he had to do...

A sudden movement across the room. Vanessa had somehow tossed the dog - *Cerberus rising to devour* – aside.

Her dress was a mass of shredded cloth, soaked in blood, stomach and chest were flayed open, bright blue and red organs, still pumping, still squirming with life, still *working*. Her right leg miraculously remained untouched but her left was flattened above the knees, peppered with bites and tears. Her head lolled along the floor to face him, held to the body by a few strips of flesh. How was she alive? Eyes clear, opened wide above two shredded cheeks, the voice that bubbled from her mouth was distorted, gargled. "Don't; he's a liar," the head said. "Let it die; let the clock die. You'll be free and all of this will end... He killed them...."

Nurse Charles recovered from the attack and bore down on her face with two of its heads, shaking, tearing. A gurgled scream, then nothing. The other head buried its snout into the open chest, chewing on a heart that would not stop beating....

"Corey!" Hank shouted from his place by the phone. "Now! Your wife is in the shed at the back of the property, stabbed and bound by our friend here. She will die, alone, if you don't stop this."

The remaining window behind the couch exploded. Glass shards cut through the curtain and cascaded across the floor in front of him. The curtains curled in flames, blackening the window frame with fire. The smoke was a swirling gray ceiling above him, falling, curling around his face but now vented outside where the lawn twisted black like the curtains. Corey tightened his throat, not wanting to cough, afraid he wouldn't be able to stop.

Then the bees poured in through the shattered window, long black wasps mixing and swirling with the smoke, a tornado circling the old man. "Now!" Hank screamed.

Corey turned the key, once, twice, the ticking at first becoming louder, then fading, softer.

Vanessa's body flipped up and down, rebuilding itself only to be beaten down by the hellish dog. Corey hesitated.

The old man closed the cab's door, sealing Corey's family inside. They pressed against the window, screaming, Help us! Help us!

No, they were waving, smiling, *the driver asking again if Corey was sure he wouldn't come, Corey wondering why he kept asking such a stupid question. Of course he wasn't coming; he had to work, had to work, had to stay and work for two more days and would meet them on vacation, Sam and Abby and... and his family was carried away, little dog in the front seat, laughing at him, wagging its tail –*

"You killed my family," he said, hardly seeing Hank through the tears. "*You* killed them!" He lifted the clock over his head, praying he hadn't wound it enough, praying he could save his family some other way.

Hank raised his hands. "Stop, Corey! I warn you, if you don't finish -"

Corey screamed and fought against the thickening air around him, forcing every bit of strength like running from the monster in a dream. Only this time he was struggling towards it, straining his arms to throw the clock. The resistance finally broke. He tossed the ugly, terrible thing to the floor. It smashed among the broken and melted window glass, blue porcelain boy shattering into a dozen irreparable shards. The clock popped free of its housing, rolled a few inches, then stopped against one of Vanessa's discarded shoes.

The dog raised its red-stained faces towards him, baring teeth the size of fingers, pieces of Vanessa hanging between them, blood and saliva in syrupy globs dripping to the carpet. The smell of its breath overpowered the smoke, nauseating Corey enough that he turned away, swallowed his terror back down. *What did he just do?*

The world fell into silence so suddenly that the echoes of its destruction rolled on in his head. The bees were gone. Vanessa was nothing but strips of skin and ribbons of intestine, white stomach having popped and excreted a stinking clear liquid. Yet the parts still twitched, twisted together, tried to become the whole again.

The world outside was dark as midnight, but silent.

Hank shook his head, stuck out his lower lip in a pout and raised his left hand with the index finger extended. One lone black bee perched atop it. He whispered, "Tell the ones in the shed to kill his wife." The wasp lifted off his finger and disappeared into the kitchen. Hank followed its progress, then turned back to the living room. He whispered, more to himself than Corey, "I'll deal with the girl."

The house began to shake again, sounds of ruin returning to the world, louder and more violent as the seconds passed. Something behind him *crack*ed! Corey turned around as the fireplace bricks fell against him. Above the mantle, the drywall broke apart from the force and weight of the collapsing chimney. He tripped over his own feet and fell backwards onto the rug, onto the broken glass and an empty box of Sterno fire logs. The final remnants of the chimney collapsed under the hammering of a hundred explosions outside. The house undid itself. The outside wall fell inward, opening the room to the burning hellscape outside.

VI

The nest had swollen to twice its original size, reaching towards the shed's broken doorway and further into the corner. Even in her panic, Sam understood that it hadn't actually grown. It had emptied. Hundreds and hundreds of black and white wasps crawled with a building excitement across its paper surface, tiny cancerous growths impatient to fly, to swarm. Samantha knew this, had stopped trying to wriggle her wrists free of the ropes. It wasn't doing any good, anyway. Her right arm was completely numb and her vision was fading, either from loss of blood or the growing storm outside. She stared at the throbbing mass in the corner then flinched at a new crash of thunder roaring overhead like a train crashing into the station, shaking the earth, rattling the old, dried boards of the shed. Each time she waited for the bees to rise up and blame her. They only squirmed and crawled over each other, a massive, black heart, beating with expectation, waiting to burst.

It was getting so dark outside! The next crashing train finally collided with the forest, sending towers of flame skyward. Sam lay on her side and watched through the door as it framed the burning woods. One wasp zig-zagged outside the door, hesitating. When it finally entered the shed, it did not join the swelling mass in the corner but circled over Sam's head. Each orbit brought it lower, and closer. She could see every detail with her one clear eye, the two sections of its bulbous body pressed together as if bound by the triple bands of white circling its abdomen, like an evil bumblebee. Long legs curled beneath it, and Sam could hear the whine of its wings.

Somehow, she understood this small creature was to be her executioner. When it landed on her forehead, touching its tiny legs to her skin a pinprick of heat spread from the poisoned barb it injected into her flesh. Then the world inside the shed exploded in a buzz saw whine. Sam cried out and wondered, even as the thousands of others swarmed over her, crawling into her nostrils and open, screaming mouth, if these types of bees died when they stung. Would *her* death mean theirs, as well? Would she be found with a thousand corpses littering the ground like a dark halo?

Then all rational thought was lost. One sting burned into a dozen, a hundred then a thousand across every part of her body, until there was only a single explosion of fire inside her, burning her down to ash.

VII

Heat like he'd never before experienced slammed into his face from the hole left in the wake of the fallen wall and chimney. Corey raised his hands, crawled backwards, hot glass pressing into his palms. Someone was laughing. He turned over, got to his hands and knees and tried to brush away the glass. The heat at his back threatened to ignite him.

Nurse Charles was a small white dog again, pacing back and forth with a terrified, uncertain whine. The strips and torn flesh and organs that once were Vanessa flipped and curled, rebuilding themselves into a whole, but still unrecognizable as human. The face was torn past recognition with two teeth dangling from the upper jaw, the bottom hanging from shredded muscle. Nevertheless, the sound, the *laugh*, came from her. More like wet gasps, but in Corey's mind still laughter.

He looked over at Hank Cowles. The old man stared back at him, defeated. "You stupid, little man."

The body across the room continued to twitch and laugh. The whining little dog spat out its sour victory with a series of yips.

The shaking of the planet continued, building; time had not stopped after all. The longer he stood in the middle of the house, the worse it cracked and shattered around him. He could do nothing. *Nothing.*

He whispered, "Sam," and stood, wavering on the unsteady floor, the back of his head seared by the heat outside. All he could do was try to save his wife one more time.

Vanessa

Vanessa couldn't move her legs or head. An invisible, unrelenting weight pressed her down, a monstrous hand she could not see. She stared at Corey, watched him resolve some unspoken conflict, then run into the kitchen. Rough squeak of the back door opening, never closing. Vanessa spit, tasted blood dripping down her cheek. She assumed it was blood, probably filling her lungs. Harder to breathe, the irresistible weight her own body imploding into itself. She tried again to move her head. It rolled, eyes lowering towards the rug. Her left arm was smeared with blood pumping from the thin valleys cut along the skin. Further past this, the knife lay discarded on the rug in the center of the room. The white handle glistened red. She focused on it as the room got cold, *winter cold*, her skin freezing over like the surface of a lake. She looked nowhere else but at the stained handle of the knife. *Shock, my body's just going into shock*. There was no little dog pacing the room beside her, whining. It was only her imagination. There had been no monster dog, either, no Cerberus' angry snarling heads. She let these thoughts roll around, convincing herself of their truth. The room was silent and cold. Something buzzed somewhere out of her line of sight. A lone bee, perhaps lost after it had fallen out of Corey's madness. Like the dog.

There is no dog.

The buzzing stopped, returned again. Was the bee cold, too? Was it falling asleep in this sudden winter like its kind always did? The third time it came she recognized the sound. Her vibrating cell phone, discarded on the couch. May as well be a thousand miles away....

Corey

When Corey burst through the back door, the world he'd seen through his car window less than an hour ago was gone. This was the world of his nightmares, darkness and fire, air like an oven, burning. His lungs seized and curled when he tried to suck it in. Pain, like broken glass filling his lungs. He grabbed the porch railing and bent over, but the porch was burning around him. Corey stumbled down twisting, wooden steps, breathing out slowly, trying to find clean air. The structure collapsed behind him, tossing him forward onto the ground, pushed and buffeted by a wind which could not decide in which direction to blow. He grabbed a handful of dying grass, took in another breath. Hurt less this time, and he tried to ignore the image of the inside of his lungs burnt and bleeding. Corey looked behind him. Something massive and bright rose in the distance beyond the house and trees, a head made of fire and clouds, rising higher....

He ran hard, leaping forward to keep his momentum towards the edge of the woods. The tops of the trees snapped and split under crowns of flame. He passed beneath them, falling now and then against a prone trunk but as quickly rising back up, and he continued deeper into the woods. Around him, branches snapped and fell, hundreds of burning tines impaled into the ground, searching him out. One would find their mark eventually, pin him to the earth where he would curl and twist like an ant under a magnifying glass. If that happened, he was done. Until then, he pushed on and tried to stay on the path. It was dark; so much smoke, hard to see any details.

Corey screamed against the world's dying groans, shouting Samantha's name, calling out for Abby –

– who spun in a slow circle in the oversized family room, hands over her ears to block out the noise around her. The tall windows bent inward, then breathed out, pushing away from flames the girl felt but never saw but which danced around the house like a monstrous snake. The air in the room was sharp, tingling and burning her skin. She imagined herself tossed into an oven by a witch who had sneaked behind the three of them when they weren't looking. Honey was like a leaf on the floor, curled and brown. The line where her charred body ended and her mother's began was hard to discern. They'd fallen together from the chair, eyes squeezed closed, skin blackening and peeling as the oven cooked them alive. Abby lowered one arm from her head and saw the tender flesh redden, darken, flake away. As if waiting for her attention, pain seared up her arms, invisible fire burrowing deep inside her. She screamed for her mother, turned around for a place to escape. The old man who had picked up Miss Charles the other day stood at the entrance to the foyer. He was grinning, his face pinched, as in pain. Abby held out her bleeding and peeling arms but lowered them when she saw the dirty old pitchfork in his hands. The stained wooden handle dripped red over his fingers –

"Leave her alone!" Corey screamed, lashing out at a branch that had whipped across his face. It swung back, insistent as a reporter's microphone, everyone screaming for answers, devouring his pain with an insatiable appetite like a dog to its food. Through squinted eyes, he saw the woods, bending down and splitting as it burned, but also Abby stepping backwards, tripping over the body of her new friend and the girl's mother. Hank ran across the room now, the painful smile stretching wider and wider and hands rising and pointing the –

"God, please help her!" Corey screamed and tripped again, right ankle twisting under a root. He thrashed free, ignored the pain in his leg, began to fear being turned around when he saw the old shed. On this he focused, nothing else, letting the images in his head, the *lies* broadcast to his mind fade to a smoldering pain, knowing they were there if he gave them attention. He could not handle the impotent shame which would paralyze him if he did. *The shed, only the shed.* It was intact but sagging amid the backdrop of the burning forest. Less than a hundred yards from the open door, a tree exploded over the roof. Embers ignited the dry wood, wild hairs of flame spreading towards the peak. Everything would be over soon. All he wanted was to be inside to die with his wife. Die *with* her, not alone like this. Never alone. Never again. Corey crawled over a trunk, managed a limping stumble into the shed.

Samantha's body lay inside. She was black, as if burned away like Abby's friend. When he reached out to touch her, however, the wasps lifted free, swarmed around his flailing arms for a second before blowing out the door and rising on heated currents away from the shed into the red sky.

Corey lowered his arms.

Above him, the ceiling boards burned in a frenzy, the single overhead beam the only thing keeping the structure together. The fire on the roof cast the room in an underwater glitter. Embers fell like red snow around Samantha's body. A section of burning plywood, curling black, fell loose and draped over her swollen legs. Her pants began to burn. Corey knocked the wood away, patted wildly at her legs until the flames died out. She did not react.

"Sam?" Even in the firelight from above, her face was featureless. Cheeks, nose, eyes, everything red and swollen, covered with tiny bruises. She looked like a badly made scarecrow. He called her name again but couldn't hear his own voice over the screaming of the dying world. Embers dropped onto his head. He ignored them. The air smelled like a campfire, like burning hair. He worked loose the knots of the rope, not bothering to be gentle because his wife was dead. His wife was dead and somewhere in the carnage behind him his little daughter was screaming. He heard it even though it *couldn't* be her, couldn't be true. None of this was real.

His hands got tangled in the rope as he pulled it free. Sam's terrible face never looked at him, never acknowledged his presence. He was alone at the end of the world. The walls buckled, then collapsed. Corey screamed and tossed the rope aside but it coiled around his head and neck. The beam above groaned and splintered. Corey looked up in time to see its massive, flaming presence draw down onto him. It looked like he was being lifted *towards* it, higher, higher, the rope tightening around his throat until he could no longer look down at his dead wife, only stare up at the beam suspended in this last moment of time.

The world died away, slowly, fading with the light.

The interior of the shed was hot and stagnant, though an occasional wisp of air circulated through cracks and fissures in the roof and walls, bringing with it traces of cool evening breeze. Late birdsong, the gradual emergence of crickets and peepers the only sounds in the this forgotten corner of the property. These, and the creak of the overhead beam, the straining gasp of the dry rope. It was a slight sound, whispering in time with the body swaying back and forth over the empty room. Corey's final, reflexive twitches subsided. Then he was calm, unconcerned with events of the world around him.

Vanessa
Saturday

I

"Vanessa? Van, can you open your eyes for me?"

Vanessa tried, but even that small action felt like it would open every slash and cut in her body. She swallowed. Her throat ached, that same cotton-dry pain as when she was five years old and her tonsils were removed. *Ice Cream*, Bill Cosby had whispered to her in those days from the stereo. She would have smiled if her face didn't feel like it was bound with tape.

"Ice Cream," she whispered, or tried to, unsure if her voice made it through the arid desert of her throat. Andrew didn't respond. That *was* Andrew speaking, wasn't it?

"Vanessa, I know you're awake. Open your eyes."

She tried again, managed only a slit at first; expected to see Corey's living room, crumbled walls, angry little dog – *no, that hadn't been real. None of it. Too caught up....* What she saw, framed within the slow rising veil of her lashes, was Andrew Booth's dark and worried face. Behind him a bright room, dull white walls, nonetheless brilliant compared to the faded house in Hillcrest. A single row of fluorescents along the ceiling. *Too bright.* She closed her eyes. When she opened them again, she focused only on Andrew. His cheeks were peppered with a day's stubble. Not like him to come to work unshaven.

Then she realized, as a dream slowly remembered, this wasn't a normal day. She wasn't sure which particular hospital this was. Didn't look like theirs, but it was a hospital. She was alive. That was something.

Andrew smiled, though the expression was pulled tight on his scruffy face. "Better. That's better. Do you know where you are, Vanessa?"

She looked around, not needing to but wanting to show him she was listening. "Hospital." Her throat ignited with the word. She flexed her hand, raised her left arm so she could see it better without lifting her head. Bandages wrapped around most of her forearm; another squeezed her bicep.

"Hurt," she managed.

Andrew nodded. He was sitting on the edge of the bed. "Yes, but you're going to be OK. Do you understand? You're going to be fine." He looked like he was going to cry. She smiled. *My sensitive hero....*

The world around her sharpened, nightmare memories of the past few hours rushing back – how long ago *had* it been? Corey running out of the house. So much blood. Her own blood.

"Corey...." She tried not to whine but that was how it came out. A sudden, terrible fear.

Andrew looked down, chin tucked against his chest. He held it long enough to tighten the knot in her stomach. His silence answered the question she couldn't ask. He finally looked up, fighting to retain a focused, neutral air and failing miserably. He said, "Do you remember, Vanessa?"

Her head felt as if it was mounted on a pole. With her right arm she reached up, touched the bandage wrapped around her throat. She tried to remember where else she'd been bitten. *Cut, I was cut, not bitten, there had been no dog....*

"He's gone, isn't he?" Speaking hurt, but she was getting used to the pain. Maybe she just didn't care anymore. Her mouth was so dry. Ice chips, why wouldn't they give her some ice chips?

Andrew stared into her face for a long time. Then nodded.

No, that wasn't enough. Corey had run from the house. *Gone* could mean anything. *Gone* could mean *ran away*. She knew it did not, but needed to say it out loud.

"Corey's dead."

Andrew's face changed, no longer as tight, less controlled. *Relief?* That he wouldn't have to say the words, perhaps, or that she was awake and talking. Maybe that she was still sane enough to say them.

"Yes. He is." He laid a large hand over a spot on her arm between two bandages. "I'm sorry." She savored the contact, let his warmth give whatever comfort she could pull from it.

Samantha was dead, and Abby. Now Corey. She did not want to ask how it happened, had a glimmer of the shed but wasn't sure why. Hank had sent him there. *No*, she thought, *Corey had sent himself*. She wasn't sure she wanted the image confirmed. Not yet. The thought wormed into her brain, found a place where it would always refuse to be ignored. She'd let him die. She'd been responsible for him, then let him wander off into the woods to –

"There was nothing you could do, Van. Do you understand that?"

"I was hurt," she said, both to the man sitting on the edge of her bed and maybe to herself. Lying on the floor, bleeding. Her memory of the attack still a mixture of truth and dream, seeing Corey Union running at her from the kitchen, holding the knife, but superimposed over that image the monstrous three-headed dog. *Cerberus rising....* A hallucination brought on by the stress of the attack. *Pulled into his world*, as Andrew had warned so often could happen. Seeing herself in the shed, Hank Cowles outside - no, seeing Samantha - not seeing, *hearing*, Corey's tale. She closed her eyes, clearing the confused jumble written across her brain.

"The dog. Kept biting me..." *Shit*, she hadn't meant to say that aloud. Andrew was worried enough already. Instead of berating her, however, Andrew only nodded.

"Do you remember the dog?"

He was being condescending. Worried she was delusional. Robert Schard stepped into view behind him. His lanky form bent over Andrew's close-cropped head. At least *his* smile was wide, and very real.

"Hey, Vanessa. You're awake! How're you feeling?"

She managed a smile, and meant it. Robert's simple question offered some light into her heart, *poured its love like iced lemonade on a hot day*, she might have written. *Samantha* might have written, if she'd been given more time in her life to do such things. She was just a baby. Just a baby.

Eyes closed again, tears running down her cheeks, soaking into the Band-aids on her cheeks.

Andrew seemed intent on keeping the mood low. He raised his free hand, palm-down as if to say, *Keep it down; keep it down.*

He said, "Vanessa, look at me. Can you tell me what you remember? Anything. Start small."

Corey had remembered, for the briefest moment, seeing the little dog in the window of the cab, watching his family climb into Cowles' taxi outside the W&G building in Worcester, on their way to the airport. Without him. Never seeing them again. He'd *remembered....*

Dog biting, laughter from behind her, Cowles screaming and raising the pitch fork with no, no... a disembodied voice as Nurse Charles bit down, again and again....

She shook her head. Corey had exploded in rage rather than face the world, deciding the only way to stop his illusions from unraveling was to stop the person responsible. He couldn't reach Hank Cowles so he'd attacked her, cutting at the only threat within reach.

But she remembered none of it, except as a dream. *Hysterical amnesia, nothing more, Vanny. Be professional about this and face the truth. You tried. You failed. Move on.*

She shook her head as a way of answering Andrew's question, a way of lying without words. *There was no dog,* she did not say. Andrew breathed out slowly, lips tight. Was he angry? Robert moved across the room and sat in a chair under a painting. She was missing something...

"Vanessa, look at me."

Tired. Too tired for any more right now. She looked towards the door then down to the bandages on her arms and his hand resting there so gently. She took this hand, turned it over to touch the pink palm to her own, wanting to hold it. He wrapped his fingers around hers. Vanessa noticed her nails were neatly trimmed, understanding the evasiveness of focusing on such minutiae.

"Vanessa?"

Tired. She held his hand but pressed her head against the pillow, wanting to escape, *needing to sleep.* Later. She'd deal with it later. Her deadline was over, Corey was dead. There was no need to rush ever again.

"Later," she whispered, "need to sleep." Her throat hurt a little less this time. Maybe she'd inherited some of the magic of Corey's imaginary neighbor.

She squeezed his hand, watching the veil of her lashes drop over him. The last thing she saw was the painting above Robert Schard's head. It was moving, swirling, re-forming into a pasture. She tried to open her eyes more, but they refused to obey. She let go of his hand.

Andrew's voice became distant, talking to Robert. "Someone should stay with her for the next couple of days, round the clock."

Robert's whisper, "That'll be tough. I'm supposed to be on the second floor...."

"...find a way. There're plenty of people who'd volunteer.... call me when she's awake...."

The painting finished its metamorphosis through the veil of her lashes, a pasture long and sweeping, one lone cow staring back. An old man stood beside it -

"Andrew," she whispered. Movement on the bed, someone saying her name as a question, as if unsure she'd actually spoken.

An old man stood beside the lonely cow, hands on hips, head tossed back and laughing, playing the victor, taking his bow as the curtain of her lashes finally dropped over the scene.

Vanessa pushed the two words out like a final breath. "Help me."

If Andrew replied, she did not hear it. She felt nothing but black oblivion.

II

The stitches had been removed from her arms and neck, plus one long gash in her side. The scabbed-over wounds felt pinched, threatening to break open with every movement. Vanessa knew they wouldn't have removed the stitches if her injuries weren't healed, so she tried to ignore the sensation. The cuts had been bad but not too deep - none required surgery. Corey could have done far worse damage, but even in his delusional state he'd held back.

Oh, don't you worry, Darlin', it's natural to worry about the scar coming loose, the nurse removing the stitches had explained with a cheery lilt, taking a macabre pleasure from each thread pulled through Vanessa's skin. *Picking at someone else's scabs*. Superficial or not, two weeks of wrapping plastic around her arm and neck when stepping into the shower was enough. She was glad for the freedom.

There would still be scarring along her upper left arm. The diagonal line on her throat would fade, but never go away completely. When she looked in the mirror which Andrew had offered the first time he changed her dressing – an act that felt more intimate than she dared admit – the wound didn't look nearly as horrific as her imagination built it up to be.

The hallway along which she now walked was as stained and dirty as she remembered. The sickness of the souls she passed infected its walls. Overhead lights flickered, slowly fading into forgetfulness under layers of dust. Most of the people behind the doors were quiet this morning, as was the security guard escorting her. She'd showed him her papers, which he'd accepted and read without comment except to say, *Follow me.*

It was barely six in the morning. The silence around her felt like expectation rather than sleep. She imagined wild-eyed creatures with large ears and curled talons hunkered behind each door, ears pressed and shaking with excitement, reading her heart, knowing her sins. Knowing also what would soon happen.

She blinked away the image as they rounded the final corner. Marty was there, as he'd promised, looking uneasy but trying to mask it for the guard, who handed him the papers. Marty was saved from speaking as the guard immediately turned around and left them alone. Vanessa wondered if Hank Cowles, or his reputation, had something to do with the rudeness. The old man had that effect on people.

Her right hand was bent at the wrist, not from any lingering injury but to prevent what hung loose in her sleeve from dropping to the floor. Fortunately no one had searched her. Why would they? She was a psychiatrist. Even Marty did not know what was jabbing into the ball of her right hand. That was a good thing. He was nervous enough after forging the paperwork and arranging this meeting without anyone but the two of them – and now the silent guard – knowing.

Most men would do anything for sex, and of course she'd had to promise herself that using it to get what she needed this time was also the last, never again, now that she'd reached this end point of her life. Anyway, she had no intention of repaying her side of the deal with Marty. Vanessa tried to ignore the conflicting emotions across his face, eyes looking her body over, face flushed with shame.

"How long are you going to be?" he asked.

She looked at the door. The viewport was closed. Silence on the other side. He would know by now she was here, was coming in.

Vanessa did not answer, kept looking at the door and reminding herself that stepping through it was a one-way trip, would mean giving in to fantasy once and for all. Hank Cowles had nothing to do with Corey's death. The man whose life and mind had been hers to save had run from the house while she lay bleeding on the rug. He'd crashed through the woods, found the old shed and an old, dried out rope, hung himself from the beam. It snapped under his weight, but not before removing Corey from her world forever.

Beyond this door was either a wildly insane man who knew nothing about what had happened, or the architect of every delusion and pain she'd been fighting in her patient. The latter was impossible. But... *but, but* and more *but*....

"Not long," she said, after what felt like an hour of staring at the door.

Marty shifted, reached for the sliding rectangular portal and moved it aside. "Mister Cowles," he said, then swallowed. Vanessa wondered if he might actually know her plan. He *couldn't* know. "You... have a visitor, sir." He opened the door.

Mister Cowles. Sir. Titles which did not belong to a monster, the man who destroyed Corey Union's world and so many others', a man who was never content, who wanted more, who found Corey's mind and finished the job.

With that thought, before taking her first step into the room, Vanessa knew there was no turning back.

"Wait outside," she said, "would you, Marty?"

He looked at her, then into the bright room. "I don't think—"

"I'll be fine. I'll knock when I'm ready to leave."

He looked down, said, "OK, but if I don't hear a knock in five minutes, I'm coming in for you."

"Deal."

He stepped back and let Vanessa walk into the small room. Hank Cowles was as she remembered, sitting on the floor, neglecting the bed and single chair, legs splayed out in front of him. Patting the invisible dog beside him and smiling.

Had he only gotten into this position when she was announced? She wouldn't put it past him. Standing in the center of the room, with the old man watching her and running his damned hand over and over the shape of a dog no one could see, Vanessa did not move or speak until the door clicked shut behind her.

Five minutes. It would be enough.

She knelt on the floor between Hank's outstretched legs, closer than she thought wise, but it *had* to be this close. He did not move, save that right hand up and down, up and down.

"Good morning, old man."

He laughed, the sound thin and without humor.

"Good morning, *Doctor Reilly.*" His eyes darted over her body. "Healing nicely, I see."

She nodded, too aware of the scar on her throat.

He continued, "Charlie is a little miffed you wouldn't stay dead. But then, she wasn't really there, was she? Just an illusion, a madman's nightmare, no?"

"You can't -" she stopped, as if a hand had closed around her windpipe. What could she say?

His smiled faltered. "Poor Corey, having to lose his wonderful family all over again." Hank narrowed his eyes. "Not exactly the kind of therapy one reads about in the medical journals." He cackled, or perhaps was only clearing his throat. The hand continued, up and down.

Vanessa blinked when the man in front of her blurred. She cursed the tears, wiped them with her left hand, tensing her right, but not straightening it, not yet. She said, "Why did you kill them? *Any* of them. What did they do to deserve that?"

His smile, when she could focus on it again, was wide, was *wild*. "They died. That's all. They died, and I made them do it. There's nothing complicated about -"

She straightened her right hand, felt the knife blade slide along her palm, slicing it open, landing with a clink against the concrete floor. With a sweeping motion she'd practiced dozens of times, Vanessa gripped the handle and slashed hard under his chin.

His words stopped. The throat peeled open, white then red then *everything* red, pouring out of the deep valley in his skin, running under the collar of his light blue scrubs, soaking and spreading *so quickly*. He opened his eyes wide, mouth spread in a mockery of surprise. "Oooh, Girl," he said, voice filling with blood, "you killed me; you killed me." He tried to laugh, but when he tilted back his head, a new geyser of blood poured out like a hose from every vein and artery.

Vanessa crawled backward, covered in Hank Cowles' blood. The knife lay discarded and stained on the floor between his legs. No sense hiding it now. It was over. All of it was over.

When she got to her feet, the dying man's hand stopped caressing the dog, then dropped to the floor.

She knocked on the door. When there was no response, she tried the handle. It opened without resistance. No one waited in the hall. Martin was gone. Vanessa hesitated, almost calling for him before realizing this would be better. She wouldn't have to explain. He would understand. They all would. The dusty lights raced above her as she turned the corner, slowed to a quick walk – *don't run; just keep moving* – down the main hall. From all sides, the invisible residents screamed and hooted, trapped in their personal hells, shouting in tongues she didn't understand, the language of the mad and lost. They celebrated the death of the demon, the Destroyer of Worlds. She rounded the final corner, saw the elevator at the far end. Vanessa curled her hands into fists to stop the incessant shaking of her arms, feeling the blood – Hank's mixing with her own – between her fingers. She opened her hands and wiped them across her slacks. The hall was dimly lighted by the elevator, becoming darker every second. She leaned on the doors, pressed the button, forcing air into her lungs, letting it out. *Do not faint, not here, not here or anywhere. Just go home*

That was the only thread of choice left to her. Go home, and wait for the police to arrive. She'd just murdered a man.

What if he wasn't dead? What if Martin came back and found him, *saved* him? No. Why would he do that? Why would *anyone*?

The elevator doors slid open with a *ding*!

Empty. She was still alone.

Ticking behind her, claws on the broken tiles. *Nothing there; don't look.* As she stepped inside the elevator, a deep, familiar voice shouted, "Vanessa!"

She whirled around, saw two things simultaneously. One warmed her heart and the other turned it to stone. Andrew Booth at the far end of the hall, staring at her with warm eyes and loving hands which would never hold her close, never keep her safe. Those hands were raised in front of him. *Stop*, they said, *come back to me.*

The second thing was the source of the clicking along the floor. Nurse Charles trotted towards her, following the droplets of blood from her palm. The adorable little Shih-Tzu, the terrible monster with its tiny paws and curly white hair and pink tongue dancing across a bottom row of teeth bared as its lips parted. Small rivulets of drool fell to the floor, stretching out behind it like a web. It ran on stubby legs towards the elevator.

Behind the dog, Andrew called her name one more time, then began to run hard. The dog was closer and would reach the doors first. Vanessa didn't dare wait and hope that Andrew could save her from those little teeth and claws which would keep hurting her while Hank laughed and laughed and never explained why he was doing this to her family. He never explained, never explained, never –

She pressed the button for the lobby. Nothing happened. Nurse Charles covered the final few feet when the doors finally jerked to life and slid closed, but the dog was inside the car. Andrew was gone. She was alone with the monster as it latched onto her right leg, claws tearing

264

her clothes, little teeth nipping the skin beneath, climbing up her body. Vanessa stumbled against the elevator wall, slipped and fell onto the floor. The elevator rose. Nurse Charles growled and bit her thigh and sliced thinly into her with untrimmed claws as it moved towards her face. She lashed out, tried to stop it but it was too late. Relentless biting, scratching, cutting her cheeks and neck and nose. Small hurts opening everywhere, never enough to kill, but pain so bad. Stinging. The nest, don't stir up that horrible, terrible nest. Why had the old man done this to them? Why was he doing this to her now? The dog moved so quickly over her from its perch on her chest the head appeared in three places at once, reflections in the blood and tears filling her eyes, like the demon it was, like *Cerberus* rising to devour her world....

Andrew

Andrew cried, "Hold her!"

Martin climbed onto the bed and draped himself across Vanessa's thrashing legs. Andrew got hold of her wrists and pulled them towards the restraints at each side of the bed, but he could do nothing else while she thrashed her head back and forth against the pillow, screaming.

He yelled, "Where's the fucking nurse?"

A tall woman with a hard face walked into the room, circled around Martin's legs as he huffed from an occasional knee in the stomach. The nurse's face concentrated solely on the needle, tapping out air bubbles then finally, *finally*, injecting the Haldol into Vanessa's upper arm. It had no immediate effect. Andrew hadn't expected it to, but he sighed with relief knowing the sedative, mild as it might be, was already working its way through her system.

Slowly, Vanessa quieted, still tossing her head side to side but less forcefully, fighting off demons like so many times before.

He was losing her again. After all that had happened, so close to breaking through. So *fucking close!*

He'd ask forgiveness for cursing later, both the spoken and not. Maybe. Wasn't like God wouldn't understand if he didn't.

His patient's shoulders sagged at last. Andrew watched Vanessa fade back into herself, into the world she'd created so many times before. Or maybe this would be a new one. Worlds rebuilt over each other. He let go of her wrists but did not restrain them. Instead he put a hand on her cheek, not to check for any damage she might have done this time – they'd cut her nails down to the nubs after she'd scratched so violently at her own arms and throat last night

– but simply to hold her. Remind her, in the only way he was able at the moment that she was not alone. The woman could come back anytime she wanted to people who cared about her.

She drifted away completely, her stress deflating into the air above the bed. Not sleeping, though. Her eyes were open slits, but what she saw.... *Shit, it could be anything.* Martin climbed off her legs and stretched, then straightened his scrubs.

"Sorry, Andrew. I really thought she was dreaming. Couldn't understand what she was saying at first. As soon as I knew what was going on I called."

Andrew didn't look at him. It wasn't Martin's fault. Not his own, either. Still, he shouldn't have left her alone so soon. He'd only been gone a couple of hours.

"You did good, Martin, calling me quick as you did. Don't beat yourself up about it."

A new voice behind him, one which tightened Andrew's shoulders. "I hope you won't argue with me about the restraints now?"

Either Jim Chen had an informant on the floor or the guy was some kind of psychic. Andrew closed his eyes. He'd run out of reasons against them.

Going forward, Vanessa Union would have to be restrained.

"No, Jim," he said. "I guess they make sense. For the moment, at least." Rather than turn to face his Chief of Staff, he looked at the nurse still stationed beside the bed. "Thanks. Sorry for yelling. Wasn't directed at you. Can you do me a favor and put them on her?"

She nodded and did so without comment. On the other side of the room Martin busied himself looking at the painting of the cow standing in the field. *Moomoo,* as little Abby referred to it in her mother's dream world.

Andrew finally looked up at Jim Chen's round, pinched face. The man made more appearances than usual this week, sitting in on Vanessa's sessions. He wasn't fooled by his boss' occasional compliments. Vanessa *had* been making progress, working through the trauma by building an elaborate world where she took on her maiden name and the role of a psychiatrist, treating her dead husband's ghost, fighting the memory of Hank Cowles. All the while, Andrew had hoped, coming to grips with the terror of what happened two years ago. Chen was simply making sure if the woman managed to find a way out he'd be seen as instrumental to her cure.

Now, so close to the top of her climb, Vanessa had slipped and fallen. How far, Andrew hoped to find out. He *had* to hope. Chen would fade into the background soon enough and let the weight of failure rest on his subordinate's shoulders.

"Is there something I can help you with, Jim?"

Chen shook his head, muttered, "No, Doctor Booth. I am sorry about this. You'll get her back." He lingered, uncomfortable in the silence. Andrew let it hang between them until Chen finally reached for his pager, excused himself, and was gone.

The men waited while the nurse finished with the restraints. Vanessa's face was softer now, calm. She stared at him through narrow eyes but Andrew was certain she didn't see him. On the bedside table was a blue plastic cup of water and a framed photo of the Union family. He reached out and took it, let it rest on his lap. Vanessa, Corey, Abby and baby Samantha. Beautiful in every way - most of all their smiles. A truly happy family.

Vanessa had survived only by the grace of God and a stray hiker lost on Cowles' wooded property. The hapless man had stumbled upon the shed, managed to dial 911 on his cell phone before Cowles, who'd concealed himself behind a tree opposite the shed door, ran him through with a pitchfork. Vanessa Union's death would have followed if the old man had realized the call went through. He did not.

Sometimes Andrew wondered if it would have been better if he had. For her, at least. Then at least she'd be with her family, truly with them. What happened to the victims in that shed was either a complete mystery, or a secret so terrible the police locked away the details forever.

And it was his job to hold this woman's sad, frightened face, and turn it towards that place again.

Andrew returned the photo to its place beside the cup. He scooted forward on the bed, ran his hand over his patient's hair to straighten loose strands, then touched her cheek.

"Van, can you hear me?"

She didn't respond except to blink once, but that was probably reflexive. How far down the hole had she gone this time? He stared into those frightened, half-asleep eyes, looking for awareness, maybe a stray image flitting across her irises, *anything* to indicate what she might be seeing right now.

There was a phrase she had written in the imaginary journal during a recent session. *Worlds in yellow*, something like that. She'd been a good poet before her world was destroyed. Andrew had read as much of it as possible from the notebooks found in her home. Hidden under the mattress. Seemed Corey never *did* know her secret. Or if he did, as she suspected, he never let on.

Worlds in yellow. Worlds within worlds. Paintings on the wall, doorways for escape. In the end, just an illusion. Andrew was still looking into her eyes when Robert Shard wandered in and mumbled something to Martin. Martin gave a quick summary but Andrew ignored their conversation. He kept looking for some opening in Vanessa's soft gaze through which he could step through, find her and pull her out.

If she *wanted* to be found. If it was even the right thing to do anymore.

Epilogue

He'd been here before. Never in person but narrated from Vanessa Union's mind. Her descriptions should not have been this accurate, not as someone who'd never stepped over these broken, stained tiles, never saw the dust caked on the caged bulbs above Andrew's head as he walked. Yes, she was a poet, or had been, could infer and draw scenes from snippets of experience and overheard dialogue.

But not like this.

Keep it together, Andy, he thought, using the much-loathed nickname as self-punishment. *There is an explanation, a reasonable one, not the inane consideration which just flitted through your mind.*

The consideration that Vanessa did not know these halls, but Hank Cowles *did*, led back and forth every day for his outdoor constitutional. And as such, Vanessa would know.

Never that. Andrew couldn't control every conversation that had occurred in her presence, couldn't be there every minute to censor the input, especially with Robert Schard on his staff. The orderly shot his mouth off in her presence far too often. *Still....* This was too much to accept.

He turned left, not needing the casual gesture from the skinny white security guard beside him to know it was the right way to go. He should let the guard lead more, pretend not to know the place so well.

Jim Chen was waiting beside Hank Cowles' cell door, second door on the left. His arms were crossed. The chief knew about his visit because of the *manager approval required* clause on the visitation form. Andrew had privately hoped Chen wouldn't feel the need to be here in person. *Of course he'd come*, he thought. *He's probably starting to wonder if his shining protégé might be getting a little tarnished.*

Chen kept his arms crossed and pretended to look stern. "You look surprised to see me, Doctor Booth."

"A little." He closed the distance between them.

Chen relaxed. "Andrew, listen. I can be a dick sometimes." He raised a hand in front of him. "Don't deny it."

"OK."

The man gave the door beside him a quick glance. "It's been three months, and Mrs. Union hasn't spoken a single word since the relapse. No recognition, no motor responses outside of reflexive. I don't understand what you're hoping to accomplish here."

Andrew sighed, looked down at his feet. What the hell *was* he thinking? His own staff had been making comments lately. *Take a few days off, Doc,* or, *Focus on something else for a while,* or the more direct, *Get a life.* The latter was from Robert Schard. Sometimes Andrew enjoyed his bluntness.

He could only think of one answer to Chen's statement. "Closure."

"Closure?"

Andrew nodded. "There's nothing else I can do for her. Before she's moved to Long Term tomorrow, the least I can do is see the man who put her there. Someday," he shrugged, "maybe I can tell her what I've seen. Prove to her he's powerless." He looked down again at his scuffed black shoes. "I should have done this a long time ago. Might have made a difference."

Chen looked away from the door. "The sheet said you're only planning to look through the viewer. Nothing else? No interaction?"

Andrew raised his hands. "Nothing else."

Chen nodded then stepped a few paces down the hall to wait beside the security guard. "Have your peep show, then."

Andrew positioned himself in front of a door which Vanessa had described so vividly. He gripped the knob on the narrow panel but did not give the man inside any warning. That rule, at least, had existed only in his patient's imagination. He simply slid the panel aside and looked through.

Hank Cowles sat on the floor, legs spread before him, hands limp by his side and stared at the door. The skin around his neck was pulled so tight it looked too scrawny to support a head. Cowles' face was stretched against his skull, no fat on his body, only atrophied muscles, blue veins under pale, translucent skin. A frightening skeleton who looked as if he hadn't moved since coming here nearly two and a half years ago.

Bloodshot eyes stared up at him from the deep sockets. The old man's right hand slowly rose from the floor, moved forward, pulled back, down, reached forward again, caressing the dog which had long abandoned him. Andrew's chest tightened. Cowles had *not* been doing this pathetic pantomime when he'd first opened the viewport. This was a performance just for him.

His jaw hurt. Tension, fighting rage and disgust seeing this near-dead thing mocking the memory of his patient. He'd once been called the *Destroyer of Worlds*, but now he was a sick old man waiting to die.

Nothing more.

It felt good to see him like this, to understand the truth.

Cowles' lips tightened then opened into a grin, his ghostly face dissected with a silent scream. Whatever teeth remained were black with decay. The grimace was unsettling; was *wrong*.

Andrew reached up and gripped the knob on the door panel. He'd had enough. Hank Cowles' grin pulled in on itself until the lips were suddenly red, puckered into a kiss.

The hand stopped moving, rested on top of the invisible dog's head.

Then dropped.

Ticking of claws on the broken-tiled floor.

Andrew slammed the window closed. He stayed like that, breathing, looking down at the light creeping under the door. No movement.

"Satisfied?"

He clenched his teeth to keep from screaming at Chen's sudden voice. Hissing out a breath between his teeth, he let go of the knob. Andrew forced himself to look Chen in the eyes when he answered, "Yes. I'm done."

"Good. Let's leave the trash behind the door for more caring souls than ours." He raised one arm in an after-you gesture. Even the guard nodded in enthusiastic agreement, going so far as to mimic the arm gesture.

Andrew Booth walked away from Hank Cowles' cell. If that one, brief encounter shook him this much, how much worse had it been for Vanessa in those days trapped alone with him? Andrew wrapped his arms around himself as he walked, not caring what Chen might read into the gesture.

He had his closure. Maybe one day he could tell Vanessa about the visit, tell her that the old man could never hurt anyone again, that he could do nothing in his cell except slowly die.

To think anything else would be insane.

As they strolled down the hall, Chen recited what he knew about the residents behind some of the doors they passed. Andrew listened intently, trying not to hear the incessant scratching of claws against the door they were leaving behind.

About the Author

Dan's previous novels include *Margaret's Ark* and the Bram Stoker Award finalist *Solomon's Grave*, both written under his other... ok, his *actual* name. His short fiction has been published in a variety of professional magazines and anthologies over the years, including *Cemetery Dance*, *Shroud Magazine*, *Apex Digest*, *Coach's Midnight Diner* and more. He's an active member of the Horror Writers Association and founding member of the New England Horror Writers. He used to be afraid of bees, but has lived in the woods so long that they've become his friends, and tell him many things.

www.ingramcontent.com/pod-product-compliance
Lightning Source LLC
Chambersburg PA
CBHW070855180626
46817CB00003B/784